# THE KING'S SEER

## BOOK 4

## THROUGH RIGHTEOUS PATHS

D1525583

L. S. BETHEL

# CHAPTER 1

SERENITY smiled at the adorable yellow outfit on the screen of her computer. She pictured a chubby-faced baby with her father's eyes and smiled. She could hear Rielle in the living room flipping through channels. Rielle had moved in with her permanently following Kang-Dae's departure after officially ending things with her boyfriend, which made Serenity proud. She continued clicking through outfits, unable to stop the bubble of excitement rising in her. The feeling was only slightly dimmed by the thought that she could not share this joy with her husband.

It had been over two weeks since he'd returned and there was still no sign of him. While that shouldn't raise many alarms to her logically, the fact that her two weeks of being back home had been equivalent to three months back in Xian was concerning. That thought had kept her up several nights. Rielle was constantly reassuring her that he was fine, that it might take time for him to work out everything. He was fighting a war, after all. Which was another sobering thought that sent her into a tailspin of worry. She tried to put on a brave face when around her family. They had been a huge comfort and support system during this time, even though they still had no idea about her pregnancy. They were still trying to come to grips with the fact that her husband is a king from another world. Serenity felt it was better to let that settle in before adding another life-changing event.

Looking at the time, she sighed and shut her laptop. Her mother was hosting dinner at her home in an hour. She got up to get dressed when a wave of dizziness hit her, causing her to stand still as she waited to get her bearings. The dizzy spells weren't often, but they were enough to make her wary. While it could easily be explained due to her pregnancy, she also still had that foreign poison in her bloodstream waiting to make an appearance. She was taking her antibiotics religiously and had not suffered any major setbacks lately, but she was always on guard. Rielle had warned that it was possible the antibiotics could become ineffective in the future, but she prayed it would hold up long enough for Kang-Dae to find the antidote. Thoughts of Kang-Dae filled her head once more. She hoped he was okay.

# CHAPTER 2

The spear barely missed Kang-Dae as it landed to his left, embedding itself in the dead body of one of his fallen soldiers. He looked down in regret at the young man, lamenting the life he would no longer get to lead. He felt someone running up behind him and quickly maneuvered to the right, causing the charging soldier to go past him. Before the soldier could resituate himself, Kang-Dae had cut him down with a swipe to his back. He let out a short cry before falling over.

Captain Kahil, leader of Lord Amir's forces, was in his own fight. He wielded his woldo expertly. Kang-Dae was blocking a vicious attack but tried to keep Kahil within his sights in case he needed help. After seizing an opportunity to knock his attacker's weapon out of his hand, he then held his opponent in place just as someone attempted to hit him with an arrow. The arrow pierced his human shield and Kang-Dae let him slide to the ground before rushing at the bowman. He was dead before he could reload.

As the bowman fell, he could see a group of his men falling to a barrage of arrows behind him. He called out to General Song.

"My king!" Song responded, stomping the remains of his opponent's head into the dirt.

"Sound the retreat!" Kang-Dae ordered.

Song blanched. "My king!" he began to argue.

"Now!" shouted Kang-Dae.

The man frowned but got his horn out and sounded the retreat. A barrage of horns went out following the sound confirming the message was received. He and his men carefully pushed back to their lines. The cheering shouts of Katsuo's men made Kang-Dae's blood boil, but he ignored them. He would not lose any more men to an endless battle today. He ordered those keeping the line to reinforce it to ensure the enemy wouldn't follow, covering them with an arrow assault as the men made it past.

Once Kang-Dae was sure all able men made it back, he demanded a count of their losses delivered to him before nightfall. The generals and captains agreed and he walked the long distance to his tent. On the way, he passed multiple screaming men being attended to by the few healers they had with them. An unpleasant sight and sound, but Kang-Dae focused on it, not wanting to ever dismiss the pain and sacrifices his men made. It made the fact that their sacrifices seemed in vain, as they were once again forced to retreat, that much worse. Kang-Dae had attempted to retake the northern parts of the western province but had been pushed back every time. Katsuo's forces were just too numerous, and they were everywhere. Every time they went to confront one force, another was waiting in the wings to pounce and outnumber them.

# CHAPTER 3

Jung-Soo stepped over the bodies, making sure they had no breath left in them. His men were doing the same. They had been able to effectively wipe out the troop in a matter of minutes.

"Mercy," a voice rasped, drawing his attention. He looked to see one of his men hoisting up the injured soldier. Without command, he passed the soldier off to his comrades so they could take the prisoner to his temporary quarters. Temporary, so that they could get whatever information they could out of him.

Jung-Soo's gaze met with Yue-hua. The older man nodded and went after them to begin his interrogation. Yue-hua's presence among the men was unsettling for many, but only because he was so efficient at what he did. The fear of the unknown is what disturbed them so. With his tactics successful a majority of the time, but nobody knowing how the man managed to do it, the mind was allowed to imagine the individual's worst possible fears. Yue-

Hua didn't make Jung-Soo the most comfortable, but few people did, so it made no difference to him. Yue-Hua was a much-needed asset. More than a few victories were only gained due to his efforts. A little discomfort was a small price to pay to win this war.

Over the past two months, Jung-Soo and his men had overtaken over a dozen of Katsuo's troops throughout the north. A feat that would never have been accomplished if he had successfully convinced Kang-Dae to give this assignment to someone else. At the time, he did not want to be away from his king and friend as he faced countless enemies.

"Once we're done, we'll go back to camp," Jung-Soo spoke to the men around him. They all nodded their agreement before continuing with their tasks. After a short time of hiding the bodies and taking the weapons, a loud cry sounded from the trees. The men looked startled for only a moment and then ignored it. Jung-Soo never looked up, knowing those screams would lead to more victories ahead.

Jung-Soo bagged the last items he collected and secured them inside the sack. After Jung-Soo tossed the bag onto the pile with the others, Yue-Hua emerged, face blank, free of any blood or any trace of the unfortunate prisoner. This fact actually unsettled Jung-Soo and the others more than if he'd arrived covered in blood.

"General." From his tone, Jung-Soo knew the man had something important to tell him. As expected, Yue-Hua's actions bore fruit. The two went off to the side to speak privately.

"We may have Katsuo's current location," informed Yue-Hua. Jung-Soo's hope peaked at the words, but he immediately calmed himself. This was not the first time they had gotten similar information. None of them had panned out. It was either plain wrong or was old information and Katsuo had already moved on.

"How can you be sure?" Jung-Soo questioned.

"I received more than just the location. I also got the next possible camps that he will move to in a month's time." It sounded promising. Too promising. Jung-Soo would not make such a move based on the enemies' word alone.

"Have Karesh see me." Yue-Hua bowed his head and left to do so. Sitting on this information was not an option but he would not act recklessly with his men's lives either. Yue-Hua returned a short time later with Karesh in tow. The young 20-year-old resembled a teenager more than a soldier. He only reached Jung-Soo's shoulder in height. The men called him 'kid' due to his youthful looks and short height. Regardless of his unassuming looks, he was a good fighter and his fastest man. Jung-Soo had never seen anyone faster.

"I need you to check an area for me."

"Yes, general." He agreed without hesitation, as Jung-Soo expected. The men he'd chosen to accompany him on this mission were not necessarily his absolute best men, but they had unwavering loyalty, not just to him or Kang-Dae, but to Xian as well. Not one hesitated to join him despite the dangers and low chance of success. They would do their duty no matter what.

# CHAPTER 4

Rielle changed the station on the radio. "I was listening to that," Serenity whined.

"Are you driving?" Serenity rolled her eyes. At least Rielle assumed she did, knowing her. "That's what I thought. Hush." Rielle turned the volume up, humming along to the song. From the side, she could see Serenity secretly tapping her finger to the beat. She smiled to herself, knowing that Serenity's annoyance was appeased. Besides that, she knew Serenity's mind was preoccupied with more than just the song choice at the moment. That was why she was joining her at her parents' for dinner... and to get some good food, as well. Rielle had been keeping a close eye on her physically and emotionally. Though she already gently informed Serenity of the dangers of her pregnancy and the toll it would take on her already compromised body, she still wanted to make sure Serenity wasn't downplaying her symptoms or struggles. She would vocalize her concerns over things, but Rielle knew she was keeping the worst thoughts to herself. Rielle made sure to reassure Serenity and distract her as needed. She did this despite her own concerns with the current situation. Like Serenity, she felt Kang-Dae had been gone too long. Even if he had yet to find another flower, he didn't strike her as the type to let anything keep him from the one he loves. She figured he'd at least visit, even if it was to say he had no luck so far. Not even sending them any kind of word or update worried Rielle. A quick glance at Serenity in the mirror showed her deep in thought, and by the look on her face, it wasn't a pleasant one. "What do you think of Moon?" Rielle asked her suddenly. The question startled Serenity out of her thoughts.

"What?"

"For my niece's or nephew's name. I think it has charm." Serenity made a face.

"I am not naming my child Moon."

"It works for a boy or a girl, and it's significant." Serenity looked at her like she was crazy.

"What about Prince or Princess?"

"So you want to name my child either after a pop icon or one of those frufru dogs that women carry around in their purses?"

Rielle held back a laugh. "I'm just trying to give you options. Boy or girl, I got you covered." Serenity shook her head.

"Not necessary, but thank you." The way she said it piqued Rielle's interest. She frowned a bit before realization hit her.

With wide eyes, she exclaimed, "You know what it is, don't you?!" Serenity quickly looked out the window. "Uh-uh, don't do that. Spill." Serenity sighed and turned back.

"Yes I know, and no I'm not telling." Before Rielle could argue, Serenity cut her off. "I want Kang-Dae to be the first to know. If he can't be the first to know about the baby, he can at least be the first to know what we're having," She explained her reasoning. Rielle felt bad for pushing, and for bringing Serenity back around to thinking about Kang-Dae. "It's OK," Serenity told her, sensing her guilt. Rielle focused back on the road.

# CHAPTER 5

The pleas of his people tugged at Kang-Dae as his men rode past. They shared similar expressions of desperation and all looked to be in a state of scarcity. Cries to be let into the capital continued, but their voices were barely distinguishable from all the others. It didn't matter how much he longed to bring them into the safety of the capital; it would be disastrous. They still had not figured out an effective method of sniffing out possible Katsuo plants among the people. Unless they wanted to end up as Illeonda and so many other Xian cities that'd fallen into capture, they could not afford to take the chance. Which meant many of his people were left to suffer. The best they could do is supply them with resources and protection from roaming bandits. It was not enough, Kang-Dae knew, and it made him sick that it came to this, but he could not give Katsuo more influence than he already had. They had come back to rendezvous at the Chungi fort. That was one of the few places they knew that had not been infiltrated.

The fort had become a beacon for the capital as a symbol of endurance and strength. Kang-Dae didn't waste time going to the room prepared for him and his generals. The map of Xian was laid out on the table for all to see. The black pieces scattered about represented parts where Katsuo's men had been confirmed to be. The gray pieces were possible sightings. The red pieces, representing Kang-Dae's men, showed where they were currently holding positions. The blue were critical lands where the enemy could and probably would go next. The number of Katsuo pieces on the board angered him greatly, but he refused to react.

"When did he get into Gao?" he questioned.

"We got word two days ago," answered general Liu.

"We've just taken that back," fussed Kahil. Kang-Dae didn't bother telling him to calm down, as he felt the same.

"My king, we should send more men to retake it for good," suggested Liu.

"We're stretched thin as it is; we have no extra men to spare," spoke Ji Sung.

"If we call in some from the capital…" Liu started.

"No." Kang-Dae refused immediately. "We cannot leave the capital more vulnerable than it already is. If it falls, we lose," he reminded them.

The men were upset but didn't argue, knowing he was right. Kang-Dae didn't blame Liu. They were slowly losing this war and had yet to find a solution to gain back the upper hand.

"Let's focus on moving forward with our plans to create a stronghold east," he continued.

"How, my king? Every time we try, we're pushed back," spoke Naseem for the first time.

Kang-Dae grabbed a red piece. "With the western plains fortified, we can afford to call on some of their men to help us. We can meet them along Yeoshi and push back Katsuo's forces in Tai-

Fie, cutting off their support. Then we can successfully retake the eastern coast."

"If we get Park's men involved, we can flank them," Kahil suggested.

Kang-Dae nodded in agreement. "Send word to Lord Park calling him and his men in," he ordered.

"Yes, my king."

"What about the refugees out there? Are we to leave potential enemies at our doorstep?" questioned Yu. Just the man's voice made Kang-Dae want to hit him.

"What do you suggest we do?" Liu asked with a scoff.

"We should push them out further and send them to the outskirts," Yu told him.

"The chances of them getting intercepted are high," remarked Hui.

"We don't even know how many of them are truly Xian. For all we know, that's Katsuo's men out there screaming for entry into our city to take it for themselves," argued Yu.

"It's possible, but not certain. We will not condemn our own on a possibility," argued Kahil.

"Would you rather take the chance and have them come through here and slit our throats in our sleep?" Yu harped.

"I am aware you have less experience on the battlefield than the rest of us," General Hui began, "but we are not so easily overtaken. You can rest easy knowing we will keep you safe, Lord Yu."

Yu shot Hui a murderous look. Kang-Dae could care less about Yu's feelings being hurt. He was only here for the use of his men and so he could keep an eye on him. He would never trust him on his own back in the palace after his failed coup. Sun either. As talented a soldier as he was, his only purpose was to manage his men. Kang-Dae refused to even speak to Sun, let alone ask his opinion on anything.

"We have considered your words, Yu, but we will not abandon the people more than we have. Once we are able to clear them of any suspicion, we will welcome them into the capital," Kang-Dae told him. He could see it in his eyes, the need to challenge his word, to refute the idea that they could ever be sure of such a thing, but he kept his mouth shut. "Make sure the supplies are distributed to them before sunset tomorrow."

"It will be done, my king," replied Hui.

After dismissing everyone, Kang-Dae finally went to his room. He made himself remove his armor even though all he wanted to do was collapse on the bed. Once undressed, he practically fell into his chair. On his desk was a small picture of his beautiful wife smiling at him. He brought it with him from her world after demanding she give him one for himself.

*"What is this doing here?" Serenity questioned, pulling the photo out of his pack. Kang-Dae quickly snatched the photo from her hands.*

*"That is mine," he claimed.*

*"Where did you even get this?" Serenity interrogated, trying to reach for the offending item. He quickly moved it out of her reach.*

*"It was a gift."*

*Serenity rolled her eyes muttering, "Mama," under her breath. The picture in question was sitting on the mantle of her parents' home. Kang-Dae had noticed it on his first visit. The "portrait" was of a slightly younger Serenity in a black robe with gold lining around the top. Her hair was straight, straighter than he'd ever seen it, everywhere but at the top. The top still showed the curls he was used to. According to Serenity's mother. The picture had been taken on something called "graduation" from her school. Serenity had been running late and had not been able to finish straightening her hair. She had decided to keep the hat on for the whole day to hide it. Unfortunately for her, when taking that picture, Levi had run by and snatched the hat off of her head just as her mother had taken the picture. Serenity's mother told him she'd chased her brother all around the auditorium to get it back.*

*"Give it to me," ordered Serenity, holding out her hand out to Kang-Dae. Kang-Dae smirked and placed the picture behind his back. "You don't even want it! You just want to make me mad."*

*"This is my most cherished possession," he claimed adamantly, holding it to his chest for emphasis, and to annoy her. Blinking, Serenity's head tilted in a way that told Kang-Dae she was a second away from taking matters into her own hands.*

*She took a step forward and he took one backward. Serenity's eyes narrowed. A tense but playful atmosphere filled the room. Serenity took a step back, confusing Kang-Dae. She gave him a sweet smile, which only raised his guard more. She*

25

walked around the couch casually. Kang-Dae did not take his eyes off her. In an unexpected move, Serenity grabbed one of the pillows from the couch and tossed it right at Kang-Dae's head. He quickly caught it with his free hand just as Serenity went lunging for the photo in his other hand. Despite the surprise attack, he managed to move fast enough and took off toward the bedroom.

"Give it back!" she huffed, running after him. He got to the bedroom only a few seconds before her but managed to hide himself behind the door. She came in, panting, stopping right by the bed. Just as she turned to look around, she caught sight of him. Her eyes widened as he rushed at her, hoisting her up into his arms. She wrapped her arms and legs around him to keep from falling. He smiled up at her while she pouted. He gave a quick peck to the offended lip. He chuckled at her attempt to keep from smiling.

"Will you please leave it?" she asked. He shook his head. "I can give you another one, a better one."

*"I do not think there are better ones."*

*"There are so many better ones," she countered, making him laugh again.*

*"If you can find one that I will love more than this one, I will concede," he offered. Pleased with his answer, she grinned and bent down to kiss him. He returned the kiss eagerly and the photo was quickly forgotten.*

Kang-Dae smiled to himself, hearing her voice in his mind. He missed her terribly. The months he'd been without her were almost as bad as when he thought she was dead. Knowing she was safe helped ease the pain a bit but didn't dull the loneliness. He had no idea how much time had passed on the other side, but he knew it was probably enough to have Serenity worried. He prayed she didn't fear the worst or think she'd been abandoned. He spent much effort showing her how much he needed her before his departure. The memory of doing so brought another smile to his lips. No, she wouldn't think he left her, but he knew she would worry for him in this war. It was another reason he was determined to remove Katsuo from his lands. He had yet to find the flower that would lead him back to Serenity. Still, he did not want her here while the war continued. She was safer where she was no matter how he missed her. It was better this way.

# CHAPTER 6

Serenity slapped at her brother Levi's hand, which was attempting to take her biscuit off her plate for the second time. "Boy, I said stop!"

"What? You not eating it."

"I'm saving it."

"You can't do that."

"Says who?"

"Table rules. Either eat it or lose it."

"It ain't my fault you ate up your food like it's your last meal."

"Can y'all stop?" Their mother finally spoke up, annoyed but gently amused at their bickering. Levi sulked back over to his seat, but not before childishly flicking Serenity's side. Without hesitation, she slammed her foot on his. He tried to hide his reaction while Serenity smiled to herself, nobody else the wiser.

"You didn't eat much," her mother remarked, concerned. Serenity froze. She didn't want to say her stomach was sensitive now and she was doing her best not to lose anything she did eat.

"It's just the antibiotic she's on," Rielle spoke up for her. Serenity nodded in agreement. Her mother appeared to accept the explanation and went back to eating. Serenity silently thanked Rielle for her quick thinking.

"Auntie Serenity, where is your husband?" Her youngest nephew asked. The room became silent. Levi was quick to reprimand the child, but Serenity stopped him.

"It's okay. He had something important to do where he lives. He'll come back when he's done," she explained. The child nodded and went back to eating, having no idea the tension he caused in all the adults at the table. Dinner continued awkwardly as everyone attempted to ignore the giant elephant that had been dropped in the middle of their dinner.

Serenity finished washing her hands and went to exit the bathroom. As she entered the hall, she ran into Denise. Figuring that she also needed to use the bathroom, Serenity smiled and moved out of her way.

"Serenity," Denise called out before she could make it to the end of the hall. "Can we talk?"

She seemed serious, so Serenity agreed. The two went into the guest room and sat on the edge of the bed.

"What's going on? You okay?" Serenity asked.

"I'm fine; I just wanted to talk to you."

Serenity's brow furrowed. "What about?"

"I know LJ can be nosey sometimes-"

"It's fine; he's curious. I understand. I'm not mad."

"But you're still worried about him," she stated. Serenity pressed her lips together, not wanting to speak her fears to her sister-in-law for some reason.

"I get it. That need to keep it all inside because you don't want everyone worrying about you. Because when they do, it just makes everything that much more real." Serenity didn't respond, but inside, she was nodding. "I felt it when Levi was deployed, even now when he's out there on the streets. It's a worry like no other cause it's always there. No matter how much you try to reassure yourself or distract yourself, you can't let it go."

"How do you deal with it?" Serenity finally asked.

"I do what I can. I make sure my kids never have to think about it. I pray and keep him covered, and I trust that he will do anything in his power to come back to us. Because we're a team, and it's just as much my responsibility to keep our family intact as it is his. So I do my part so he can do his, and vice versa."

"I know he would come back if he could. I can't help feeling like he can't, and the worst thoughts go through my head wondering why."

Denise nodded her understanding. "You don't have to keep those feelings yourself. I've got enough worry for us both. If you need to talk, or just need some encouragement, I'm here."

Serenity smiled softly and hugged her. "Thank you."

The two walked out to see everyone out on the front porch saying their goodbyes. Serenity hugged each of her nephews. Levi held out his hand. She smiled and made it seem like she was going in for a hug before side stepping him for Denise. Levi sucked his teeth and murmured under his breath. Rielle shoved past him jokingly, and Levi pushed the back of her head.

"Levi!" their mom scolded.

"Why you always gotta take their side?" He whined.

Serenity hugged her parents goodbye, promising to call when she got home. She finally hugged Levi, who refused to hug her back out of principle, which didn't matter to her. Towards the end, he seemed unable to hold his anger and embraced her.

"Call me if you need me, alright?"

She nodded in his chest. With the final goodbye, she joined Rielle in the car and then she headed home.

*The crying baby in her arms was barely being soothed by her rhythmic rocking. There was no one around, but Serenity still felt she needed to be quiet. She scanned the area, which looked vaguely familiar but still gave her no clue as to where she was. Anything that could've given her clarity was either burnt out or destroyed. There was no human, animal, or anything living she could hear or see. She continued walking but stopped short once the smell of death hit her nostrils. The smell was so strong her eyes began to water. She continued walking, trepidation filling her with every step. In the distance, she could make out the palace in the darkness. The sight should have relieved her, but instead, her fear increased. The baby in her arms was wailing now. The urge to keep the child quiet was replaced by her need to get inside. She ran, crossing fields of dead grass and entering the gates. Once inside, she froze. A sea of soldiers were scattered along the grounds, kneeling and completely unmoving. They all wore foreign armor. Serenity wanted to turn back, to run away, but she forced herself to push forward. Not one soldier moved or even turned their head to look her way. She clutched the baby to her. After entering the palace, she went straight toward the main hall. Inside, there were broken Xian swords scattered on the ground all the way to the steps leading to the doors. There were so many she couldn't avoid stepping on them. The doors themselves weren't just open, but busted open. Serenity knew nothing she found ahead would be good, but she needed to see. Upon entering, her dread turned into full-on horror.*

*Hanging on the walls were the armor of at least a hundred Xian soldiers in various states of array showcasing how each soldier most likely met their end. A figure sitting on the throne had her rushing toward it, eager to see if it was Kang-Dae, but once she got there, the figure was gone, and the thrones she once shared with her husband were just a pile of debris on the ground. She reached inside and pulled out Kang-Dae's crown. She shuddered seeing the specks of blood on it, marring the once flawless headdress. She wiped desperately at it trying to remove the stains. A man appeared in the reflection. It wasn't Kang-Dae, or anyone she knew, and she was too afraid to turn around.*

Serenity awoke with a gasp, tears rolling down her cheeks. It took her a while to calm her racing heart. She reached out for her notebook in her drawer and quickly began writing everything in the dream, everything she saw, everything she felt. Just recalling it all had her eyes blurring with tears once more, but she kept writing, determined not to miss a single detail. She went through it all, picking apart any and all symbols and meanings she could pull well into the morning.

# CHAPTER 7

A frustrated Rielle watched helplessly as
Serenity kept packing. She had been moving nonstop since Rielle had got up, babbling about a dream
she had and how she had to go back now. Rielle had
been trying to get her to slow down to talk to her
and think things through more, but Serenity barely
acknowledged her.

"Can you please stop for a second?" Rielle
tried once more. Once again, she was ignored as
Serenity continued packing up her medicines.

Deciding on another tactic, Rielle said,
"Even if you're right and something is wrong, what
if Kang-Dae isn't coming back yet because he
can't? Maybe it's not safe. You have no idea what
you're going to run into – what danger you'll be
exposing yourself and your baby to."

She emphasized the word "baby" hoping it
would break through the fog of determination
surrounding her. When Serenity finally paused, she

felt hope that she might've gotten through to her, but she also felt guilty for having to go there. Serenity looked up at her for the first time all morning.

"I know," she said without much concern, which bothered Rielle. "I know there's danger. I know it's crazy to just walk into that. But I have to. The last time I ignored a dream, Kang-Dae suffered for it. I can't af- he can't afford for me to ignore this one. I don't have these dreams for no reason. If I get one, it's because I can do something about it. The dreams aren't informative; they're strategic, and if I don't listen to them, things go wrong. God trusted me with the dream. I can't just sit on it. If he thinks I can do something about it, who am I to say no?"

Rielle remained silent, not knowing what to say. She was feeling a great deal of admiration for her friend but also genuine worry as well. Serenity meant every word she said, and nothing she said would dissuade her, Rielle knew.

"What about the baby?" she whispered, feeling like she had to at least make a last attempt to keep her here.

"I'm going to protect my baby and trust God will keep us both safe. But I have to do my best to make sure Kang-Dae and our home are safe. Cause it's not just about us. I owe it to those people – my people – to do everything in my power to keep it from falling."

Right then, is when Rielle saw it. 'Queen Serenity.' That had always been the part of Serenity's tale that she had found hard to swallow. Serenity had always been strong, but a leader Rielle had never seen, until now.

"What about your parents?"

"You can tell them if you want. It's just going to make them worry, and they can't stop me," admitted Serenity. Rielle stayed quiet for a moment before sighing and helping her pack.

# CHAPTER 8

Like most nights, Kang-Dae lay awake, allowing his mind to fill with memories and thoughts of his wife and queen. Only in these rare quiet moments would he take the time to remember her. He hoped she was happy and safe. As he had not made much or any progress in finding an antidote to the Gi poison, he prayed she was alright still. Now that Katsuo had taken the upper western region, getting there to search for the remaining family was close to impossible. Once he had permanently dealt with the invader, that would be his first stop. He fiddled with Serenity's necklace, recalling when she'd last had it in her hands.

They'd been lying in bed, nude, as they had been the majority of the time he'd spent in her land. A smile ghosted his lips at the memory. She told him then how the necklace brought them together, not once, but twice. She told him to keep it, declaring it would always bring him back to her. He kissed her head and told her, "I will always return to you." She'd kissed him in return and they'd made love for the second time that night. More than anything, Kang-Dae wanted his wife back.

Movement outside his tent drew his attention. Multiple shadows moving about on the outside raised the hair on his arms. He quietly rose, reaching for his crossbow. He didn't bother with his armor. Checking to see if his weapon was loaded, he was relieved to see that it was. He kept the shadows in his sight as they circled his tent. The figures paused. His heartbeat was strong but steady. With controlled breaths, he stayed quiet, barely moving. One of the figures came toward the entrance; Kang-Dae took aim.

"What are you doing?" a familiar voice spoke.

The figures quickly moved from his tent. He could hear a scuffle outside. Not knowing the situation, he wouldn't just run out. Instead, he crawled under the flap in the back of the tent and circled around to the front. Officer Jhang was on his

knee trying to fight off two attackers while the other
was dead on the ground. These men were dressed in
Xian armor. They must have snuck in during the
retreat. Kang-Dae took aim and hit the one closest
to Jhang in the throat. The second tried to rush him
but was dead with a bolt to the heart in a second.
Kang-Dae rushed over to Jhang. He was bleeding
out of his side from a clear sword wound.

"My apologies, my King," he began.

"Quiet. I'm taking you to Hui."

Kang-Dae shouted for one of the patrolling
guards. They came over quickly, eyes widening as
they took in the scene.

"Sound the alarm. Clear the camp of any
other possible intruders and prepare to set off," he
ordered.

Since Katsuo's men knew where they were,
he would not take the chance that this may be their
only attack. They could be on the verge of being
surrounded at the very moment he helped Jhang
over to the healer's tent. Most of the cots were full,

but he found the closest one that was empty and helped Jhang onto it.

A healer came asking, "What happened?"

"Just help him," Kang-Dae said, not having the energy for anything else.

Once he was sure Jhang would get the help he needed, he left the tent to search out any more infiltrators himself. The camp was now fully active and awake, still unsure as to what had transpired. Kang-Dae's anger and frustration at it all was overwhelming him. Their plan to take the fight to Katsuo was costing them. Not only that, but if they didn't find a better way to defend against his underhanded tactics, they'd be taken out before they ever got close to him.

# CHAPTER 9

Serenity felt surprisingly calm as she walked down to the water. In her haste, she'd walked ahead of Rielle who'd gone back to get something she claimed Serenity needed. Serenity wasn't concerned about any of that; her focus was singularly on getting back. There was no fear or worry this time. Even if the theory of the baby keeping her safe was just a theory, she believed it whole-heartedly. She was no longer questioning her dreams. It was clear to her that they were what would guide her and save Xian. She tightened the strap of the backpack, making sure she wouldn't lose it in the water. Steps behind her let her know Rielle had arrived. She turned to say her goodbyes and to assure her that she'd be all right, ready to have to argue with her one last time, but stopped short to see Rielle dressed in a similar fashion, along with her own pack. For a moment, she was confused, until realization hit her and she began to shake her head profusely.

"No," Serenity told her.

Rielle tied her locs back, and Serenity suddenly noticed her new bracelet with a locket on her wrist. Serenity had a sneaking suspicion of what was inside.

"You can't," Serenity insisted.

"I told Mama Pat I was taking you on a girls' trip to take your mind off of things. That gives us at least two weeks before they get suspicious," she explained, ignoring her protests.

"Rielle, you can't. It's not safe for you."

"If you have to do this, then I have to go with you. Whatever you need to do, you need someone who can have your back and look after you and the baby. You may know what you know, but I know you need me with you."

Serenity felt anxiety peaking its ugly head. She was okay with her choice; she trusted in it. But bringing Rielle along, putting her in the same danger, filled her with anxiety. But she couldn't stop her. Even if she left her behind, she would just follow her through.

Rielle took Serenity's hand. "If you believe you'll make it, then so will I, cause I'm not leaving your side," she stated.

Serenity could feel her tears well up at her sincerity. She pulled Rielle into a hug, which she returned.

"Are you sure?" She sniffled. Rielle nodded.

They pulled back and shared determined smiles before turning to the water. Together, they walked into the water. Into the lake. Into the unknown.

# CHAPTER 10

Jung-Soo's eyes moved over the letter he was reading. If anyone was watching him, they'd never know how amused he was reading Amoli's words. True to her word, she continued to write to him consistently. Sometimes about important matters, other times personal. He found her inability to admit her relationship with Amir, despite how she wrote about him constantly, amusing. She probably hadn't noticed how prevalent the council member had become in her life. He was glad she had someone with her to care for her, as well as keep her safe. He was hoping she'd find someone worthy of her admiration. He was a poor choice and uninterested in such things. She was young, beautiful, and innocent. She deserved the fairy tale. He could never be that, and he didn't want to be.

"General," Tae-Soo called to him.

He rolled up his parchment and put it away before addressing him. "What is it?"

"Tan has returned."

Jung-Soo quickly followed Tae-Soo, who led him to a small group of men gathered around the recently returned Tan. He looked winded – sweat poured down his face as he drank the water that the others must have provided for him. Other than his fatigued state, he looked to be unharmed. Seeing Jung-Soo arrive, Tan stopped drinking to properly greet him, but Jung-Soo stopped him.

"Are you well?" he asked him. Tan nodded.

"I wasn't spotted," Tan told him.

"What did you see?" Jung-Soo asked.

"He's there; I'm sure of it."

Jung-Soo looked at Tae-Soo. "Get the others; we're moving out."

Tae-Soo nodded and went off to do just that. Jung-Soo dismissed the others so they could prepare.

"What did you see?" Jung-Soo asked Tan.

"We were right. He's in the northern mountains. There's a stronghold in the center. It'll be difficult to attack outright. Infiltration is probably best."

Jung-Soo had to concur. "I need you to send two of your best runners to the King. Get this information to him."

Tan nodded his understanding. If Kang-Dae could send more men to meet them in the north, it could better their chances of taking out the would-be conqueror altogether. But knowing Kang-Dae, Jung-Soo was sure he would come himself, though he hoped he didn't. This new plan was built on maybes.

# CHAPTER 11

Serenity gasped as soon as she breached the surface of the water. The night sky shone above her, confirming her arrival. The heaviness of the pack was making it difficult to keep afloat. She looked around for Rielle. The two held on to each other as the whirlpool drew them in but lost touch right after. She looked around, desperately hoping to see her somewhere in the lake. Finally, her eyes hit the grass and she released a sound of relief seeing Rielle on the sand. Using what energy she had left, she swam over to her. Once she hit land, she crawled on all fours over to her friend. Rielle was lying on her stomach, face lying in the grass. Serenity, fearing for her, immediately checked to see if she was breathing. Great relief filled her when she saw that she was. Serenity rolled Rielle onto her side and began to try and wake her.

"Ri Ri, wake up," she called to her.

Rielle's skin was cold to the touch, and Serenity suspected it had little to do with the water.

She remembered how rough her first time was. She prayed Rielle would not take days to recover as she did, hoping the freshness of the flower would help alleviate some of the worst symptoms. Soon, Rielle began to stir.

"Hey," Serenity said softly to her.

Rielle's eyes opened slowly just a bit. She let out a soft moan.

"Cold," she croaked.

Serenity nodded. "I know."

She took her pack off and pulled out the towels they packed and covered Rielle with them. Serenity sat with her while she got herself together, slowly trying to bring herself out of the lethargy she knew Rielle was feeling. Serenity was grateful she wasn't feeling it nearly as strongly as before. She had her baby to thank for that. Soon, Rielle was able to sit up with their help.

"How are you doing?" She asked her.

Rielle took slow breaths, and with a small shake of the head responded, "Fine."

Serenity rubbed her towel-covered shoulders, attempting to give her as much warmth as possible.

"It'll get better," Serenity told her. Rielle tiredly nodded.

Serenity looked around and spotted Rielle's pack a few feet away. She went and brought it over to them.

"Let's change into some dry clothes; it'll help," She suggested.

The two, with effort, clothed themselves in the appropriate attire that they packed so as to blend in as much as they could, considering their skin tone.

"How far is the palace?" Rielle asked.

"We can rest more if you need it," Serenity offered, seeing how much effort it took just for her to dress herself. "It's more than a three-day walk without horses."

Rielle let out a noise of disbelief. Serenity agreed it wasn't ideal, but they didn't have much of a choice. If she could have driven a truck into the lake she would have, hell, even a skateboard would have been good. The loud sound of a horn let out. Both women looked up in the distance. It sounded far off but not that far. The women shared a concerned look and quickly gathered their things.

"Do you think it's Kang-Dae's people?" Rielle asked hopefully.

"I can't tell. Safest thing to do would be to just head straight to the capital. We'll know for sure we'll be good," Serenity told her.

They put their bags on their backs and rushed toward the road to begin their trek.

# CHAPTER 12

Kang-Dae rode with the other generals ahead of his men. They had ridden through the night for two days and needed to rest. Still not confident enough to set up camp in their usual places, he decided a passing village was a better option for the time being. It was small, less than two hundred people, he expected. They looked as though these hard times had not left them unaffected, but what interested him were the stares they were giving him and his men. He was dressed like the other generals, so he didn't think they knew his true identity. He wasn't sure why they looked at him this way. If he were honest, more than a few of the stares were full of disdain.

"Sir, can you have the leaders of your village meet with us?" He asked one of the villagers standing about. The man gave him a hard look before nodding shortly and walking off.

"I feel as though we are not very welcome here," Kahil spoke from his left.

"It is not just you," Kang-Dae responded. He dismounted and the others followed.

"Have the others create a perimeter and rest up in the neighboring woods," he told his men.

As Kang-Dae looked around more, he realized it was worse than he initially thought. The village had been dealing with its own issues of lack. A line of people stood waiting to be given what looked like a small cup of grain and another cup of rice. The people walking about avoided their stare and rushed to get back to their homes.

"Have some of our stock brought up as soon as possible," he ordered one of his generals, who nodded and walked off.

"This way," the man from earlier called out upon his return.

He led Kang-Dae and Kahil to a building close to the center of the village. There, he was met with two men seated at a table. They did not stand or even greet him as he entered, but he dismissed it.

He greeted both men respectfully, but they did not return his greeting.

The man on the right coldly asked, "Why are you here?"

Kang-Dae and Kahil shared a look before Kahil responded.

"We need a place to rest our men for a day or two. We won't cause you any trouble," Kahil tried to assure them. Neither man seemed pleased.

"May I ask why you all are still here? These lands were meant to be evacuated. The enemy is roaming about. It isn't safe," Kang-Dae spoke up.

"And go where? The capital?" The man in the turban scoffed. "We've already been turned away from there. If the king wants us to move, he can come and move us himself." It was said with such contempt Kang-Dae was taken back. "We will stay in our home. We cannot move you any more than your king will move us. Do what you like."

"'Our king'?!" Kang-Dae sputtered. "Have you already declared your allegiance to Katsuo?" Kang-Dae asked sharply.

Kahil had to put a hand on his shoulder to calm him. The men were unconcerned with Kang-Dae's ire.

"We do not have any allegiance to anyone. Not anymore. What difference does it make to declare loyalty to one or another? It would not change anything for us. It has been made clear to us neither spared us a thought."

Kang-Dae was outraged at the assumption and was a second away from revealing himself and demanding an explanation, but Kahil's calming hand tightened on his shoulder, silently warning him against further arguments. Kang-Dae wanted to ignore him but knew that in the grand scheme of things, it was not important. He turned and stomped out of the room with Kahil following behind closely.

"My king," Kahil quietly called after him.

Kang-Dae continued, knowing that if he stopped, he'd go right back to those men to speak his mind.

Kahil caught up to him and matched his speed. "I'd recommend keeping to the outskirts of the village for now. We'll have lookouts keeping an eye out."

Kang-Dae didn't say anything back, his mind still on those men.

"My king?"

"Fine," he said shortly.

"Don't take it to heart," Kahil told him. "They do not have the same privilege of information as others."

Kang-Dae was not comforted, and as Kahil continued to the rest of the men, he wondered to himself how many others felt the same way.

# CHAPTER 13

Panting and on wobbly legs, Serenity and Rielle struggled to keep up their pace as the noises they attempted to flee from seemed to get closer and closer. The ominous sound was not exactly following them, but it was clear the women were in its path. There were several groups in the surrounding area it seemed, and trying to avoid them was becoming difficult. They were everywhere, and Serenity had a sick feeling they were not the Xianians. Given her dream, she shouldn't have been surprised to see how far they'd infiltrated, but being in the middle of it made it that much more real. They'd walk through the night, and as daylight reared over the horizon, the masses of smoke in the surrounding skies clued them in to how surrounded they were.

"We might need to get off the road," Serenity suggested, seeing even more smoke ahead.

"Can you find your way if we do?" Rielle asked.

Serenity was quiet because she wasn't sure, especially once night fell, but she didn't like their chances on the road. They would be sitting ducks. With their looks, the chances of their being able to bluff their way out if caught were slim. Rielle took her silence as her answer but headed into the trees anyway. Seeing how much Rielle was wobbling, Serenity decided they needed a break.

"I'm fine," Rielle argued.

"Then why are you huffing and puffing like a special edition soul train?" Serenity snorted.

"Shut up."

Serenity chuckled and the two sat side by side against one of the many trees. Serenity handed Rielle her water bottle and she took two long sips.

"You really want to live here full-time?" Rielle asked. Serenity knew it was just a joke, but she could detect a hint of curiosity in their tone.

"I missed it a lot when I was home."

"Hmm."

"I was surprised... You've always been the woodsy one – trying to get me to go camping all the time, making me bring you when daddy took me and Levi out..."

"Exactly. That's why I find it weird you're all for it now."

"This isn't a big part of it. I actually didn't spend much time out here. That palace life just hits different," she joked, making Rielle laugh.

"I'm sure."

The two sat quietly for another fifteen minutes before deciding to continue on. As they walked, Rielle's eyes were on the different trees and plants. She was surprised by how many she recognized. She always figured a different planet would at least have some different things but this place looked remarkably like Earth. Looking in the tree, she spotted something strange. It definitely didn't belong. It took a few minutes for her to realize it was a line, almost identical to a fishing line. She followed its path behind a large tree and stopped short.

"Rielle?" Serenity called to her. "What is it?"

Rielle couldn't answer, her eyes were glued to the scene. Serenity's gaze followed hers and a horrified gasp left her lips. Ahead was a line of unfortunate souls strung up by their feet. They had been caught in some trap and had never been found or worse, had been cruelly left there to die. Serenity grabbed Rielle's hands and began to drag her away. It took a few pulls, as Rielle was frozen in shock, having never seen such violence in her life outside of her television. Serenity kept hold of her hand as she began to lead them back to the road. Rielle assumed because there was less chance of them ending up in a similar predicament. As they moved, Rielle barely felt her feet, still too shocked to think of anything but the awful image was now imprinted in her brain. She wondered how long they'd been there – if they died of dehydration first or if the animals got to them. She was so in her thoughts that she hadn't realized they had stopped moving until Serenity's hand went over her mouth to stop her talking. She hadn't even realized she had been saying anything out loud. Rielle's focus was ahead of them to a large group of men clad in armor, marching together in the very direction they had been heading. They were still deep enough in the trees that they wouldn't be immediately noticed. In unison, the two took slow steps back until they found refuge behind a tree.

Neither of them moved. They stood completely still, doing nothing but breathing as the group marched past. Seconds turned into minutes. Rielle's heart pounded so hard in her chest that she felt like she could hear it. She was sure it was broadcasting to those around them, leading them straight to her. As the footsteps retreated up the road, she could feel her breathing ease, and her tension slowly loosened. Next to her, she could see Serenity who had her eyes closed, mouth moving silently in prayer. Once they could no longer hear the steps or the clanging of armor, they finally relaxed their bodies. Rielle's ankles were burning from holding her stiff position for so long. They stepped off from the tree, not sure of the best direction to go. Taking the road while knowing what was ahead of them seemed unwise, but the image of what awaited them if they were to fall into one of those traps wouldn't allow them to continue through the woods carelessly either. Rielle looked into the wilderness in the same direction as those bodies. Though she could no longer physically see them, they were clear in her mind.

Serenity pulled on her hand and looked her in the eyes. Serenity's eyes were surprisingly calm. "When the sun goes down, we will get as close to the road as we can."

Despite what just passed them by, Rielle was thankful to hear that, not believing she could take another step into that.

# CHAPTER 14

Sunset came and went. Serenity and Rielle gathered their things after eating some of the food they brought. Serenity took out her small battery-operated lantern and led them closer to the road but behind the line of trees. She kept the light angled to the ground on a low beam to minimize the light's reach. They walked silently, somberly, in the darkness. The cool winds made her shiver as they hit her face. It was a jarring difference from the summer temperatures they just left back home. She would have loved to have her leather jacket right now. The crunch of the leaves on the ground was the only accompanying sound to their trek. Their steps were purposeful but careful. Serenity made sure every step had been preceded by the flashlight's beam to avoid any traps or obstructions. Serenity estimated if they traveled mostly at night this way and hid away during the day, it would take at least a

week to make it back to the palace. She
hoped she wasn't too late by then.

Laughter hit her ears, and she
stopped along with Rielle. She quickly shut
off the light, leaving them in complete
darkness. She listened hard, trying to
determine what direction the sound came
from. She tried not to think the worst. It
might be a random citizen traveling and
resting for the night. The laughter sounded
again, but this time it was accompanied by
loud male voices overlapping. The noise
seemed to be coming from their left further
ahead. Serenity weighed their options. Rielle
looked at her and gestured to the other side
of the road. Serenity concurred with her
silent suggestion to get to the other side and
try their luck there. Without light, they made
their way to the road. Rielle checked one
direction while Serenity checked the other
before making their run for the other side.
As quickly and quietly as they could, they

sprinted to the other side, hoping to disappear into the trees.

They slowed their pace to minimize the noise of their footsteps, unsure if this side was any clearer of people. They went deeper than they had before into the other side, but still close enough to the road to feel safe from traps and being seen. They walked much slower, taking care with every step to make as little noise as possible. Serenity didn't dare turn on the flashlight, just praying for God to guide their feet. They walked another five minutes before they heard it. First Serenity, then Rielle from the way she froze as well. It was a noise that otherwise could have been explained away by a number of small animals or normal night noises, but the steadiness of it and the way it appeared to be heading toward them had them believing the worst.

They began to run, weaving through the trees, hands interlocked. As they feared, the steps also picked up their pace. They ran as fast as they could, legs screaming, almost burning. Logically, Serenity knew they couldn't outrun their pursuers indefinitely. They needed to hide and if worse came to worse, fight. Serenity pulled Rielle to a tree and motioned for her to stay quiet while she planted herself by another. Serenity quietly removed her backpack and dug around. Serenity found what she wanted. The footsteps slowed only a few feet from them. From the sound of the steps, there was more than one. She knew they were searching for them now. Her hands tightened around the object in her hand. She saw the dagger first and waited until the hand came into view. Pressing the button, she dug the taser into the pursuer's hand and didn't let up until the dagger dropped and he jumped back falling onto his knees. As she prepared for the other to descend on her, she looked up to see Rielle on the back of the other, her taser pressed into his throat, making him convulse heavily. Serenity stared on, impressed, and almost sympathetic to the soldier. He fell to his knees and face-planted just as Rielle jumped off. The two didn't wait around and took off running once more. If the men managed to get back up to come after them, they could no longer hear their pursuit, making Serenity believe that they had outrun them. They were feeling halfway relieved when the light appeared ahead, making them stop.

Serenity wanted to cry in frustration. What would they do now? They were everywhere. Noises behind them let her know her previous assailants were catching up. Rielle suddenly went to her knees. Serenity feared she was hurt but became confused when she went into her bag and began pulling out certain things – small things, important things – and storing them in various places on her person. She took

Serenity's backpack from her and did the same. As the steps grew closer, Rielle led them deeper into the woods where she tossed both packs one by one as hard as she could and led them in the opposite direction. They ran back across the road and onward. Through the noise of their steps, Serenity realized in despair that there were now multiple men after them, but she didn't dare look back, afraid of what she'd see. But in the end, it didn't matter. Ahead of them were multiple burning torches being held by menacing men in armor. With just one look, Serenity knew they were Katsuo's men.

The woman finally stopped, defeated. Not long after, the footsteps stopped right behind them. Serenity was roughly grabbed from behind, and from Rielle's grunt, she knew she had been handled the same way. They were led further into the trees until they came upon a clearing and a medium-sized camp full of soldiers. Heart pounding, Serenity prayed for God to show her how they could get out of this. They were taken to a small group of people who Serenity assumed had been captured as well. They were tied together and pushed into the dirt. The men grumbled to themselves about having more mouths to feed and how it'd be better to kill them. At the moment, she was glad Rielle had no understanding of the Xian language. They were left on their own with a couple of guards standing over them. Tears welled up, but she pushed them back. She wouldn't cry; she couldn't, and she didn't have to. They would make it out of here. They had to.

# CHAPTER 15

Jung-Soo removed an arrow from the departed's back and tossed it on the pile they gathered after their attack ended. Once again, his men received no casualties on their side and none of the enemy had been left alive. As per their routine, the fallen would be stripped, and anything deemed usable, or more importantly, wearable, would be collected and put amongst their other spoils. The armor he wore had been confiscated a few months ago from one of their captains after he fell to Jung-Soo's sword. This deception had awarded them many victories in the past few weeks. Jung-Soo surmised that if Katsuo could use deceptive tactics to take their land and subjugate their people, he'd use those very tactics to eradicate them all. This particular group had no inclination of who they were or their motives when they arrived, claiming to need more supplies after being raided. Once they were all comfortable and relaxed, Jung-Soo's other men who had been hiding in wait attacked with their forces. Jung-Soo and the others cleared them one by one until none were left standing. They were still days away from Katsuo, but Jung-Soo wanted to remove as many of his men on their journey as possible. Something shiny caught Jung-Soo's eye. He could see something peeking out from beneath the body. He roughly kicked it to the side and looked closer. It was a sword beautifully made with clear markings. Whoever the owner was must have been one of Katsuo's elite. Jung-Soo took the sword into his hands and inspected it. The steel was well-made, sharp to the touch, and well-balanced. It's probably the best he'd ever handled. He took ownership of the sword, even swapping it out in his sheath. It only pushed the narrative of his allegiance to Katsuo more, so he figured, why not? His men continued their cleanup, and he went back to join them. Eventually, they managed to salvage over a hundred new weapons, fifty pounds of rice, ten undamaged breastplates, thirty helmets, and three barrels of water. Not a bad haul to start the day. Every bit would be needed. They would not stop until they reached and killed Katsuo.

# CHAPTER 16

Kang-Dae stared down at the village leaders, fighting back the urge to scream. A scout had arrived, warning of a large troop coming their way. Kang-Dae along with Kahil had been trying to convince them to leave, even offering to personally escort them to safer lands. They refused.

"You all may go on your way," one leader said dismissively. "We'll take care of ourselves like we've been doing."

"This is not something you can just wait out. If they find you, they will not leave you untouched," Kahil said.

"We are aware of what they are capable of," the other leader spoke.

"I do not think you are, or you wouldn't be risking the lives of all your people over your pride," Kang-Dae shot back, not understanding these men's distrust for them.

"Sir, we care more for these people than you or those in the capital. We have already tried entrusting ourselves to those like you and we were left behind, forgotten. We were made to fend for ourselves, so that is what we are doing."

Kang-Dae opened his mouth to say more but stopped. With a scoff, he walked out of the room.

"We need to move on. We can't waste any more time here," Yu spoke.

"And prove their accusations right? That we would abandon our people without care?" Kang-Dae retorted.

"It's not our job to change their minds. We have more important things to worry about. They've made their choice," Yu rebutted.

"I agree," said Sun. Kahil made a sound in the back of his throat that perfectly vocalized Kang-Dae's feelings about Sun's opinion.

"We are soldiers of Xian. It's our duty to fight for everyone," General Shum spoke up.

"They don't want our help. Our labor is better suited for those in need," said Yu.

"They may believe they don't need us but that doesn't change the fact that they do," Shum responded.

"Leave!" shouted Kang-Dae, unable to take any more of their bickering. The men all left him except Kahil.

"I take no pleasure in saying this, but Yu is not completely wrong. There are bigger battlefields we're needed on. Every moment we spend here trying to convince these people to move on is another moment Katsuo has to push further in."

Kang-Dae shut his eyes and sighed. "Our goal is to expel him from all our lands, even the smallest places," Kang-Dae reminded him.

After a moment of pause, Kahil nodded. "I understand, my King."

"Tell the men to prepare for a fight. We'll fortify the area as best we can, and try to lead them away from the village. Hopefully we'll be able to keep them from setting foot here."

# CHAPTER 17

Rielle was leaning against Serenity. Both women had not been able to sleep well in the night, only nodding off here and there. The night before, there had only been two guard shifts. When the sun rose, another three men came to relieve the others. No one spoke in their sad group of captives. It was mostly women and children, and a couple of men. There were no more than fifteen of them. They looked to have been there for a few days, judging by their appearance. Serenity stirred, letting Rielle know she was waking up.

"Hey," Rielle whispered as soon as she sat up.

Serenity looked a bit dazed at first, trying to get her bearings. She could see her eyes darkened at the reminder of their situation.

"How long was I sleep?" She asked.

"Only an hour or so I think." Keeping time without a watch or clock was very hard.

"Did any of them come over, or say anything?"

Rielle shook her head. One of the soldiers shouted at the guards, and one guard went off to meet them. Rielle looked back to see if anyone else was behind, looking for an opening. Serenity got her attention and shook her head.

"We wouldn't make it far and we'd only end up making them mad. We gotta get a huge head start if we want to have a chance," she surmised.

Rielle knew she was right. Serenity looked around the enemy's camp. There were at least fifty men she could see, not counting however many more there were walking in the woods, possibly in search of more captives. She wasn't sure what they wanted them for. From the guard's words last night, they weren't exactly wanting guests. Someone with more authority wanted them alive for some purpose. Serenity believed it would be best to escape before they found out what that purpose was.

The current guards on duty were taking glances at them. The way one of the man's eyes lingered in a way that made her skin crawl, especially the way they slid over Rielle. Yeah, they needed to get away sooner rather than later. They needed the right moment and the perfect distraction. The other guard returned with a small sack. He reached in and pulled out pieces of bread, which he coldly tossed onto the ground. The other prisoners descended on the food, quickly fighting over the scraps. Only one landed near Serenity and Rielle, which she picked up before a male captive could snatch it. She split it in half and gave a piece to Rielle. It was tough, overbaked and hints of dirt tainted the taste, but she scarfed it down regardless. She couldn't afford to get weak, not now. Rielle discreetly handed her something. Serenity looked and saw one of her antibiotics. That must have been one of the things she had taken from their packs before their capture. She was grateful. She had not even thought about it in the moment. She ate it with a piece of bread and forced it down with some difficulty. The guards began speaking to one another.

"It'll take another three weeks to make it back," one said.

"Even longer with these pests," said the other.

"If we show up empty-handed, the king will have us demoted or worse. Remember the decree. No less than twenty. We can only hope we find more on the way," the guard continued.

'Katsuo,' Serenity thought to herself. Were they going to take them directly to the invader? She listened, hoping they would drop a clue to where he was so she could give the information to Kang-Dae when she found him. Unfortunately, they offered no such knowledge. The men went off on more personal conversations – the one with the creepy stare was complaining of an itchy, swollen foot for days. Serenity tuned them out and looked to Rielle, who was barely eating her bread and was looking at her expectantly. Serenity shook her head, letting her know she hadn't heard anything worthwhile.

"They're going to move us soon," she whispered.

Rielle let out a defeated breath. She took hold of her hand and squeezed silently, letting her know they would not be stuck here.

# CHAPTER 18

Kang-Dae walked the defensive line his men made at the road. In such a short amount of time, they had done well. The ditches and barricades looked cheap but sturdy. Scouts reported the troop was less than two days away.

"We have to be sure we have all the defenses covered," he announced to the men around.

"Yes, my king," they responded.

"We need at least half a day to complete the barricade around the village," Sun came up to report. Kang-Dae nodded.

"Get it done." Kang-Dae ignored the sneer on the man's face.

"How do we replenish the supplies once we're done here if we are to go on to Piang?" Yu asked, masking his frustration poorly.

"Once we meet up with Park's men, they'll be able to help," Kang-Dae responded, not up to dealing with Yu's cynicism at the moment.

"These people won't thank you for this. They made it clear they do not care for anything we're doing for them," Yu ranted.

"I'm not doing this for thanks," Kang-Dae gritted.

"Then why risk ourselves, our mission, for this?"

"It is our duty! It's what we are meant to do. You always saw this position as a means to your end!" shouted Kang-Dae.

"And what is it to you?" Yu challenged.

"A duty – a charge to do what's best for everyone under our care. Not some, or the rich, or those who can do for us. It was never about us. We are here for them," he finished, eyes blazing, standing at full height and towering over the smaller man. Yu had a flicker of intimidation, but it disappeared quickly.

"Then how do you justify your decision to abandon them for your own personal wants?" Retorted Yu, staring him straight in the eyes.

The statement quickly stifled Kang-Dae's anger. The longer he contemplated the words, the less anger he felt. Feeling his point was made, Yu walked off, leaving Kang-Dae with his inner struggle. Kahil was suddenly by him, breaking him from his thoughts.

"The leaders are waiting to see you," he reported. He must have noticed the disturbed look on Kang-Dae's face. "My king?" He questioned.

"I'm coming," he told him, forcing himself to snap out of it. Kahil led way, and he was once again in front of the same angry man, only now, Kang-Dae was looking at their anger in a different light.

"We have asked you to leave, yet you refuse, and now you tear up our lands for your war," the man huffed.

Kahil began to explain, but Kang-Dae cut him off. "I apologize." The words caused not only the leaders to look at him, but his men as well. "I should not have done so without your permission."

The men looked as if they had no idea how to handle this admittance of guilt.

"I understand how you see us as interfering with your lives, your home. Your feelings about those in charge are not without merit. You are victims of those in charge's unwise decisions. This should not have happened. The king should not have allowed it. You are right to be upset. But this isn't about us throwing our weight around or trying to make up for what was done. It is doing what we should have been doing in the first place. Protecting the people. Giving you all your best chance to live," Kang-Dae spoke vehemently.

The two men looked at one another. They even looked to Kahil, trying to get the assurance to see if he was truly being sincere. Kang-Dae bowed in respect. One man sputtered while the other stared wide-eyed. The first man turned and stomped off with the other slowly going after him. His men were looking at him mystified.

"Is the work done?" He asked suddenly. The men rang out in a chorus of 'no's. "So, get to it!" He ordered, and they were off.

# CHAPTER 19

Serenity and Rielle fell over in exhaustion once they were allowed to stop for the night. They had been traveling all day on little food and whatever breaks the soldiers took for themselves. The journey was filled with nonstop work for them and the other captives, as they had been put to work preparing and serving meals, serving water, and cleaning any clothing or weaponry they were given under watchful eyes. Not only that, but it was clear she and Rielle were getting forced to do more work than the others. At first, she chalked it up to good ole racism, but the way they repeatedly called them "Assani dogs" had her thinking there was more to the men's disdain. Serenity knew very little about the country across the sea, only that it was inhabited by people who shared her skin tone. In Xian, she'd gotten flack for being a foreigner, but it had never seemed country specific until now.

Serenity's feet were killing her. She longed for the padded sneakers she had before Rielle tossed them away. She knew it was for the best. The last thing they needed was to draw even more attention to themselves for having strange things. While the slip-ons she had were plain enough to pass for the land's apparel, she couldn't imagine making this trek in the flimsy flats the other captives were forced to endure in. Rielle had gone into her hair in what looked like a simple attempt to straighten the locs, but Serenity knew better. She was soon proved right when Rielle slipped her another one of her pills. Serenity didn't know when she had done it, but at some point, she'd hidden more than a few items in the mass of hair. 'A trick from the ancestors,' she told Serenity. Serenity discreetly swallowed the pill as the soldiers looked elsewhere. Once again, they were given a piece of bread and a cup of water each. She ate slowly, hoping that taking her time would trick her brain into thinking she was eating more than she did.

A soldier came and forced two of the men up, demanding they go gather wood for the fires. The already weak men struggled to stand and were pushed in the direction of the trees. Serenity winced when one was pushed hard enough to fall face first into the ground. Without offering any assistance, the man ordered him to stand while kicking at him. Serenity had to turn away from the scene. When she did, she saw the guard from before once again staring at Rielle. She tried her best to keep Rielle from him, offering to be the one to give him water and walking in front of her to keep her from his view. She didn't know if Rielle could tell what she was doing or if she even noticed the man's stares, but she hoped that she didn't. She didn't want to burden her with that knowledge on top of everything.

"Hey you, come help me take off my armor," he directed at Rielle.

Not knowing what he was saying or that he was speaking to her, she didn't even look up. Serenity saw his nostrils flare at the supposed disrespect.

She quickly stood up and said, "She's tired and can barely walk right now." The man sneered at her.

"I wasn't speaking to you. Hey!" He shouted again at Rielle. By now, Rielle had picked up on the conversation and was looking intently between the two. "Get over here," he ordered her.

Still not understanding him, Rielle didn't move. He moved toward them, probably meaning to snatch her up. Rielle scooted back as Serenity got between them.

"How long will you keep that gold hidden in your satchel?" She asked suddenly, but quietly enough for him to hear and no one else. The man froze. "Does your captain still not know about it? What about the other men?" He quickly began turning red.

"You-"

"You may want to find a better place to put it. He's going to start checking tents soon."

"How-"

"Raizo! Over here!" A soldier called out. The man stared down at Serenity with animosity in his eyes, then turned and walked away. Serenity released a breath.

"What just happened?" Rielle asked worriedly, which made Serenity's heart clench.

"It's okay. He'll leave you alone for now."

"What'd you tell him?" She asked.

"I basically let him know I know he's stealing gold and valuables from the places and people they've been raiding and not sharing with his boss."

"Did you dream that?"

Serenity smiled. "No. Elham told me he took some from her and a couple others when no one was looking."

"Elham?" Questioned Rielle. Serenity pointed to the older woman with her teen daughter.

"We had to clean buckets together. We had a little time to chat," she revealed, and Rielle grinned.

"I don't want to wait any longer. We need to go. During dinner is the best time, less guards, men drinking. It's our best chance," Serenity reasoned.

Rielle nodded. "That's usually when the one with the scar is on duty. He is starting to limp more, you notice?"

Serenity nodded and relayed what she'd heard him say to his fellow guard about his foot.

Rielle raised her brow. "Sounds like gangrene."

"Really?"

"If no one treats it, he'll be dead in less than a couple of weeks."

Serenity filed that information away just in case it came in handy and the two proceeded to plan out their escape.

# CHAPTER 20

The scouts returned, shouting about approaching enemies. The men moved to get to their assigned positions. Kang-Dae was in the tree line with the other bowman lying in wait. They had hoped some reinforcements would arrive in time, but they hadn't. Still, they would pursue victory without them. A rustling behind them had all the men turning and prepared to fire, only for Kang-Dae to yell out "Hold!" once he saw who it was. One of the village leaders had arrived along with other male villagers, armed with their own weapons.

"We cannot in good conscience allow you to fight and die for us alone," the man said.

"Sir-" Kang-Dae began.

"You do your duty, and we'll do ours. My brother is already evacuating the rest away from here with some of your men. We must buy them time."

Kang-Dae felt more respect for the adversative leader and nodded his approval. The man took up with them and they went back to watching for the enemy. The riders were the first to arrive on the road, a gang of at least a hundred marching behind. Kang-Dae would wager there were more coming through the woods as well. Kahil interacted with the Captain and leader of the troop on the road from behind the barricade.

"If you wish to continue, I tell you now: it's only hell that you will get," Kahil warned confidently. The captain chortled.

"I've heard this before from the last Xianian dogs we put down. You're a proud bunch, that much is true," he spoke. "If it's death you seek, we will oblige."

Kahil removed his sword and pointed it forward. "Take them!"

"Now!" Kang-Dae screamed as he and his men let an onslaught of arrows out on all of them.

More than a few went down instantly, while some attempted to shield themselves and their superiors. Shouts came from beyond the trees as more enemy soldiers came into their sight line.

"Archers!" Kang-Dae shouted, ordering them to take aim.

On the ground level, Kahil and his men held back the surviving men, not allowing any to pass the barricades. The men who made it past the arrows quickly engaged with them. Kang-Dae took two more out with his crossbow before pulling out his sword and slashing at the legs of a charging soldier while blocking the blade of the soldier following the now crippled man. Seeing another coming for him, he changed his position, making the attacker change his, which, unfortunately for the attacker, put him in the direct path of Kang-Dae's oncoming blade. By the time the man realized he erred, Kang-Dae had stabbed him through the chest, dealing a killing blow. On the other side of him, Kang-Dae saw the villagers struggle to keep up with the seasoned soldiers, but they were determined. He went over to lessen their load, pulling an enemy away and taking him out with a slash across the chest. He dispatched two more the same way, giving the men the edge they needed to overcome their opponents. The men panted as they attempted to catch their breath, but the enemy didn't give respite and continued to attack. Kang-Dae and his men were quickly able to take them on.

Hands full with the enemy, he couldn't keep an eye on the villagers as he put more men down. He slammed one soldier's head into a tree. He could feel the crunch of bones breaking beneath his hold as released the man's neck before almost fully bisecting him with his long blade. The enemy's numbers dwindled. It wasn't much longer that only a few were left and they began to try and flee. Kang-Dae sent his archers after them, making sure none of them made it. His men in the villages shouted in triumph. Kang-Dae smiled. The victory felt good after so long. He had the men sweep for any survivors and begin to clear out the evidence of their victory, gaining spoils and much-needed morale.

# CHAPTER 21

It was dinnertime at the newly settled camp. Elham and her daughter were serving the broth to the growing line. While Serenity had been assigned to wash clothes near where they kept the prisoners, Rielle was on the other side of the camp with another couple of captives gathering more wood for the campfires. Tonight, was the night. They'd gone as far north as Serenity was comfortable with.

She got up under the pretense of getting more clothes from the pile. In her hand, which she hid, she carried a lit match that she'd struck before standing. Not looking up from the pile she tossed the match under the carriage, while the men were occupied with food and conversation. It hit its mark, catching the grass by the wheel. Serenity went back to her seat, continued washing, and waited. It wasn't noticed for a while. The small flames barely reached three inches at first. The woman opposite of her noticed and her eyes widened, but Serenity shook her head, warning the woman not to speak yet. Seeming to understand, she nervously went back to her task, singularly focused on the shirt in her hands.

"Look!" A man shouted. Instead of men hurrying over to the now foot high fire Serenity caused, they were rushing over to the other side of the camp where black smoke was rapidly rising. One of the men came to snatch the bucket of water Serenity and the woman had been using, but stopped short at the sight of the carriage that had now become inflamed. He let out a shout of alarm and threw the water on the carriage with a shout, in a feeble attempt to stop the blaze. When the fire only blazed brighter, he screamed in fear, falling backwards. Serenity kept from smiling, knowing the wine she accidentally knocked into the water had done its job. By now, another team of men came over to try and combat the fire. Serenity looked at the woman and quietly told her to run. Serenity crept away without hesitation, while the woman did the same. Serenity backed away slowly and snuck behind one of the tents. Once she was out of sight, she took off running. After running about a quarter mile, she came to the road. Instead of continuing, she whistled a tune to a familiar song her and Rielle loved when they were in college. The returning whistle finishing the song was heard from across the road. Smiling, she ran toward it and hugged Rielle as soon as she saw her. Not wasting any more time, the two took off south through the woods. The possible traps were still a concern, but they opted to take their chances. They traveled a good distance from one another just in case one was unlucky enough to fall into a trap, the other could help them out. A female scream echoed in the night sky and both women froze. The soldiers must have noticed their prizes were gone and were getting them back. They sped up their movements, trying to put as much distance between them and the soldiers as possible.

Rielle ran as fast as her feet would allow. She knew if she were retaken it would not be good for her, especially knowing that disgusting guard and his leering gaze were waiting for her. It was why her match's target had been his bag and tunic. He carelessly left it against his wineskin. Once the flames sprouted, that was all she wrote.

Something caught her foot, sending her crashing to the ground hard with a startled cry. For a moment, she thought she'd been caught in a trap. In her fear, she began to cry, but there was no following pull of a trap. She looked back and saw she had only tripped on a large root. Massively relieved, she almost laughed herself silly until the pain in her ankle began. She carefully pulled herself up into a sitting position. She looked at the offending foot. Seeing no outside damage, she tried moving it around. She could move it but there was some pain.

"Are you okay?" Serenity asked, making her way over. Rielle nodded.

"It's not broken. Just a sprain." Minor though it may be, both women knew it was a huge setback at the moment. Serenity looked up and blanched. Before Rielle could look as well, Serenity was helping her up. Serenity quickly looked around and saw that the tree Rielle had tripped on was massive and had a narrow but deep gash in the center. She checked it and saw it was a tight squeeze but not enough room for both of them. Serenity started shoving her into the hole.

"Wha-." Rielle started, but Serenity pushed her fingers to her lips to keep her quiet. The glimpse of the soldier walking across the way told her they could be found at any moment.

She continued pushing her in and whispered, "Stay down, wait a day until they're gone."

"Ser-" she began again, but Serenity cut her off.

"They won't spend longer than that searching. When you leave, head that way," she told her, pointing south. "Keep the road on your left and you'll make it to the capital. Find the first Xian soldier you can. Tell them you have a message for General Jung-Soo. Tell them it's about Katsuo.

Once you see him, tell him who you are and what happened."

"Serenity, no, get in," Rielle pleaded, eyes shining with tears. Serenity shook her head.

"Remember, General Jung-Soo," said Serenity. Rielle tried to pull her in but Serenity pulled back.

"Say it," she demanded once more.

"General Jung-Soo," Rielle cried softly.

Serenity kissed her head and took off away from her, hoping to lead the surrounding soldiers away. Her intention wasn't to get caught, but to at least get them away from Rielle. But she knew being caught was a real possibility. As far as Serenity was concerned, it would be better that she be taken back alone than with Rielle. She didn't know the language or the customs. If they deemed her useless, she didn't want them opting to use her in other ways. Besides, she was only in this land for Serenity. Serenity would keep her safe no matter what.

# CHAPTER 22

Rielle cried silently in the suffocating tree she'd been left in, with nothing but the sound of the night to comfort her. The pain in her foot was forgotten, only replaced by the hole in her heart and the knot in her belly out of fear for Serenity. She wanted to go after her. If she were caught, she wanted to be with her, but her fear and Serenity's words stopped her. She may be able to save her friend better by following her instructions. If Kang-Dae knew she was here and in enemy hands, he'd move heaven and earth to get her back. Telling this Jung-Soo person about Serenity would lead her to Kang-Dae, Rielle surmised. She repeated Serenity's words in her head over and over, imprinting them in her mind, as well as praying they would not be the last words she heard from her friend.

Somehow, as impossible as she would have deemed it, she fell asleep against the tree, and morning light hit her. It was still quiet. She couldn't see anything from her hole. She was stiff, itchy, fatigued, and probably had more than a dozen ant bites on her arms and legs, but she did not vacate the tree. She continued to wait, not only to follow Serenity's instructions but in a hopeful attempt to see if she would return.

Serenity made it half a mile away from where she left Rielle before the rushing feet of multiple soldiers came behind her. Her feet were aching, her legs wobbly, her chest was burning, and her eyes were blurred. Once she slowed, it was over, and she collapsed to the ground, unable to go any further. The men were on her instantly. She was hauled up and dragged back to the still semi-burning camp. She was tossed onto the ground atop the woman who she told to run. Her eyes were swollen shut and she was quietly sobbing. Serenity was dismayed to see more than half of the captives had been recaptured, but she found comfort in not seeing Rielle among them. The general came up to them, face red screwed up in anger.

"Is this all of them?" He asked the men. It appeared none of them wanted to speak up, but when his angry eyes moved to them, the hesitant shake of their heads was all they did to answer him. "How many?"

"We lost six, General," the only one brave enough to speak answered.

The general let out something akin to a snarl. His eyes turned back to the captives. Serenity's heart pounded as his eyes roamed over each of them. She felt her anxiety spike when he paused on her for longer than a second. His gaze shifted to the older woman who was clutching her son to her. He pointed at them.

"Bring her," he ordered the man.

Serenity and the others cried out in protest, pleading for her to be left alone, but they were ignored. The boy cried and pleaded for his mother as she was ripped from him and brought before the general. The general took out his sword. The boy's screams were unbearable. The woman sobbed and pleaded for mercy, then began begging the others to look out for her son. Serenity moved before she could think to stop. Her body covered the woman, shielding her. She heard the general demanding she move, but she didn't. When he ordered his men to move her, she was suddenly covered herself. First by one person, then multiple. She could hear the general screaming, and she felt the soldiers attempting to pull them away, but their determination must have transferred to physical strength because they could not be moved.

"I'll have you all killed!" The general threatened. The sound of a sword unsheathing hit her ears.

"We don't have the time to find more, Sir," one reasonable voice rang out.

Serenity continued clutching the woman, praying for all of them. The general released a string of curses. Serenity then heard him put away his sword and the sound of receding footsteps.

"Up, now!" A voice commanded.

They finally released one another slowly to ensure the danger had passed. They were ushered as a group back to their containment area. Walking back, Serenity caught sight of the general reprimanding the two on-duty guards.

"We'll have to move out sooner now; our position is exposed," he finished.

"What about waiting for that group of Xian soldiers?" One inquired.

"It's too risky now. I'll have to let the king know about it when we arrive." Serenity was pushed forward, cutting off the conversation.

Rielle walked through the trees, careful of her foot. She spent another night in that tree before finally moving on. It was the hardest truth when she realized Serenity would not return. She quickly spun her grief into action and started her journey south. The last few days felt like a bad dream she couldn't escape. Not only was she in this dangerous foreign land, she was now alone and had no way of knowing if her best friend was alive. Rielle also didn't know if she would even succeed in her mission. She couldn't be one hundred percent sure she was going the right way. The chances of her finding the right people were impossibly low. One of her locs fell over her eye, so she moved it back in place when something fell out of it onto the ground. She bent down to pick it up and her heart stopped. The tiny pill in her hand turned all her worry and anxiety into overwhelming dread. Serenity was not only back in captivity, but she also no longer had her antibiotics.

Immediately, she began to figure out how long it would be before the poison started to rage in her blood once more. It had taken over two weeks before she ended up in the hospital. They had already been a week from the capital before they'd been marched in the opposite direction for several days. Even if she traveled day and night, by the time she made it there and convinced someone to go after Serenity, it would be too late. No, she couldn't leave her, not now. She had to go back. Maybe she could get her away. The worst thing that could happen was that she'd be recaptured, but she'd be able to take care of Serenity if her health began to fail. She apologized to Serenity in her head for going against her wishes and turned around. She doubted they'd made it too far.

Rielle heard the sound of water and was reminded she hadn't had anything to eat or drink in a while. She took a glance toward the road before heading toward the sound. It took her about 10 minutes to locate the small strain. She cupped her hands in the cold water and drank her fill. She hadn't realized how thirsty she'd been until she started drinking. Even in med school when she was struggling every day, she'd never been this hungry or thirsty. 'All that struggle just to give up,' she thought bitterly. Her decision to drop out of med school in her final year always haunted her. She knew it wasn't smart. Rielle had worked so hard to get in, finishing her Bachelor's in 3 years just to get ahead. She'd taken dual courses in high school, and even took summer and night classes. Serenity had begged her not to give up all she worked for just for that man, but she was too in love to listen, and he needed her. At least that was what he told her. Just thinking of Darrel made her seethe, but she had no one to blame but herself. She let him convince her to take a break for their relationship and go back later once he was stable. That break turned into two years. It took two break-ups and an affair before she finally left him. So broken from that hurt, she clung to the first thing that made her feel better, which is how she ended up in a relationship with a man she barely liked. She had used Serenity as an excuse to finally break away from Marcus. If she were honest with herself, she knew the only reason she was not throwing herself back into another relationship was because she had been hyper-focused on Serenity. When she watched Serenity and Kang-Dae, knowing what they'd risk to be with one another, it made her rethink what she wanted in a relationship.

Thirst satiated, she sat for a minute or two, wondering if there were fish in the stream so she could satisfy her hunger as well. She peeked in the water hoping to see something, anything swimming by. She saw a ripple ahead of her and went to see. She got a quick glimpse of something red going by.

Not wanting it to get away, she followed it upstream. Pulling her scarf from her head, she thought she might be able to catch it if she could just get in front of it. She followed it for a couple of meters before it began to slow. She was about to make her move when another ripple sent the fish driving back the other way. Rielle frowned as she watched her potential meal go off. She started to look back in the water to see if she saw another fish, when what looked like a cup came floating in her eye line. Curious, she pulled it out of the water to examine it. Suddenly, she saw movement in her periphery. She looked over and stopped breathing. Three men in armor were staring at her.

# CHAPTER 23

Kang-Dae and his men helped load up what resources the villagers had, along with what he'd rendered his men to give them, along with a few horses they could spare. Now that the battle was over, he was able to send a small troop to safely escort the rest of the villagers to a safer location.

"Thank you general," the leader said to him once more. Smiling, Kang-Dae accepted his thanks. "We know you are one of the ones who care, and we'll remember this."

Kang-Dae didn't respond, allowing them to think he was just another soldier. His decision had not been about changing their opinion of him, so he would not mention it.

"The men from Yario have arrived," Kahil announced while walking up.

"Good," said Kang-Dae.

The men were pulling up on horseback. Their captain was the only one to dismount and come towards him. He immediately bowed and greeted Kang-Dae.

"Sorry we were too late, my king," he said remorsefully. Kang-Dae made him rise.

"It is not your fault. We all had our hands full," he told him.

The man looked relieved. His brows furrowed as he looked beyond Kang-Dae. Kang-Dae turned to see the village leader and several villagers gawking. 'The secret is out,' he thought to himself.

"My apologies for the deceit, but out here, I am just another soldier," he said. The men rushed to bow and Kang-Dae stopped them.

"It is alright. You can go in peace," he assured them. The leader continued to stare in disbelief.

"You fought beside us," he spoke, more to himself than to Kang-Dae.

"I didn't do anything more than I am charged to do as my title demands."

"What- what I said…" he began to sputter, obviously worried about the consequences of his badmouthing the king to his face.

"What you said were words of a worried and frustrated leader. Nothing more," Kang-Dae cut him off.

The man appeared relieved. But for a moment, he looked as though he wanted to say more but seemed to think better of it. He bowed and went off with his people.

"My king, our men ran into a messenger of general Jung-Soo. He's here with us." The general spoke, motioning to the young man.

"Come forward," Kang-Dae called out to him. The messenger came forward and dropped to his knee.

"My king, General Jung-Soo has obtained Katsuo's location. He's on his way as we speak."

"They went on their own?" Kahil questioned incredulously.

Kang-Dae understood. If Jung-Soo could not succeed, he wanted the information to get to Kang-Dae so they could still have a chance.

"How long will it take us to meet them there?" He asked the messenger.

"At least a fortnight," he responded.

"Let's prepare to move out," Kang-Dae ordered.

"Yes, my king!" the men shouted.

# CHAPTER 24

Rielle kept struggling against the men dragging her toward the tent. At the stream, she'd immediately tried to run from them, but with her foot, she didn't get far. They didn't look like any of the soldiers from before, which meant she'd been captured by another group of Katsuo's men, which really sucked. As soon as she was pushed into the tent, she was forced to her knees roughly. She imagined the roughness was payback for the kick she'd given the man between the legs when he first put his hands on her. The man said something to her in Xian with a smug smile. Of course, she had no idea what he said but jumped to the obvious conclusion it was not good for her. The smug soldier left her along with the other two. She kneeled in silence, stomach in knots, not knowing what to expect. This troop seemed a bit smaller than the previous one from what she saw. Maybe she could escape once more. She still had the matches on her and, thanks to one irresponsible soldier, a stolen hidden knife by her inner thigh.

After a few minutes, the soldier returned with someone else. This soldier was slightly bigger but just as tall. However, the way he carried himself made her think he was in charge. He had armor like the others, except the sword on his side was much flashier than any of the others she'd seen. As soon as he looked at her, his eyes widened just enough for her to notice before turning to normal.

'Was that recognition?' Rielle dismissed the thought. He didn't know her; he couldn't, and she sure as hell didn't know him. He spoke to her, probably asking who she was or something to that effect. She didn't respond. It wouldn't do her any good, anyway. Maybe playing dumb would make them let their guard down. He repeated his question, and she stayed silent. Giving a slight tilt of his head, he opened his mouth again to speak.

"Who are you?"

The surprise at hearing English had her flabbergasted, and her jaw opened before she could stop it. Trying to save face, she closed her mouth and looked at the guard with her best blank expression to pretend that she had not understood, but she knew she'd given herself away. He said something else in Xianian and the other men exited the tent, leaving the two alone and Rielle on edge. She thought about the knife, wondering if it would be her only hope now.

Jung-Soo stared down at the woman his men captured, claiming her to be a servant or a spy of Katsuo. She must have figured out they were not true Katsuo soldiers because she immediately tried to flee, perhaps to go report back to her masters. When he entered the tent, he was immediately taken back by her appearance. The hue of her skin had reminded him of Serenity. Only this woman was a shade darker. Her hair was also unlike Serenity's, bound together like ropes wrapped up into a ball atop her head. But something about the texture of it also reminded him of Serenity. However, that was where the physical similarities ended. She was taller and thinner. Her eyes were not round, but almond-shaped. When he questioned her in his language and she stared back blankly, a small sense of deja vu filled him. It hit him suddenly. The idea seemed ridiculous at first, but he figured it couldn't hurt. He didn't know what to expect, but he was surprised when the woman showed reconnection at the old tongue. She understood it, he knew that. It didn't make sense for a spy not to speak the language of those she chose to spy on. But she could also just be a servant who lost her way or became separated from her people, which could make her useful.

He watched her carefully, trying to determine the best course of action. He knew his men wanted to give her over to Yue-Hua. Jung-Soo didn't think he was comfortable subjecting her to him just yet, at least not until he knew her motives for sure.

"Where did you come from?"

She didn't look at him, but he could tell she was purposely avoiding looking at him. He bent down to her level. She shied away from him, trying to make herself small. He noticed a mark on her shoulder that looked like writing. He moved to pull her shirt out of the way to get a better view. In hindsight, he realized this wasn't the smartest move and could easily have been misconstrued. The prisoner suddenly shoved at him hard, and he felt a sharp pain in his shoulder. While he looked down at the dagger protruding out of his flesh, the woman sprinted towards the exit. Unfortunately for her, he was still faster. His injury did not slow him the way she may have hoped, and he captured her by her waist as she screamed and fought, trying to hit him but unable to. More of his men came at the sound of the chaos and took her back into the tent. Tae-Soo looked at Jung-Soo's injury and called for their healer. Jung-Soo's focus was on the woman still screaming in that tent, probably giving his men as much trouble as she'd given him.

# CHAPTER 25

*Serenity was playing chess alone. The pieces on the board were strategically placed. She moved the purple piece ahead a spot. On the other side, the green piece moved automatically. She switched spots, now playing for the opponent's side. She moved a piece, causing a purple piece to move as well. Thousands of people were watching her from the stands, waiting anxiously for the end of the match to see who would be victorious. The purple king stayed at its position despite the oncoming green pieces. From Serenity's position, she knew she had the advantage and power to either give the green side victory or help out the purple. A hand appeared on the side of her, displaying a gold ring. She slowly looked up.*

"Up! All of you. Let's go!"

Serenity's eyes shot open. The sliver of sunlight made her close them again, but she began moving nonetheless, knowing if she didn't, she'd be kicked or worse. She gradually began to sit up when a hand appeared in front of her eyes. She looked up thoughtfully at Elhaim before putting her hand in hers and allowing herself to be pulled up. It had been two days since she'd been recaptured. They'd been traveling almost nonstop since. She was handed a piece of bread that the woman saved for her, as she must have slept through breakfast. Serenity thanked her sincerely before taking a bite. One of the other women, the one with the son, handed her a small cup of water. Serenity now knew her name was Il-Nam and her son was Pyeong. The others had become more open with her after the failed escape. Despite being recaptured, the others seemed to trust her. Perhaps they were hoping she would be the one to get them free. It made her feel anxious, and slightly guilty, because she had no idea how she could do that, and she was now terrified of not only disappointing them but getting them killed. To give them an edge, she gave them all the simple instructions which were: Listen; pay attention to any and all conversations between soldiers; and share anything that might be important.

"Move!"

Serenity was shoved hard enough to stumble. Luckily, both Il-Nam and her son were there to steady her. She stared back at the creepy guard from before, who obviously blamed her for the escape and probably the loss of his target, Rielle. His watch partner walked beside him. The way he stood, keeping his weight off the left foot, reminded Serenity of Rielle's grim prognosis. They were walking past him when he grabbed her by the hair. The pain made her cry out.

"I will enjoy watching you break when we arrive," he sneered in her ear.

"That's enough," the other guard warned.

Serenity was given relief when he released her, and she regained her composure. She turned to look him right in his eyes.

"You will not make it back," she said without emotion.

The man scoffed at first, but she held her gaze unblinking, conveying her belief in the statement. "Before the next full moon, you will fall before your brethren, and not one tear will be shed." She continued, seeing the scene flashing in her mind.

By now, the area around them was silent and they had several onlookers. The guard was no longer smirking. His angry stare slowly fell, and there was uncertainty and genuine fear in his eyes. Not giving him any clarity, she turned and walked on with the others following behind her.

# CHAPTER 26

Kang-Dae and his men were about to start their journey north. According to Jung-Soo's messenger, they had moved on a week ago. Kang-Dae had not gotten another word from Jung-Soo, so they would go on as planned. The village had been completely evacuated, with the exception of a few able-bodied men. They had volunteered to fight with him, not having any family and wanting to do their part in saving their country. Kang-Dae tried to deter them, but they would not change their minds. He put them in the care of Captain Li, who managed the rear lines, hoping to keep them as far from danger as possible.

"What route do you recommend?" He asked the newly arrived general.

"We barely made it through Sana. They would have reinforced it by now, so avoiding it would be best," he began. "Our scouts report few enemy sightings by Galie, but with Silou being destroyed, it's a risk."

Kang-Dae's head shot up. The lake with the gateway to Serenity's world came to mind.

"Destroyed? What about the villages?" He asked worriedly.

"From what they saw, there's no one left there. Whether they fled or were taken, it's overrun with enemy forces." Kang-Dae wanted to curse. If the village had truly been taken, then his only path to Serenity would be lost to him.

"My king, shall we go back and take it?" The general asked, sensing his king's distress.

Kang-Dae wanted to lead them all there right now – take it back while it was still possible with the number of men he had. But was that a move for the people or for himself?

Kang-Dae forced his answer out. "No. We do not have the time," he reasoned with the man and with himself.

The best thing for Xian and Serenity would be to win this war. Once they did, the land would be safe, and he would be able to bring her back to a peaceful Xian.

*Serenity's mother and sister-in-law laughed at Levi's shouting as he ran in fear with Serenity chasing after him in her white gown.*

*"Quit playing, quit playing," he kept repeating. "Mama!" He shrieked when she looked to be gaining on him.*

*He'd been on the run since he dared to shove a piece of cake in her face, claiming Kang-Dae had not done it right and offering to remedy it for him. Now, he was trying to dodge an irate Serenity who had a handful of cake in her hand as she chased after him.*

*"I can't help you!" Her mother shouted back with a laugh. Their father was chuckling beside him.*

*"Y'all get him!" Serenity ordered her nephews.*

*"That's cheating!" Cried, Levi.*

*The boys didn't agree as they began targeting one leg, holding him still. The sinister look on Serenity's face was amusing as she slowly approached her prey.*

*"I'm sorry, OK?" Levi pleaded, eyeing the cake in her hands.*

*"Are you?"*

*"Yes."*

*With a smirk, Kang-Dae watched in anticipation, knowing how it would end. He could honestly say this was one of the more peaceful moments he's had in years, and not just since he arrived. There was no threat of enemy attacks, no one plotting or scheming to grab for power because there was none to take. It was just him and the woman he loved. He understood more at that moment why Serenity fought so hard for this. He wanted her to have it, not just here, but back home as well. He vowed to do so, to make Xian just as safe and peaceful as her home.*

Kang-Dae would fulfill his vow. He just hoped she'd wait for him to do so and wouldn't do anything to put herself in danger.

# CHAPTER 27

The marching had stopped, and they'd been ordered not to move as the conversations in front of the caravan brought some of the rear guards past them to check out the problem. Before long, Serenity didn't have to wonder what was happening as a group of men came by carrying something – no, someone. Two men were holding up the barely conscious guard with the injured foot. He was dripping with sweat and his eyes had dark circles under them. He couldn't even move his feet. They took him toward the back, possibly to the wagons, to lay him down for the rest of the journey. One of the captains walking behind them glanced right at Serenity as he passed. Serenity forced herself not to look away until he was gone. When she did turn away, she noticed he was not the only one staring. Word of her prediction to the guard must have spread throughout the camp, as more than a few were stealing glances at her. She didn't know what made her speak that day, but now she was wondering if it had been a mistake. Would they blame her when he did die? Would they accuse the others? When they did stop for the night, she didn't see the guard or the captain.

Serenity and the others were picking up wood under heavy guard. The soldiers were acting odd, though. None were willing to make eye contact with her. Sorting through wet wood for something dry, Serenity noticed a line of fire root on the tree nearby.

*6 months ago*

*It was nice being outside the palace, Serenity thought to herself as she wandered aimlessly between the trees. She had to practically beg Kang-Dae to bring her out. His overprotectiveness following her war injury had dimmed quite a bit, and this was the ultimate test to prove that. Serenity continued walking about, feeling his eyes on her. She supposed she should be grateful she was able to get this far without him breathing down her neck. They weren't even that far from the palace, less than a mile, but it felt like a country away given how she'd been under such restrictive circumstances as of late. So desperate just to have a little bit of alone time, she told Amoli to stay behind. They'd still brought the guard with them at Kang-Dae's insistence, but they were far enough away that she could pretend that they were alone. She came to a tree so big that even if her arms were three times as long, she couldn't wrap her hands around it. But it wasn't just the size that struck her. All along its base was a thin red vine circling around it all the way up to the top. She'd never seen anything like it. She leaned forward to get a closer look when she tripped on a root and began hurtling toward the trunk face first. Quickly, she put her hand out to keep from smashing into the tree. She straightened up, slightly embarrassed. As she pulled her hand away, her eyes widened and she felt a gasp escape her lips.*

*"What is it?" Kang-Dae asked, suddenly beside her.*

*She didn't answer, too concerned with her hand. The red vine that was on the tree had now latched on to it. She lifted her hand to show him.*

*"Is it poisonous?" She asked fearfully.*

*He looked at her hand and then at the tree. His face was blank, which scared her more.*

*"Come," he said, grabbing her by her other hand and pulling her away from the tree.*

*They walked back towards the road where the horses were waiting. He grabbed his water pouch off the satchel and pulled her back towards the trees. He knelt in the grass and dirt, pulling her down with him. He looked into her eyes; expression grim.*

*"You will need to trust me," he told her.*

*She quickly nodded, her anxiety going up more and more. He began digging at the ground with his dagger, making a small hole before pouring the water from the pouch inside. He stirred up the dirt into mud, then he asked for her hand and she obliged. Using the dagger, he smeared the mud all over the vine and her hand, and like magic, the vine began to release its hold. He pulled the mud off, and the vine came with it. At first, she was relieved and then she frowned.*

*"That's it?" She asked.*

*When she looked at him, she saw he had the most mischievous grin on his face. She suddenly realized she probably had not been in any real danger. She pushed his shoulder.*

*"Really?"*

*He let out a laugh. "It is fire root," he told her. "It grows in this region when it gets warm. It attaches to whatever living thing it can so it can continue to grow."*

*"And it's not dangerous?" She asked to make sure. He shook his head.*

*"No. At most, it would cause some redness, maybe some itching. But it is fairly easy to get rid*

*of. It sprouts from the ground, and it is the ground that remedies it."*

*"Don't scare me like that," she told him with a shove. He just smiled.*

*He turned her hand over and gave it a quick kiss. "My apologies."*

*Ignoring the butterflies in her stomach, she pulled her hand away and stood up.*

*"I think I've had enough of nature for today," she said, going back to the horse.*

Getting an idea, Serenity moved toward the root, acting as if she was picking up more wood. She discreetly stepped on the plant and slid it towards her. She packed it up with her wrapped hand and put it in her pocket. Luckily, the woman saw what she was doing and moved in front of her, keeping Serenity from sight. When they were done, they were taken back to camp and ordered to wash and set out the clothes for the next day. Serenity had the woman hide the piece of the wrapped root within their sleeves and rub it inside various items from shoes to helmets. They even left small pieces of it in them to ensure some would attach to the unsuspecting captors.

"You!"

Serenity froze, fearing the worst. She dropped the shirt and rag she had been using, along with the fire root within it. She stood to face the captain from earlier.

"I have men in my camp that believe you are a sorceress."

Her breath caught and her throat went dry. She didn't say anything, only keeping her head down submissively.

"What did you tell my soldier?" He demanded.

"I don't remember," she lied, trying to sound as meek as she could. He took a step toward her, pointing a dagger in her face. She took a step back.

"Do not lie," he warned. "Did you know he would die?"

She hesitated. Serenity knew if they felt threatened by her, she'd be tossed on the pyre faster than she could blink. She needed to make them think she was not only useful but that she could also still be controlled. She nodded slowly.

"Yes."

"How?" he demanded. "Did you curse him?"

She quickly shook her head. "He cursed himself."

The man's eyes widened, then narrowed.

"You all did when you picked up these people."

He roughly grabbed her by the neck. "What foolishness is this?"

Serenity winced as his grip dug into her skin. "The place you found them, there was a small temple. Your men burned it didn't they?" The man's eyes narrowed, but he didn't answer. "You've angered their ancestors. They will take their vengeance out on you all. The curse will spread to your men as long as you hold them," she continued. His eyes flashed and he threw her to the ground.

"Ridiculous," he sneered. "Keep your wicked tongue silent, or I'll have it removed," he threatened, storming off.

Serenity took a second to calm down before rejoining the others, just trying to breathe evenly. 'Just wait,' she told herself. 'One step at a time.' She got back to work, rubbing the root even more vigorously than before.

# CHAPTER 28

Jung-Soo kicked at the abandoned and spent campfire. Around him were signs of a very empty but obvious camp. From the looks of it, they'd missed them by a day. This group had been moving slowly. They had been tracking them for a few days. This particular group had a consistent pattern, but they suddenly were moving faster. The last camp they came across looked like they hadn't been there but a day. Was there someone else in pursuit of them? They hadn't picked up any signs of anyone else. Maybe they had caught on to them and were trying to shake them off their trail. Jung-Soo wanted to take this group out when it became clear their path was leading to Katsuo. It would have been easier to infiltrate if they were expecting a troop to arrive. One of his men came up to him.

"The tracks on the west road stop after three miles. They've covered them well." He informed Jung-Soo.

Jung-Soo cursed inwardly. They were not far, but going in the wrong direction would cost them time they couldn't afford. Not to mention, if the soldiers knew they were being pursued, they couldn't catch them off guard.

"Maybe that spy will know which way they went," the officer offered.

The thought had crossed Jung-Soo's mind. His wound ached at the thought. Apparently, she had tried to escape two more times since he'd last questioned her. His guards were getting frustrated at having to deal with her. they pleaded with him to give her to Yue-Hua already to make short work of it, but Jung-Soo still couldn't bring himself to do it. For some reason, he didn't want her harmed, despite her violent attack on him.

"I'll ask her myself," he said, prompting his men to block him.

"General, it's not safe," said Tae-Soo. Jung-Soo gave him a look.

"I didn't ask you to go. If you're fearful, stay here."

Tae-Soo quickly stood up straighter.

"She has already hurt you; you want you to be careful," spoke Hae-In.

"I'll be careful," he said, walking past them.

The walk back to their camp wasn't long, but his thoughts played out how he expected this conversation to go. She wasn't afraid to hurt him and she was stubborn. It probably would take painful persuasion to loosen her tongue, but he didn't want to do that yet, and that hesitation worried him. He's done much worse to others, women and men, so why was he so reluctant now? She had even proved to be dangerous to him. Jung-Soo's steps faltered only the tiniest bit as he approached the tent. Pretending it didn't happen, he walked in head high.

The woman in question sat on the ground, hands shackled at the wrist. Her legs were tied as well. As soon as he entered, she stared up at him.

Her anger was apparent, but beyond the anger, he could also see the fear. She was afraid of him. 'Good,' he thought. After what she did to him, she should be. She's lucky he had not returned the favor.

Rielle looked up to see the man she stabbed earlier, unfortunately still alive. The other soldiers didn't scare her as much as this one. They treated her as an inconvenience, never doing more than adding more bindings to her when she misbehaved. This one, though, she didn't know what he'd do. What if he tried to attack her again? She held her restrained hands to her chest, just waiting for him to make a move so she could strangle him. He wore less armor now, but he still carried the same sword. He spoke to her in Xian, and she inwardly rolled her eyes. 'This again?' She thought as she pointedly looked away from him. She knew it was petty and probably not the smartest thing to do. Why antagonize someone who held all the cards? But she couldn't be bothered to care about that. She was too tired, too hungry, too everything. She wished she was home. At this point, she'd take living with

Marcus again over this. Rielle caught the tail end of a question that she realized was English this time. He must have caught on. However, she didn't look his way, instead choosing to pick at the rope around her feet. She had tried loosening them, spending hours and only ending up with blisters and sore fingers.

"They haven't gone far. You came from them; we found you near the latest camp," he continued with his questioning that she hadn't paid attention to.

'Were these men trying to reunite with their fellow soldiers?' She wondered. She wanted to smack him for the audacity. Take her prisoner after she just escaped one captor, only to want her help to return to said captors? This time, she did roll her eyes. But she thought of Serenity still stuck with those men alone without her medication. She was caught either way. Maybe helping them to the others will lead her back to Serenity. That would be better. Maybe if she played nice enough, they'd let their guard down, and she'd be able to get away. Either way, it seemed like the best option.

"Untie me and I'll tell you what I know," she said, surprising him with her voice for the first time.

He looked genuinely surprised she'd given up the silent charade. He looked to consider her offer before moving a dagger from the side, making Rielle's heart stop. He approached slowly, making her attempt to scoot away. But with her limited mobility, all she could do was an awkward scoot back a few inches. He grabbed her feet in hand while she struggled, trying to kick him off to no avail. With a quick slice, the rope fell. Once free, he stood to his feet and stared down at her expectantly. Feeling embarrassed at her initial reaction, she kicked out the remaining line of rope, stretching out her feet. She rubbed at the rope burns with her still burning hands. She stood on wobbly legs, having been stuck to the ground for so long. She raised her hands to his, waiting for him to remove those as well. The insufferable man had the audacity to raise his brow. She tilted her head and glared at him with wide eyes.

"I'm still tied up."

"Considering your past actions I think that's generous enough," he reminded her.

While she logically knew he had a point, it still pissed her off.

"How about this? I tell you where they are, you let me go," she offered. "You won't have to worry about me anymore."

The corner of his lip quipped for a second. It was so quick she thought she had imagined it. Was this jerk laughing at her? She wished she still had her knife so she could wipe that sad excuse of a smile off his face. Just as she finished that thought, he spoke.

"Where are they?"

# CHAPTER 29

Serenity was being dragged into the center of the camp. The other captives looked on fearfully. The general and some of the men stood angrily in front of her. But when she looked at the others, their expression looked more like fear. Judging from the redness in one of their necks, she had a good idea why.

"Whatever dark magic you are doing, remove it," the general demanded. Serenity looked down at the dirt.

"It's not me," she lied. "I already told you. This is not my doing, only your own."

"Lies!"

"You know how to remove it. I told you how what happens to your men is up to you," She told him, playing with her hands.

The man glared down at her. After a few seconds, he finally opened his mouth to say, "What do we have to do?"

"I already told you. You need to let them go. Once you do, I can ask the spirits of their loved ones to accept your offering and hope they give an answer on how to remove the curse."

He gave an order, and his men pulled their weapons on the others who cried and whimpered.

"I can kill them all now if you delay."

"Then you and your men will die," she said quietly but clearly.

She looked him right in the eyes as she spoke, knowing it was up to her to sell her lie. If she didn't, both the captives and Serenity's lives would be in peril. The general grew still, his jaw clenching. He pulled out his sword, pointing it at her throat. She felt her heart pound in her chest and she shut her eyes, waiting for the killing blow.

"If you fail, I'll have you begging for death," he threatened. He ordered his men to drop their weapons.

She heard the men shouting, "Go! Get out of here!" When she reopened her eyes, the sword was gone, and she saw the retreating forms of her fellow captives. Her eyes met with Elhaim, who turned back, apprehension etched across her face. She nodded to the woman, letting her know she should go. The woman nodded back her thanks and caught up with the others. Once they were gone, she was pulled up to her feet.

"Cure them," the general demanded. She asked for water, a bowl, and a crusher. She took dirt from the ground.

"What are you doing?"

"You want to break the curse from this land; I need the land to break it," she told him, impressing herself with the lie.

She poured in the water. She pounded it all into a paste. She called forth the first man. She spoke made-up words, mixing up words they wouldn't understand, including the names of some rappers she knew. She smeared the cool paste

151

directly on his rash. The happy look on the soldier's face let her know the remedy had worked. She gave them all instructions to purify their clothes and items with soap boiled in a "holy" flame using special wood. At that point, she was just making things up at the top of her head, but they were eating it all up. She spent the next hour smearing mud on various soldiers under the general's eye.

"In a few days the curse will fade," she told them.

The men were extremely grateful and thanked her with a bow, which annoyed the general the most. By the time she was done, the men were off, eagerly doing their assigned tasks. The general just walked off without a word, leaving her with only a few guards who no longer looked hateful toward her, but cautious, still not willing to make eye contact. She thought about pushing her luck and demanding her release as well, but already knew he'd never go for it. For now, she took comfort in knowing the others had been released.

# CHAPTER 30

Eight days later, they arrived at the mountains. Some were massive, reaching all the way to the clouds. They squeezed through a very narrow path between two mountains. The path led upward to a steep incline. As they climbed, Serenity felt fatigued but was forced to continue. A couple of the guards helped her along, which she appreciated. One of the side effects of her "power" was some of the troops had begun to treat her with small amounts of decency. They climbed for hours, not stopping even for a few minutes. Serenity's stomach was battling between growling and eating itself, giving her sharp pains that she had no choice but to ignore. When the group came to a stop, she had to keep herself from falling to the ground. There were voices speaking ahead. It sounded like a check-in. Soon, they were moving again. Once Serenity turned toward the mountainside, her eyes widened and she froze. A huge ridge was before her, but it was the sight of the hundreds of people that shocked her.

She had expected to see a sea of tents. Instead, carved into the mountain were layers upon layers of homes and buildings. While there were some tents, it looked like the majority of people were coming in and out of the mountains. It was like a city, only these weren't villagers. They were soldiers – a lot of soldiers. They had suspected that with Katsuo's men in various places, he couldn't have a great number of forces with him. They were wrong. Very wrong. From what she could see, this army alone would be almost a match for Xian, and this was not his full force. Even if Kang-Dae managed to remove the smaller forces, they still had a strong and formidable force left.

She was walked further in. The tents that were there varied from simple to extravagant. There were also quite a few blankets and pallets scattered about, and from the looks of the people on them, it was clear those meager options were for the captors/slaves. She couldn't tell if those captured were all Xian or if any were brought from Katsuo's land. There were no noticeable differences in their clothing or treatment that she could see. It did look as though there were quite a few young people, teens, and kids.

A memory of her conversation with Queen Priya of Kah Mah came to her mind. 'He asked you for something, something precious.' Was it the children? Serenity wondered. Was that the line she'd refused to cross?

"I'll take her." The general's voice shook her from her thoughts.

He motioned for her to follow him, and she obliged. She kept a record of her surroundings, marking possible escape routes if she ever got the chance, but given the number of soldiers around, she didn't like her odds. They walked toward the back of the massive camp. There were fewer people moving about. They came to rows and rows of unmoving guards – not one made a sound or even scratched. They stood straight and still with staffs in hand as the general walked through. Serenity feared one would reach out and grab her, but no one did.

Ahead, she could see the largest tent she'd seen in this land. It was the size of a revival tent, green and black. Two men guarded the entrance. Unlike the others, these men blocked the general from entering.

"I need to speak with him," the general told them.

"He is busy and not to be disturbed," one guard spoke.

"He'll want to know this immediately. If he thinks you or I have kept something so important from him, we will all bear the consequences," The general warned. "I have an Uranaishi."

The word was not one Serenity was familiar with, but it made her nervous.

"He'll want to meet her personally."

Her breath picked up. What had she gotten herself into now? The man looked past the general at her skeptically.

"Are you willing to bet your life on it or ours if you're wrong?" The man asked.

"She's real. I've seen her power."

Serenity wanted to throw up. The guard cast one more look at her. With a sigh, he went inside. The three of them stood outside the tent for a long stretch of time. Serenity called on God to help her survive whatever test she was going to go through. So engaged with her prayer, she jumped when the guard returned.

"Go in," he told them.

The general looked at her. "Keep your head down and don't speak unless spoken to," he ordered.

The warning coming from him made her even more nervous. They entered the tent and Serenity did as she was told, only watching her feet and the ground before her. The ground was covered in soft black fur, not a speck of grass or rock she could see. She stopped only when she saw the general had. Still, she did not look up. Two seconds later, she was forced to her knees.

# CHAPTER 31

Jung-Soo and his men were falling behind. The route the woman gave him appeared to be correct but ineffective, only leading to an empty, burnt-out camp. The troop was moving faster than anticipated. They'd never catch them before they reached their destination. The storm they'd been forced to take shelter from had delayed them. Jung-Soo looked around to see the woman surveying suspiciously with her hands still bound. He had no fewer than three guards on her at all times. He wouldn't trust that she was not plotting her escape constantly. And as sure as he was about her desire to escape, he was that much more unsure of her allegiance. For a spy of Katsuo, she didn't seem very happy to go back to them. Maybe she feared for her brethren, but that wasn't the feeling he got from her. There was a slight disappointment when they failed to find the troop, but there also was a lack of concern, like she didn't care that they would massacre the men once they found them. If that was true, what did she want to get back for? Why had she left them?

Rielle impatiently searched for signs of Serenity but found none. She hadn't expected to. She knew it was ridiculous. She wasn't going to find a note on the ground addressed to her, but she still hoped. She had also hoped that jackass and his men would bring her to Serenity, but it looked like he couldn't even be good for that. Something was off about him, all of them. They didn't act like men trying to return to their buddies. The way they would come to the abandoned camps – it was like they were prepared for a fight. It had her questioning exactly who they were. Serenity was telling her about how the soldiers who'd taken them were trying to lure out an enemy to ambush. They claimed to have lost a number of men. There were even talks of ghosts making them disappear. Were these the ghosts that they had feared? She needed answers. If these were not Katsuo's men, then she may have made a mistake, and they could help her more than she thought. She took a step forward towards the serious one, only to be stopped by one of the guards watching her.

"I need to talk to him," she explained, but they didn't respond. She wondered if they spoke English.

She pointed at the one she wanted. "Him. Talk. Me," she said but it was ignored.

Rolling her eyes, she put her fingers in her mouth and whistled. The sound had all eyes on her, including the one she wanted.

"Hey! I want to talk."

He looked for a minute like he was going to ignore her but seemed to think better of it. 'Good,' she thought. He took his time walking over, which only annoyed her more. Stopping in front of her, he did not speak a word.

"Who are you guys? Who do you fight for?" She demanded.

He remained silent, his expression blank.

"Hello?" She demanded. "I gave you what you wanted. You can answer one question."

The man turned to walk away. Rielle scoffed loudly. At that point, she didn't care if he was team Katsuo or Kang-Dae – he was just an ass. Deciding to take a page out of his book, she decided to test her theory in a different way.

"Do you know General Jung-Soo?"

The question had the desired effect. He froze mid-stride. He turned back and began walking toward her, saying something in Xian. The three guards he had watching her walked off.

"How do you know that name?" He asked.

Rielle didn't answer immediately, needing to be sure before giving anything away. If she was wrong, she couldn't afford to give away any info that would compromise Serenity.

"Do you know who that is?" She asked.

He stared her down. "Who are you? Where did you come from?" He asked.

"Where do you think?" She countered. His jaw clenched and his eyes narrowed.

"Useless," he muttered. The insult stung for some reason.

"Go to hell! I hope Serenity has all of you demoted!" She shouted. Jung-Soo's eyes widened. Realizing she probably said too much, she pressed her lips together.

Jung-Soo wasn't sure he'd heard her right, but her reaction confirmed he had.

"You know Serenity? You have seen her?" He asked.

She looked at him with anger, but weariness as well.

"Answer me!" He demanded, needing to know the truth.

Had this woman been in contact with Serenity? How? She was safe in her world, wasn't she? His eyes went to the mark on her shoulder that he had seen before. He had never gotten to see the whole thing but recalled the letter 'R'. The way she spoke, her attitude, now her connection to Serenity… It couldn't be.

"Rielle?"

# CHAPTER 32

On her knees, Serenity didn't dare look up. She heard the general speak softer than she'd ever heard before. The reverential fear he had for the person he was addressing only made Serenity more nervous. She noticed that the accent was a bit different, almost a different language, but she was still able to keep up. The voices stopped. Her heart beating in her ears blocked her from doing much else other than breathe. Two shoe-covered feet came into her sight. A hand grabbed her chin in a tight grip, forcibly raising her head. She tried to fight against it, unable to resist the urge but was slowly forced to look up. She saw black and green robes first, adorned with gold decals. Unable to hold back any longer, she looked up into dark brown cold eyes. The gold crown on his head told her exactly who she was facing. Katsuo. He looked younger than she expected, probably slightly younger than Kang-Dae. All his hair was pulled up beneath the crown, making his cheekbones very noticeable. His skin was slightly darker, and his chin came to a slight point. He was handsome. Why did that surprise her the most? Had she really been expecting some old, decrepit, obvious villain?

"Pretty," the word passed through his lips with an unsettling purr, showcasing a deep but smooth voice. He finally released her face. Not liking the way he spoke about her, Serenity lowered her head in an attempt to hide her face.

"Where did you find an Assani beauty?" He asked. Though the words were complimentary, they were said in such a tone that it was anything but. The general who was kneeling in front of her spoke without rising.

"Southwest, after we were driven back."

The invader's eyes never left her as the man spoke.

"And she's the reason my orders were not followed?"

Serenity's eyes went back to the ground.

"I thought it best to come back without losing any more men. If not, we wouldn't have been able to return with servants or without," the general made excuses. "It was her magic that forced us into such an offense."

"That's not true," she spoke out, not allowing the man to throw her under the bus to save himself, even if he was technically right. She had a baby to protect. The invader's brows raised at her outburst. She quickly lowered her head once again.

"Is that so?" He asked.

"All I did was save them from the consequences of their actions."

"And my tribute? What of them?"

Serenity chose her next words carefully. Truth mixed with lies would be her best defense.

"I wanted to save them. I saw a chance to do so, so I did. They deserved to be free," she admitted with conviction.

"What of you? What do you deserve?" Katsuo asked, stepping into her space. She fought to hold her ground.

"My general thinks you're a sorceress – a dangerous one," he continued. Serenity swallowed.

"I'm not," she said quietly.

"Then what are you?"

'Seer' was in the back of her mind, but she decided against it. It could expose her true identity. If he found out who she was, she started to think about how he would use her against Kang-Dae.

"I don't know," she lied. "I just see things when I sleep. My people, my village, thought I was cursed."

"What things do you see?"

She hesitated to answer.

"Do you get visions of the future?"

She nodded.

"What about the past?"

167

"Sometimes," she answered.

"Prove it."

Serenity's head shot up.

"What?" She asked without propriety. The invader smirked.

"You claim your vision saved my men. Tell me something, something no one can know."

Serenity fought not to panic.

"I-I- don't-" she stuttered.

"Would you like to go home?"

The question confused her. She expected threats, and physical violence, but not that. The look on his face and her gut told her he didn't mean it. If she proved her power, he'd never let her go, but if she didn't, they would probably kill her for deceiving them and costing them their slaves. Serenity thought back to the dream she'd had right before she'd come to this place. When she woke up, she had no idea what it meant and what she was meant to do with it, but now she realized that maybe God was giving her the means to survive this very moment.

"I dreamt of a child with curly hair."

The amused expression dropped, and his eyes darkened. Despite this, Serenity continued.

"He was alone and crying, reaching out for someone."

He held up a hand to silence her. It was so quiet she could hear the wind outside.

"Iko!" He called out.

A woman came over, dressed in the same clothing as the other slaves she saw.

"Have her cleaned up and set up in General Fichi's tent."

The woman hesitated, looking at the general, but quickly nodded and went to Serenity. Serenity looked to Katsuo, then to the general, and back to Katsuo. The invader was staring at the general, who had yet to get up, but from the way his body was tensed up, she could tell the general was hiding his anger. From the way Katsuo stared, he was waiting for some type of reaction. Serenity didn't bother asking about his word to let her go. She could tell he was waiting on her to do just that, but she refused to give him anything else he wanted. She'd known it was false. She followed behind the woman, leaving the two behind.

The tent she was brought to was about the size of a small bedroom with its own bed and a small table. The woman named Iko left her, promising to return with a basin to wash up and fresh clothes. Serenity didn't care either way, too focused on how she could get herself out of this situation. Was she being set up to be the enemy's seer? Hell no, she wouldn't do that. She didn't care what that man threatened her with. She wouldn't betray Xian or Kang-Dae, even to save herself.

A young teen emerged. His head was wrapped in a grey bandana. He carried a large basin of water with a washcloth hanging off the side. The teen placed the basin on the small table in the center.

"Hello," she said in Xian, testing the waters with the newcomer.

The teen didn't respond and only continued setting things out for her to wash with.

"How long have you been here?" She asked.

"I do not recall."

Serenity felt he was lying, but she didn't blame the boy.

"Where are your parents? Are they here as well?"

The boy quickly rushed out. Serenity worried she scared him off. She remembered a time when she was worried anything she said would cost her. It seems she was once again in the same position. But she knew more this time around and had gotten better with her dreams. That would be a big help in getting out of here. She needed to do so before her time ran out.

# CHAPTER 33

Jung-Soo entered the tent with a bowl of rice and water. It was his version of a peace offering to Rielle. Though she had refused to confirm her identity to him, he knew he was correct in his assumption. Now, he needed to earn the woman's trust to find out what he needed. Rielle sat on the pallet he made for her. He'd had her shackles removed but still had the tent guarded, just in case. He placed the food down in front of her. She only spared it a quick glance before going back to rubbing at her red wrist. He supposed she wanted an apology for her treatment, but that was not something he was going to do. He had every right to take the precautions he took.

"Do you need to see the healer?" Jung-Soo found himself asking despite his thoughts.

She ignored him, grabbed the water, and slowly sipped it.

"How did you get here?" He asked.

She pulled the cup from her lips.

"You put me here, remember?" She responded flippantly.

He was a second away from taking back the food he'd brought.

"Did Serenity send you?"

She ignored him, reaching out to grab the bowl. Having lost his patience, he snatched it up before she could reach it.

"Oh, are you angry because the woman you tied up doesn't want to answer your question? No wonder you guys are losing this war. Stupid soldiers making stupid decisions that everyone else has to pay for," she spat.

"So says the woman who has been captured twice, and that's just by my stupid soldiers."

"If you weren't out here dressed like the enemy, maybe you could have saved yourself from getting stabbed by a stupid old me."

Jung-Soo refused to argue tactics with this woman. She was irrational. Nothing like Serenity.

"She would not send someone like you," he murmured.

That only increased her ire. She closed her eyes like she was trying to calm herself.

"Don't do it, Rielle," she muttered low to herself, but he heard it.

His guess confirmed, he bent down to face her. Doing so seemed to interrupt her bravado. She shrank back.

"Get away from me," she warned.

"Is Serenity still in her world?"

The question seemed to have calmed her enough for her shoulders to ease.

"Who are you?" She demanded.

He thought about it for a moment before deciding to take the risk.

"Jung-Soo."

Surprise came over her face. She looked to be about to say something but stopped herself. She met his gaze.

"How do I know you are who you say you are?" She challenged.

"I could say the same to you," he retorted.

"The only reason I know your name is because Serenity told me. She told me when she first met you, she tried to save Kang-Dae from assassins and had to kick you in the-"

"That's enough. I believe you," he said quickly, not wanting to recall that embarrassing memory.

She gave a half-smile, making her appear softer somehow.

"I guess you're you," she admitted.

"How is Serenity?" He asked now that they were finally in agreement.

Her smile fell away, and the grim look on her face worried him.

"We don't have much time."

# CHAPTER 34

*Hands that were aflame, were stitching a
flag with a stopwatch winding down.*

*A young teen was walking hand in hand with
a little boy with curly hair towards a cliff.*

*A sick older man with half his head missing
was holding onto a scepter for dear life until his
symptoms caused the thing to fall onto the floor and
roll to a young man's feet.*

Dream after dream had plagued her when
she had been able to shut her eyes. With no journal
to keep track of them all, she did her best, repeating
them to herself over and over to burn them in her
memory. They were all short clips of different
scenes with no real plot. She paid special attention
to the details of them all, knowing they were
important.

In her new garments adorned with silver and
teal, Serenity was led back to Katsuo. Tense after a
night of restless sleep. As she entered the tent, she

didn't hide her eyes this time around. She saw the throne in the front with Katsuo lazily draped on it. There were more guards, two on each side up there with him. Another older man with a staff stood by Katsuo. He wore heavier robes and had a long gray beard, but a shaved head. Even from a distance, she could somehow tell he was staring at her with disdain.

"Hello, dream walker," Katsuo greeted.

She didn't know how to respond and settled for a low bow.

"I imagine you had some interesting dreams."

Serenity stared down at her feet, not before answering in a quiet voice, "One or two."

She admitted to them, hoping to feel out his intentions. The invader smiled and stood in front of his seat.

"There is very little entertainment during these trying times; I do find myself getting bored often as I take hold of this country. Sometimes, we must find our own means to keep our spirits up," he said.

Serenity was getting more anxious with every word.

"I thought we could play a game."

Serenity dreaded to think what he found fun.

"What kind of game?" She asked. His smile widened with a childlike glee that chilled her to the bone.

"Bring them in!" He shouted.

Several soldiers entered, herding in three people with their hands bound and all clothes removed except for their pants. They were all adult men, the youngest looking no older than his early twenties. The oldest had longer hair with a swollen eye. The second's body was bruised and hunched as if he couldn't bear to stand straight. The youngest looked down, never lifting his head, and holding his hand to his chest.

"I've had a traitor in my camp for some time," Katsuo spoke. "We know it's one of these men – we're just not sure which."

Serenity could feel her nausea coming on before he even got to the worst part.

"I want you to tell me which one it is. He'll be killed, of course, but it'll keep us from having to execute them all."

He said it so casually that Serenity wanted to call him every vile name she could think of.

"That is your idea of a game?" She gritted out in English, unable to hide her disgust.

The invader's eyes widened a bit, and a dangerous smirk came upon his face.

"As I said, it gets boring here."

Serenity wanted to hyperventilate. What could she do? If she did as asked and was right, she was condemning someone, a possible ally, to death. If she chose wrong, one innocent, albeit enemy soldier would lose their life. She glanced at the invader, who was watching her intently, not paying any of the men any mind. There is no way he didn't know who the traitor was, she realized. This wasn't a game; it was a test. A test of not only her power but of her allegiance. It wouldn't be much of a test if he didn't already know the answer. If she failed, she would lose her life right along with them. She could not save any of these men.

She shut her eyes and thought back on her dreams. She remembered a pair of hands sewing a flag. Not just a regular flag – a Xian flag. The hands completed their task and draped the flag over their chest and heart. As soon as it touched his skin, an arrow pierced it and him. Serenity opened her eyes. She could feel the tears building for what she was going to do but forced them down. She had her answer. Praying for strength and forgiveness, Serenity lifted her finger to the youngest on the left, with the birthmark on his chest, just above his heart. The poor man tried to deny it, screaming his innocence, but the guards hit him in the stomach, forcing him to be silent. Behind her, clapping could be heard. She couldn't bring herself to look.

"Well done," he praised. "Go ahead," he told his men.

To her shock, all three men were run through in front of her.

"They failed to notice their fellow soldier was moving against me. That kind of incompetence can't be allowed," he told her, but Serenity was too focused on the slaughter she just witnessed to even react to the knowledge that the other two had been loyal men.

She felt a tug on her hand as Katsuo raised it to his lips. It took every ounce of strength for her not to snatch it away and slap him.

"You are special indeed," he gushed. "Come, eat with me. You're too entertaining to let go."

# CHAPTER 35

Kang-Dae's men were making good time for their numbers and stops. Kang-Dae made it his mission to have any populated areas they came across evacuated. He wanted to save as many people as could as he and his army moved through the land. As they approached the latest village, they slowed. Black smoke was seen ahead, filling them with ominous dread.

"Si-Jin, Ya-min, with me," he said softly.

The three men in their squadron came with him. They had weapons drawn, preparing for anything. The burnt-out village came into view. Kang-Dae's anger almost got the best of him at the sight. There were bodies strewn about, Xian and Katsuo soldiers alike. Most of the civilians' bodies were males. Thankfully, there were no children, but it shed light on a new horror. Had they been taken? And for what purpose? The city Illeanda, as Jung-Soo described, had been taken with most of the civilians under Katsuo's soldiers' reign, but there had been no children. The Duke claimed they were used as leverage against the soldiers, but that didn't appear to be the case here. These were simple people, not soldiers. They posed no threat, so why take their children and women?

"Check for survivors," Kang-Dae ordered his men as they fanned out.

The surrounding quietness of the area had Kang-Dae on edge. He hated that he could not feel safe in his land. Katsuo's infiltration was too great, and he was spread too thin. He feared that even if he did find Katsuo and his army, they would be outmanned and only be going to their deaths. They underestimated him. He should have been more diligent about rooting him out, and now it was Xian that suffered.

"My king," a soldier came running. "We found a survivor.

Kang-Dae allowed the man to lead them deeper into the village to one of the burnt-out homes. A couple of these men were helping a still bleeding Xian soldier. His armor was stained with blood and so disheveled to the point it was falling off of him. He had blood falling from his lips.

"Get Hui!" he told the soldier, who wasted no time and ran from the house.

"What is your name?" Yae-Min asked.

"Ji," the soldier rasped out, followed by a weak cough.

Yae-min gave him water from his pouch. The men carried him out and sat him on the ground.

"When was the attack?" Kang-Dae asked.

"Less than two days ago. We were ambushed – I got separated from my squad and came upon this village. I didn't think they'd attack everyone," he said regretfully.

"Do you know which direction they went?" Kang-Dae questioned. The man nodded.

"My king," Si-jin began.

"They couldn't have gone far. We could take them down before they do this to anyone else."

"General Jung-"

"We cannot do nothing," he argued.

"And Katsuo, do you expect him to wait for us?" Yu spoke up. His tone had everyone growing still.

"My king," he pressed in a softer tone. This opportunity is too great to risk it on another endeavor."

"And what of the people? Do we leave them to their fate?" Kang-Dae snapped.

"For the good of all Xian. It's not a pleasant choice, but a right one."

Kang-Dae turned from the selfish ex-Councilman. What would he know about what's right?

"Have the men ready to move. We'll leave at noon."

"My king," Yu began, but Kang-Dae walked away.

# CHAPTER 36

The chicken was the best thing she'd ever tasted. Maybe it was because she hadn't eaten anything of real substance in days. She was so hungry she couldn't even force herself to slow under Katsuo's scrutinizing stare. She deliberately skipped the wine for obvious reasons, opting for water.

"I must apologize for the treatment you've endured," Katsuo said, probably in response to her ravenous hunger.

Serenity ignored it; he didn't mean it, and even if he did, it didn't matter. There were hundreds of others he allowed to be treated just as badly or worse because they didn't have the good fortune of having a skill he could take advantage of.

"Tell me: how did you end up in this land?"

Serenity froze mid-chew.

"You are not a native of Xian. Your accent is different, as is your speech."

'What, you want me to be impressed? That's pretty obvious,' she thought bitterly. She forced herself to swallow.

"I don't remember where my home is," she started. "I was sold to a rich merchant when I was a young child. I don't remember my parents," she lied effortlessly, borrowing bits of what Jung-Soo had told her about his childhood. "He brought me here, but once he realized what I could do, he became frightened and abandoned me. A village took me in."

As smooth as she was with her delivery of her fake backstory, her body was not in sync with her verbal confidence. Her heart was pounding and her leg nervously jiggled beneath the table. Thankfully, it was out of his view.

"Did they know of your gifts? How did they feel about it?"

She thought quickly. What type of story would be best to sell her hopefully non-threatening personality? Was she going for pity, trying to impress, or did she try to scare him into releasing her immediately? She could never pull off the intimidating persona, and impressing him could risk more tests.

"I was forbidden from speaking of them unless it was about any danger the village would face. I was not accepted there, only tolerated." She took a bite of bread with honey.

"So you have no husband?"

The question almost made her choke. She took a large sip of water as he looked on with amused eyes. She thought fast – the last thing she needed was a sociopathic conqueror trying to woo her.

"I dreamed long ago that as long as I remain pure, my visions will remain."

She'd gotten the idea from a movie she saw once. She prayed he believed her. She watched him beneath her lids, trying to gage his reaction. He didn't smile or give any outward reaction, only tapping the outside of his wine glass as he stared.

"Shame," was all he said, which sickened and relieved her. "My future queen doesn't have the same open-mindedness as me when it comes to these arts. I think if she met you, she would change her stance."

'Queen?' She thought to herself. Did he leave her back home?

"Where is she?" Serenity asked.

"She rarely visits me here. It is not the most fitting place for someone as delicate as she is. Her grace and beauty alone would cause a stir with the men." The way he described her was not with love but like someone listing the best features on their new car. "Her beauty is unmatched and her loyalty has been tested." Serenity frowned at the statement not quite sure what he meant. "Perhaps you will meet her."

"You said you would let me go if I did what you asked," she reminded him.

She didn't expect him to honor his word, but he didn't need to know that she had zero faith in him. He had the audacity to look cocky.

"You are simply too valuable to let go."

Serenity clenched her fist.

"I promise you that you will be well cared for. You will not want for anything."

'Except for my freedom,' she thought, a second away from saying it out loud.

"Why do you need me? You appear to be doing fine on your own," she countered. Katsuo gave a slight nod and took a sip of wine.

"It would be an honor to say it was all due to my great planning; I'm afraid my victories are not of my own making."

Serenity sat up a little straighter. "What do you mean?"

Seeing her finished water, he had a servant refill her cup before answering.

"This conquest of mine was set on me before I was born. I was chosen to be the sole ruler of all. The gods saw fit to help me to fulfill my destiny."

'Great, he's insane,' she thought.

"How do you know it's your destiny?" She couldn't help asking. If he was willing to enslave a country and kill thousands for his so-called destiny, she wanted to know why.

"The 'soothsayer' that performed the blessing over me while I slept in my mother's womb all but declared itself. He said I would accomplish a great victory following years of strife and tragedy."

"Was he right?"

"The country was attacked the day of my birth. We were set upon by barbarians who took what they wanted and killed all those who stood in their way. We warred with them for 15 years before we were chased from our homes completely and forced to flee." There was genuine anger in his tone. His eyes stayed glued to the candle in front of him.

She could see the tiny flame in his eyes. "After two years we were able to return and we took our home back on the anniversary of my birth. I knew then what my fate was. We spent years rebuilding our country, getting it back to its glorious state. When we did, I vowed to never let it fall into ruin again."

The emotion and the way his voice wavered exposed his sincerity. Maybe he wasn't just a cruel invader. Perhaps there was more to the enemy than she thought.

# CHAPTER 37

Serenity sat in the corner of her tent, in her cot, fanning herself. Considering the coldness of the mountain she imagined the heat she was feeling was not a good indication of the poison's stability in her body. She was feeling warm on and off throughout the day.

The servant Iko came in with a tray of food. Serenity was about to greet the woman when she realized that Iko could barely hold onto the tray. Rushing over she grabbed the tray from the woman and set it on the table. The poor woman began apologizing profusely but Serenity dismissed it. "It's fine. Are you okay?" she asked the woman. The woman shook her head in an attempt to shoo away Serenity's concerns but from the circles under her eyes, her chapped lips, and the way she was barely standing up straight Serenity knew she was not. She led the protesting woman to a chair and had her sit before pouring her a cup of water and handing it to her. The woman tried to decline at first but Serenity wouldn't have it. "Please," she begged the woman. Giving in, she began to drink, slowly at first but the longer she drank the more desperate her sibs became. It was apparent that she had not been given much to drink in a while. She hated to see her in such a state. Though not elderly, she was an older woman who definitely should not be put in such conditions.

Serenity took some of the food that was brought to her and put it on a plate to give to the woman. Once again, the woman began to protest. Serenity pushed the plate in front of her. "Eat. You need your strength." The woman looked longingly at the food but still was hesitant to eat. Serenity put the chopsticks in her hand and encouraged her once more. Iko seemed to struggle with herself for a moment before finally giving in and taking the tiniest bit of rice. Once that hurdle was over, Serenity encouraged her to eat more. She sat down with her, eating just a little bit herself so that Iko wouldn't have to eat alone and maybe be less nervous. The young teen entered carrying a jug of water. He froze at the sight before him. Casting a dark look toward Serenity he placed the jug down and rushed over to Iko.

Though they whispered amongst themselves, she could still make out what they were saying. He asked her if she was alright and the woman assured him that she was. He called the woman "aunt". She had wondered about their relationship as he never seemed far behind her and she clearly cared for him. He began to whisper to Iko that Serenity wasn't to be trusted and that she had no idea what Serenity could have done to the food. Iko smartly remarked that she was the one who brought the food in the first place. He questioned why Serenity would do such a thing and claimed it must be some sort of trick. He told her people like Serenity are capable of anything. Iko chastised the boy for being rude and then turned to Serenity to apologize, knowing that their conversation had not been private.

Serenity dismissively waved her hand. "I understand," she told her. "It's hard to trust anyone in this place." The woman's warm smile was offset by the boy's scowling.

Serenity offered some food to the boy who only stared at her. Iko gave him some of hers which he declined wanting her to eat it all. The two women made short and pleasant conversation while the angsty teen watched on, refusing to engage or eat. When the woman said she had to leave to do her duties, Serenity made sure to pack up some of the food for her to take with her. The woman thanked her once more sincerely. Serenity packed some food for the boy as well and tried to hand it to him but he once again just stared. The woman took it from her hands thanked her and then left.

# CHAPTER 38

Rielle marched, or speed walked, with the men. She was only able to keep up with the back, but to her, that still counted as keeping up.

*Earlier that day*

*"I'm not going," she protested, tossing the pack to the ground. Jung-Soo glared up at her.*

*"You cannot come with us," he said for the third time, or maybe the fifth; she lost count.*

*"If you're going to get Serenity, I need to be there," she told him adamantly.*

*"You will only slow us down and get us caught."*

*"No, I won't. I've done five different 5ks; I can do this."*

*He gave a blank stare at her mild flex, but Rielle would not back down over this.*

*"She needs me. I'm the only one who can help her," she told him, reminding him of the poison in Serenity's blood.*

*She could just give him the pills and tell him how to help her manage it, but he didn't need to know that. She was not going to let him ship her off with strangers so she could go crazy in the capital, not knowing if they had succeeded. She came to this land to protect Serenity and she was going to do that. Jung-Soo gave her a bag before pushing past without another word, which she took to mean she'd won.*

Rielle was so focused on keeping up that she never noticed Jung-Soo slow his pace enough to walk right next to her. He never told her, but she impressed him with her determination. He also expected her to fall behind and need to stop frequently, but, true to her word, she kept up with his men. Her stamina was admirable. He knew of some soldiers who would have complained by now. He could never imagine Serenity doing it.

"Why did you come here?" He asked Rielle, startling her once she realized he was there.

"What?" She asked, confused.

"Why make the journey here at such a dangerous time?"

She looked ahead. "Was I supposed to let her come alone?" She asked.

Despite her attitude, he admired her answer and her loyalty to Serenity. From the stories he'd been told, Rielle did seem like a very good friend, if not a bit unreasonable.

"Even at the risk of your life?"

She didn't respond right away. "She'd do it for me."

'And she has,' Rielle thought. There was a time in her life when she didn't want to live anymore. Without Serenity, she would have completely given up. She gave her support, love, and even a new family. If she lost Serenity, she didn't know what she'd do. She glanced at Jung-

Soo, who wasn't even breaking a sweat. 'Show off,' she thought. With what Serenity had told her about him, she didn't know what she pictured, but it wasn't the person next to her.

"You're nothing like I thought you'd be," she said out loud.

He looked at her. She couldn't tell, but he seemed almost insulted. Did he think she was insulting him?

"I just meant, you're younger than I thought," she tried to clarify.

Cuter too, she thought, then pressed her lips shut. She caught a glimpse of the bandage peeking beneath his clothes and felt guilty.

"Does it hurt?" She asked, trying to sound casual.

"You did no real damage," he claimed, which she knew was a lie.

"I could clean it later if you want, to keep it from getting infected," she offered, looking ahead.

Jung-Soo didn't accept or decline the offer.

# CHAPTER 39

Serenity had to stop drinking her tea as the coughing fit came on. She had a small cough the other day and was hoping it was just a run-of-the-mill cough but she was starting to believe it was worse than that. She knew without her antibiotics it would only be a matter of time before the poison began to rage once more. She was doing her best to supplement her meds based on natural remedies Rielle had told her about. She'd been requesting lots of tea with honey. Also, under the guise of a ritual to bring on more visions, she asked the woman assigned to her to find her some ginger. According to Rielle it wouldn't get rid of the poison or work as well as the pills but it could still slow the spread and give her more time, how much was up for debate. She was glad she hadn't been summoned by Katsuo recently. The last thing she needed was for him to notice her symptoms and have his physicians check on her. If he knew she was pregnant, her lie about being a virgin would be discovered and she dreaded to think what would happen then. She used her free moments to go over her dreams to determine which ones she felt would be safe to reveal to Katsuo. She had no intention of helping Katsuo ravage the country but she also needed to stay useful enough to survive. It was a hard line but she would walk it as long as possible.

"Bring him down," she heard outside her tent.

"Please no!" A woman's voice cried out.

Serenity let her curiosity rule and went outside the tent for the first time in two days. The first thing she saw was several soldiers holding someone down while one man, dressed in ranking clothing, stood above them. To the side was the same woman who'd been assigned to her, looking on, trying to reach them all. She was being held back by another soldier.

"Give him thirty!" The man shouted.

Serenity watched, horrified at the large paddle that had been brought out. Serenity recognized the person they held as a young teen who had first served her when she arrived.

Before the first blow could connect, Serenity cried out, "Stop!"

"You do not order us!" the officer spat. "This thief was caught stealing from private stocks. The punishment is thirty flogs."

"It's my fault. I asked for more food. He's only doing what I asked. Ka- the king," she caught herself, "ordered him to do so. Are you going to punish him for following the King's orders?" She accused.

The man's eyes darted away as he pondered. She could see the soldiers' grip loosening on the teen's shoulders.

"I can ask him myself if you like," Serenity pushed, hoping to scare them enough for them to drop it.

To her relief, the tactic worked, and the official had the teen released. The men quickly left them both. The older woman rushed over immediately to help the boy up. Serenity went over to assist. He pulled away from her slightly, opting to stand on his own, so Serenity backed off. He wiped at his eyes discreetly, refusing to look her way. Sensing he was already feeling some embarrassment, she decided against asking him if he was alright.

"You got to be careful," she warned.

She didn't care about his stealing, but she would hate to see him face the harsh consequences of such behavior. The boy looked at her with a gaze full of distrust.

Their interaction was interrupted by Iko, who kneeled down in thanks to Serenity. Serenity helped the woman up. "Take care of yourselves," was all Serenity told them. The boy continued to stare until Iko slowly dragged him away.

Later she was back in her tent retwisting her hair for the second time as she had nothing better to do. A guard announced from outside that she was being summoned. he immediately wondered if word had gotten to him about what happened and she became anxious. She was once again escorted to the main tent she visited before. There were only guards present, no one else when she arrived.

She took the time to examine the tent, especially the throne. She wondered if he'd brought it with him or had it built when he'd arrived. Even the design of it was so different from Xian's. This chair was designed with comfort and flash in mind. Gold made up the base foundation of the chair and an assortment of jewels and jade was decorated into it. The seat itself had a large black cushion lined with fur along the back as well. Even the furs leading to the throne were lined with gold thread. The spots on it had her guessing it was made from the pelt of a panther. The crown was sitting in the middle, showing off its glamor as it shimmered. She had yet to see Katsuo without it, so she was surprised. Not as surprised as she was when she heard a quiet, "Magnificent," in her ear. She jumped with a gasp, almost knocking into a chuckling

Katsuo. Before she could stop herself, she was rolling her eyes but stopped mid-roll as soon as she remembered her place. Desperate to fix her error, she dropped to her knees.

"Apologies, your majesty," she rambled. "I did not realize it was you."

Judging by the laughter from above her, her fear was misplaced. Katsuo stood her up, his smile making her uneasy. He led her to sit on the ground in front of the throne, but he went to go take a seat in it, placing the crown to the side of him.

"Did you want me to tell you of any visions I've had?" She asked, wanting to get this over with so she could leave.

Ignoring her question he asked, "You had some trouble in camp earlier?"

Feeling her fears were manifesting, she quickly began to explain with her rehearsed excuse that she worked on during the walk over. "I am sorry. I just didn't want them punished for my mistake."

"Why?" He asked; the genuine confusion of that made her hate him all the more. Was he that callous?

"He didn't deserve it," was all she could muster, knowing further explaining would tempt her into saying what she shouldn't.

"Life isn't about what is deserved, but what is necessary," he countered in a surprisingly thoughtful tone.

"And you believe this war is necessary?" She asked, needing to have that answer. He looked nonplussed by her boldness, maybe even a little impressed.

"Sometimes we have to make the hard decisions for the sake of everyone involved. Peace is never achieved through peaceful means. It is only ever earned through blood and sacrifice."

"We had peace," she said.

"Did you?" He questioned. "True peace? True peace is knowing you will never have to worry about the people on your side or across the sea coming for you. Anything else is false. As long as we're all divided, we're all potential enemies. But if we unite, fight under one order, we have no enemies, only allies."

"You started a war to bring about world peace?" She asked, disbelieving.

"If you are not the one starting the fight, you will be the one who falls to one," he said with conviction.

She remembered what he said about his land being overtaken. She was starting to understand the root of his madness and narcissism. Twisted as it may be, he convinced himself what he was doing was right. Not only did he think it was right, but according to others, it was his destiny – his birthright. He reminded her of Jae-Hwa in a way. Someone who was brought up since childhood to fulfill a purpose that was forced on them by others. She was sure she was meant to be Kang-Dae's bride because she'd been told that her entire life. She believed so much that she was willing to do anything to get it. Otherwise, what was her life's purpose? She imagined Katsuo was the same way. He would never question his birthright, as it was as much a part of him as his heart. He could never be a villain in his eyes because he would be a hero to the world according to the soothsayer. She had some choice words for whoever that person was. But was Katsuo lost to his illusion? Maybe she could steer him back to his true purpose.

"It's easy to make sacrifices with other people's lives. But if the sacrifice isn't your own, is it a sacrifice? Does that type of sacrifice lead to true peace?" Serenity questioned.

She brought it up wanting to see where his head was at. Silence followed her prodding. She took a peek at him. He was facing forward, eyes unblinking, face blank, but the way he swallowed looked like he was fighting his emotion back.

"I've had to make sacrifices for my destiny. I have done things that would break a lesser man. Not out of desire but necessity, for the good of all."

Serenity thought back to the little boy she had seen in her dreams. Was whatever haunting Katsuo related to him? Was the child still around? If not, what had happened to him and who was he to Katsuo? She felt no closer to figuring him out, as only more questions filled her. However, the oddly vulnerable expression on his face made her want to pity him.

"I'm sorry," she apologized without thinking. "I should not have assumed."

She wasn't sorry, at least she didn't think she was. Serenity ignored that speck of pity she could feel trying to emerge for this conqueror. He looked at her, and just as quickly as the somber expression came it was gone, replaced by the overconfident rogue she was used to.

"Tell me… what dreams have you had?" He asked. Ready to end this whole interaction, she obliged.

# CHAPTER 40

Her baby was crying. On the other side of the wall, she could hear the wailing of her baby. Serenity pounded on the walls with her fists as hard as she could, as there didn't seem to be a door in the room. She beat and kicked at the wall, desperate to get inside. With a loud yell, she hit the brick with all her might, and it flew into the room, leaving a hole. She looked at the damage she did. For a second, she worried she'd caused too much damage, but then she remembered her child. She looked inside and saw that it wasn't her baby inside, but scared captives huddled together, crying in fear. She realized all her pounding had frightened them. She tried to reassure them that they were safe when the walls began to crumble. She looked up and saw that she was at the front walls of the palace. In her panic, she'd caused the whole thing to fall. Panicked that she had caused such a disaster, she went running for help.

*She ran into Kang-Dae, who had a grim expression, but he held her gingerly.*

*"We knew it had to come down to this eventually," he told her.*

*She was confused as to what he meant. She turned to see not only the wall was destroyed, but the entire palace was being torn down with green and black bulldozers. Serenity cried at the sight and begged Kang-Dae to stop it, but he only watched.*

*"We have to wait," he said.*

*Before long, the palace was nothing but rubble. Suddenly, she was walking the very same halls of the palace, but they now looked newer, with specks of gold flickering in the walls. Everything seemed to shine. As she walked hand-in-hand with Kang-Dae to the main hall, she cradled her now very large belly.*

Serenity felt something wiping at her cheeks. She opened her eyes and started to scream seeing a face right by her. The person jumped back.

Serenity realized it was the same boy she'd saved earlier.

"You were crying in your sleep," Ami stammered out. She touched her cheek and felt wetness.

"What are you doing in here?" She asked without accusation, just genuine curiosity.

"I heard you coughing. I wanted to have your tea ready when you woke," he explained.

Now that he said it, she did feel the harsh tickle in her throat. Her coughing was getting worse.

"I can get the healer for you. "

"No," she quickly declined. "It's alright; I'll be fine."

Because someone up there thought it might be funny, no sooner had she said that when her first true bout of morning sickness reared its ugly head. Reaching for the wash basin by her bedside, she vomited into it. She saw the teen going for the exit in her peripheral.

"Wait!" She shouted, followed by a horrid dry heave. "Don't get anyone, please," she begged.

After it was over, she asked him for some clean wash water and he obliged. After washing out her mouth and washing her face, the teen brought her honey tea. She thanked him as she accepted it.

"Are you sick?" The teen asked in a small voice. Not knowing if it would be better to lie or be truthful, she didn't answer at first.

"I'll be okay," was all she said. "I just don't want anyone to check on me," she vaguely explained.

The teen looked unsatisfied with the answer but remained quiet, only giving a small nod.

"Thank you for checking on me," she said to him sincerely.

Given the dim light, she could see the tiny flush on his cheeks. He gave a short bow before running off. She looked at the table and saw he'd also brought food with the tea. From the looks of the extra portion of meat, she figured he'd stolen it. She shook her head at his boldness and went to eat when her dream came back to her memory. Was she going to do something that could bring tragedy to Xian? Was it her fears and wild actions that would make them fail? The implications were making her already unsettled stomach worse. That dream couldn't be taken lightly. She would sit on it to understand it more. She suspected if she interpreted any of it wrong, it would be disastrous to Xian.

# CHAPTER 41

Rielle held out her bowl for more stew. The man serving the food seemed more interested in staring than filling her bowl. Annoyed, she grabbed the ladle out of his hand and filled her bowl herself before walking off. She passed at least a dozen staring eyes. They were constantly staring. It was driving her crazy. She didn't care if they weren't used to women being around, or just a black woman, but they could at least have basic manners in this place. She got enough of this when she was younger. She hated it then; she hated it now. She was about to go sit as far from them and their prying eyes as possible when she felt a tug on her forearm. Jung-Soo pulled her towards his tent, not roughly, but with no gentleness either, which made her try and wriggle out of his hold. She failed, of course, and subsequently was dragged inside. She hadn't been around him in a couple of hours. When the tent went up, she figured she wouldn't see him for the rest of the night due to his sudden need for privacy. She didn't know what that was about. He hadn't put up the tent in the past few nights. Once inside, he loosened his grip enough for her to snatch her arm away. He paid her attitude no mind and went to sit on his mat to eat his food. Seeing that he wasn't sitting on it, she decided to claim his cot as her seat. They ate in silence, neither even bothering to look in the direction of the other.

"I thought time was of the essence," she repeated his words back to him in an overly mocking impression. "Why set this up?"

She knew he had no problem sleeping with his men. Comfort was not an issue for him; she figured that out off the bat.

"It is not for me."

The implication of his answer made her stop eating. He set this up for her? Jung-Soo continued eating, not sparing her one glance. Rielle felt a bit warm at the gesture. Serenity had told her the two of them had been friends. She might be starting to see why.

"You and Serenity were close?" She asked.

A simple innocent question she thought, but the way he choked on his current bite of food led her to think it wasn't. Jung-Soo grabbed a drink of water.

"I just meant you were friends," she said, not sure why he'd had such a reaction. Jung-Soo recovered and tried to recompose himself to give the illusion of stoicism, but that ship sailed.

"I know her well." His vague response and refusal to look her way increased Rielle's curiosity.

On the surface, he was a stone-faced soldier, but she had a feeling there was more to it. The way Serenity spoke about him, she never suspected anything other than friendship. After all, it was abundantly clear to her that Serenity only had eyes for Kang-Dae, and she knew Serenity would never be the type to stray. Thinking back on those stories, she just figured he was a good friend, and an even better general, who put himself on the line for his queen like a good guard. Was it more than that? It wouldn't be a surprise to her. She had years of experience watching the men go after her friend while barely glancing her way. Jung-Soo was no different. Small pangs of what felt like disappointment rose in her.

Needing to change where her thoughts were leading her, she decided to ask, "how much longer till we get there?"

"A week, possibly, maybe days if we forgo the woods."

Knowing what lay in wait in the woods, Rielle didn't object to it.

"What's the plan? How do we get Serenity out?"

Jung-Soo set down his now empty bowl. "If we can cut them off before they get back to their base, we can free her and anyone else. We have to scout the land first. There were many marching north. Since that is where Katsuo lies, it will not be easy to infiltrate."

"If?" She asked, realizing the wording. He let out a sigh.

"There is a chance we will not catch them before that."

"What happens then?" She asked, almost tossing her bowl on the ground. "By then, won't it be too late? If you think she's heading towards this Katsuo guy, won't he have a ridiculous amount of security?" Her words seemed to confuse him. "Soldiers," she corrected herself.

"I imagine he'd have many."

"Then how will you save her?" She demanded, not liking the turn this conversation took.

"We will," he said, probably in an attempt to assure her, but Rielle wasn't buying it.

"This man has been taking this country bit by bit. How exactly do you plan to go against him with just a few men?"

She didn't care how high-pitched and hysterical her voice was starting to sound. How had she managed to convince herself that getting Serenity would not be an impossible task? She looked at Jung-Soo, looking completely unbothered, lacking any type of concern. It was him. Somehow, he and his impassive attitude had tricked her into thinking Serenity would be saved by him. Hell, even Serenity must have thought so, as he was the one she told Rielle to ask for by name.

"You don't know that," she said, voice rising. She pushed herself up to her feet. "You don't know anything!"

Rielle didn't know where this irrational panic came from, but it was quickly consuming her. She stormed toward the exit. 'I'll find her,' she thought to herself. The rational part of her knew that this was ridiculous, but she wasn't functioning in that state of mind at the moment. The very real and possibly horrible things that Serenity could be facing were piling up in her mind, making it hard to focus. She had come with her to protect her. How had she failed so spectacularly? Arms around her waist stopped her most likely disastrous plans, and she was pulled back. She tried to fight against Jung-Soo's hold, but his grip didn't loosen. She was forced to sit on the cot, but as soon as her bottom hit it, she tried scrambling around the muscled soldier, only for him to catch her and push her back down. He held her down by her arms securely, but without hurting her. He bent down to stare into her eyes. Rielle didn't fight anymore, not only because it was pointless, but because of the look on his face. That stoicism, that look of nonchalance, slowly slipped before her. She thought, at first, that it was an unintentional and uncontrollable slip that was forced out with her outburst, but with the way his eyes bore into hers and how he continued to hold her in place, she realized he was revealing himself to her. He was showing her what Serenity meant to him. The concern, the uncertainty, his sincerity, she saw it all. It was so real she could feel her eyes water.

His point made, he slowly replaced his mask and released her, backing up to stand a few feet from her.

"I won't leave," she spoke quietly. He gave a short nod before pushing himself up to stand.

"Sleep. We leave at first light."

He was out of the tent a second later. Rielle, now alone with her thoughts, reflected on what had just transpired. Her opinion of the general was taking on a new perspective.

# CHAPTER 42

Serenity nervously approached the main tent but forced herself to keep her head high. She needed to present confidence even if she felt none. She informed the guards on duty that she needed to see him.

"He is not to be disturbed when meeting with Lord Sho," the guard told her. She frowned, finding the name familiar. Had Katsuo said it in passing once or twice?

"It's important," she pushed.

If she missed the chance, she didn't know when another would arrive. The guards looked at one another, neither wanting to be in this position. The one she spoke to opened the flap for her.

"Bear the consequences," he warned, effectively washing his hands of any repercussions he could face.

The warning was meant to frighten her off, and though she was really anxious, she walked in.

Katsuo and a man she believed she'd seen before were in conversation. The man stood before Katsuo, his back facing Serenity. He was draped in heavy gray robes. The man's raspy voice gave age to the currently faceless man. His hair was hidden in a gray wrap sitting atop his head. Katsuo noticed her presence, and his eyes were now focused on her. The man, realizing he no longer had his attention, turned toward her. The long-faced man's tan skin sported a couple of wrinkles, which could have been a scowl seeing as his expression had become one of pure disdain. Serenity remembered she'd seen him standing near Katsuo once before, holding the same thick staff he was holding now. The staff was made from dark wood with the top carved into the head of a lion. The eyes were made of green jewels.

"Dream walker," Katsuo called to her. "How are you?"

His lack of annoyance at being interrupted gave her some relief. Serenity bowed her head before answering.

"I've had a vision about some men of yours. They are in danger," she forced out. The dream came last night, following the disturbing one she'd had before. Unlike that dream, this dream had been more hopeful. She had been content to keep it to herself and let it take place but that other dream and the reappearance of her illness put her in a time crunch. If she was stuck here, she would use it to Xian's advantage. That meant gaining Katsuo's trust. She figured it would be best to use the dreams she believed were harmless enough to prove her worth but not give Katsuo too much of an advantage. The vision had been clear to her as soon as she woke. A troop of Katsuo's would be ambushed in the pursuit of slaves in a village in the eastern province by the river. She relayed the dream and the message to Katsuo, not leaving anything out. When she was done, Katsuo was sitting up straighter; his eyes went to the older man.

"Have you seen anything like this?"

His inquiry alerted Serenity. Was he the Soothsayer he'd been relying on? He had admitted to believing in the ability of such men, which explained his willingness to believe her. The soothsayer's eyes narrowed at her.

"No, your majesty." He turned toward Katsuo. "I have not seen any such thing."

"You believe she is false?" He questioned.

She watched as Sho looked her way before turning back to Katsuo.

"I know your majesty finds the girl interesting," he spoke condescendingly. "But relying on her in such important manners would be unwise. What little ability she has cannot be counted upon."

'Oh, he wants to go, we can go,' Serenity thought to herself. Nervousness gone and replaced with a confident fury, she marched past the soothsayer and stood in front of him, blocking him from Katsuo's view given his short stature.

"You do not have to believe me," she began in English. "It's your choice what you wish to allow.

I don't care either way. Your people are not mine, and I gain nothing by helping you."

"Precisely why you should have her removed," the little man harped, but Serenity continued as if he had never spoken.

"I believe in my dreams; I believe it is my responsibility. I honor the dream, not you. So, if you choose to ignore it simply because my eyes see further than this man, the consequences of that choice will not be my responsibility."

She faced him head-on as she spoke, forgetting her demure act under the weight of her anger. She could almost feel the soothsayer bristling behind her, incensed by the claim she was more powerful than him. Her focus stayed on Katsuo, who went through several emotions, from interest to uncertainty to bewilderment, and, finally, to amusement. His face broke into a half-smile, and he sat back down on his throne.

"Did you hear that, old friend? It appears my entertainment believes herself to be more powerful than you."

The lilt in his voice showcased his utter glee about the whole thing. The mischievous glint now in his eyes should have put Serenity on edge, but she kept her cool.

"Maybe we should put this to the test?"

'Another one?' She thought.

"If you prove your sight to be…" he hesitated, giving a sly smile to Sho, before continuing with, "…more open than Sho, I will trust your word today."

"Your majesty, we shouldn't waste time on an ignorant girl with this matter." Sho objected.

"The mission is what matters, correct? Shall we not take advantage of every possible asset?" Katsuo counseled. "If she can indeed give us leverage over the enemy, she should be utilized."

"If not?" Sho pressed, his desires clear.

"I am sure I can find her useful in other ways," he murmured, raising her anxiety once more.

"You can't keep such a person around," Sho scolded.

"Yes, yes, I understand," Katsuo said dismissively. Turning to Serenity, he said, "If you fail to live up to your words, you'll be expelled from this camp. And I warn you, it's a long way down."

His insinuations clear, Serenity's heart dropped. 'God, help me through this.'

# CHAPTER 43

Rielle paced back and forth for the hundredth time. The past few hours were filled with nervous pacing, nervous sitting, accompanied with uncontrollable leg shaking, obsessive peeking outside the tent, and desperate praying. Jung-Soo had left her with a few men to go after the soldiers they had spotted. According to Jung-Soo, there was a chance they were the ones who had captured her and Serenity. But if they weren't, that meant they probably had already returned to their base and Serenity was in even more danger. She hoped that Serenity would be there and that they'd find her so the nightmare could be at least halfway over. In her prayers, without meaning to, she covered Jung-Soo pleading for his safe return. As sick as she would be to not find Serenity, she would be upset if Jung-Soo didn't return as well. He wasn't a bad guy and Serenity cared for him is what she told herself to justify her compulsion.

"If I do not return, Tae-Soo and Hae-In will take you back to the capital. The Dowager will look after you until Kang-Dae's return," he told her.

"But Serenity," she started to interrupt.

"You must heed my orders," he stopped her. "If you are captured or killed, it helps no one, least of all Serenity. Keep yourself safe," he reiterated. It was strange, someone other than Serenity or family showing concern for her. After Rielle's parents were gone, she'd only been able to rely fully on Serenity. No one else had cared. The thought made her unexpectedly emotional but she hid it well. She nodded to him letting him know she would do as told.

A voice shouted out something in Xian. Rielle wasted no time rushing out of the tent. She stopped only a few feet out as the men filed into camp looking exhausted but otherwise free of injury. A few were sporting blood on their armor but it was clear it was not their own. She kept looking around them and through them hoping to spot Jung-Soo. The longer she went without seeing him the more nervous she became. 'He would make it back,' she thought to herself. If these guys did he definitely would. She'd never seen him fight but she figured what he lacked in social skills would be made up for in battle. He wasn't a general for nothing. Before she could whip her mind into a frenzy, he appeared through the tree line with the last of the soldiers. They were carrying a couple back. The relief she felt was quickly overshadowed by the realization that Serenity was not with them. Her heart sank. Jung-Soo handed the injured soldier to others. He came up to her with his eyes downcast, probably as apologetic as he'd ever been. She didn't let him speak, not believing either of them could handle it at the moment.

"Do you need me to look at your injured?" She asked, her voice tight.

"No, our healer would do that," he told her still avoiding her gaze.

"What about you?" She asked looking over him.

"I am unharmed," he said and then he walked off most likely to tend to his men but mostly to avoid her. She knew he felt guilty for not returning with Serenity and being around her probably made him feel worse so she tried not to feel offended but she was disappointed to have to suffer and her sadness alone.

# CHAPTER 44

Her hands wouldn't stop shaking. Serenity held them together in an effort to get them to stop while also combatting the growing nausea in her belly. She didn't know if she was feeling symptoms of pregnancy, poison, or just nerves. With the looming test coming up she was sure it was the latter. The fear she was experiencing had her almost wishing the poison would go ahead and take her out. How was she going to get through this? She knew in the back of her mind that her mom would say, God would work it out, but that did not dull the worry and fear she was currently suffering. A cup of honey tea came into her view. She accepted Ami's offering but could only manage a sip.

"What will you do?" The teen asked, looking almost as anxious as she was. She took another sip just to do something.

"Use my dreams," she said simply to trick herself into believing it was that easy.

"The soothsayer has visions," the teen responded as if she needed to be reminded.

"I know." Somehow, she needed to prove hers with stronger or at least more accurate.

"I heard he uses the blood of sacrificed animals to see into the future with his staff. Some say he uses humans sometimes," he claimed. Her nausea increased. What if he were more powerful? What did she know about these things?

"Does he always use the staff?" She asked, finally noticing that bit of information.

"I believe so."

Does the man have the power or was it in his staff? She wandered. Sensing where her thinking had led her the teen spoke up.

"Maybe I can steal it for you."

"No!" She said almost harshly. "They'll kill you without thinking twice."

"They would not catch me," he insisted.

"No. You're not risking your life like that," she said strongly leaving no room for rebuttal. The teen looked like he wanted to argue more but wisely stayed quiet. She set her tea down knowing she wouldn't be able to finish it.

"I'll get some more for your stomach," he told her. She thanked him as he left grateful to have one person in the camp she could count on.

Ami stepped out of the tent. Instead of heading toward the physician's tent to steal more herbs, an act the woman had no idea about, he went towards the high rise in search of the soothsayer's tent.

# CHAPTER 45

Kissing her felt like home, more home than he'd ever felt inside the palace walls. Kang-Dae wrapped Serenity up tightly in his arms. She giggled into his mouth, making him smile.

"What?" He asked, going for her lips again. She kissed him back.

"You," she said. He flipped them over hovering above her beaming form. She was dressed in white silk, her curly hair adorned with white petals framing her round face.

"What about me?"

She smiled, causing him to kiss her again. She pushed gently at him.

"You are so good."

"Really? I haven't even undressed you yet," He joked. She smiled and rolled her eyes.

"You do what's right even when it's hard," she clarified. He tilted his head.

*"What brought this on?" He asked out loud.*

*They were in their bedroom in the palace. There was nothing going on at the time. It was quiet outside the doors and the windows. But as he turned to look, he could see the fire raging outside, overtaking what looked to be a city right outside their bedroom. He turned back to her, but she looked unbothered. She stroked his hair.*

*"What is good isn't always what is needed," she told him. He frowned.*

*"What do you mean?"*

*She played with her necklace that dangled from his neck. "To get the things we need, we have to let go of the things we want."*

*The sound of something falling in the distance drew his attention. A building had collapsed. When he looked back down, Serenity was no longer beneath him.*

*"Serenity!" He called out.*

*Looking around the room, which was no longer the bedroom but the throne room, he began to panic. He ran out, shouting for her, only to end up outside. A sea of thousands were coming towards him.*

Kang-Dae awoke with a gasp, sweat coating his body. The men around him were still sleeping. He remembered they had stopped for a few hours to rest that night, not bothering to set up a camp, as they would restart their journey to pursue Katsuo's troops soon. Kang-Dae took time to calm himself. He had not dreamt like that since before he left for Serenity's world. Was Serenity trying to tell him something? Or was it her God? He could chalk it up to his stress due to his current situation but knew he shouldn't. If Kang-Dae learned nothing from the past year, he knew the power of the dream. It should not, could not be ignored. But how he wished Serenity was there to help him understand it.

He got up, forgoing any more sleep, and walked the camp. The soldiers on guard duty greeted him as he passed. One of the men on duty was a village volunteer. He took their courage and gratefulness to heart. They wanted to fight for their home. He wanted that as well, but mostly, he wanted to fight for the people affected most by this war. As the sun rose, more of his men did as well. They gathered their things quickly, and within half an hour, it was like they were never there. They continued in the direction the survivor, Ji, had told them. He led from the front to avoid known traps and ambushes they'd marked. Ji was good at spotting them.

"Hold!" Someone called out.

Kang-Dae and his men immediately took hold of their weapons. Kang-Dae rode off to the front to see what was going on. Ahead was a galloping horse with a single rider coming towards them.

"Lower your weapons," Kang-Dae ordered, recognizing the messenger. He was one of Jung-Soo's men. "Karesh," he greeted once he made it to him.

"My king. There's a slew of Katsuo's men, not two leagues from here. They're heavily armed and have a good ground for defense and offense," he told them.

Kang-Dae's brow furrowed at the information. He looked at Ji, who appeared to be just as confused.

"Do you think they're the same men?" Kang-Dae asked him.

"I do not know, my king. Maybe they left scouts to report on our movements," Ji suggested.

It was possible. Luckily, Karesh showed up when he did. Or they would have run straight into an ambush.

"We will head back and draw them towards us," Kang-Dae said.

The leaders agreed and went to order their respective men. As he looked around, he paused at the disappointed look on Yu's face. The man said nothing and walked off. Despite it being Yu, something in his stance made him feel ashamed.

# CHAPTER 46

No one glanced his way as he moved
through the camp. It was a benefit of his low status.
Ami just walked with his bucket giving the illusion
of running a task to serve the men like any other
day. Like the many others who'd been captured to
serve, they were seen as nothing but tools, tools
under the army's complete control. A slave
wouldn't dare try to escape if they knew the penalty.
If you were caught you risked the chance of
watching the one you cared for be killed in front of
your eyes. Many had been taken with their families
and loved ones just for that purpose. It was a price
he'd never pay no matter how desperate he got.

As he neared his destination, he kept his
pace not wanting to give off any suspicion. Instead
of going straight to the tent he went around
avoiding eye contact with the guards in front. He
found a spot far enough away to keep his eyes on it
but not close enough to be noticed. He started
washing, using the clothing he'd stolen as props for

his act. He kept it up for over an hour before he saw Lord Sho exit the tent. Just the sight of the soothsayer brought bad memories. He hated the man almost as much as he hated Katsuo.

When Ami saw that Sho was empty handed he was relieved that his plan could go into action. He waited for the man to get further away until he was completely out of sight before making his move. He took the clothes in hand and walked purposely in plain sight until he made it behind the tent disappearing from any onlooker's view. He tossed the clothes aside.

The tent sat right on the wall of the mountain so he had to squeeze his way through. Back pressed against the mountain, he shuffled sideways feeling the fabric of the tent walls with his fingers searching for the right spot. Once he felt no resistance, he took out his small knife and slowly cut into the tent making an incision large enough for him to crawl through, but small enough not to be noticed. He didn't fear anyone being inside as the Soothsayer allowed no one into his domain believing it interfered with his magics. Ami stayed low until he was inside and climbed to his feet.

Immediately he felt the urge to crawl back out. It was a dark feeling, an atmosphere of ominous intention saturating the place. It felt like every bad feeling he had about magic. If he'd never met the dark woman he'd still believe that all of those that played with those types of forces were just like Lord Sho.

He pushed past his trepidation and searched out the room. It took less than a second to locate his target as it sat on the other side of the tent. It was surrounded by burning candles, propped up on an altar-like table. He approached the object slowly, cautiously. He wanted nothing more than to break it into pieces and burn it along with the whole tent but he feared the thing. He felt like the closer he got to it, the stronger the dark feeling became. Ami stopped altogether when the feeling became almost too overwhelming. It almost felt like he was being watched and conspired against. His eyes watered and his heart pounded. Without meaning to he took a step back. Beads of sweat broke out on his forehead. He couldn't take it. He doubted he'd even be able to grab it with the way he was feeling.

'Don't give up.' He took several breaths and forced his feet forward.

# CHAPTER 47

The breeze felt nice. Serenity would've appreciated it more against her increasingly hot skin if not for what lay ahead. The guards walked in front of her leading her into what could very well be her end. She fought to put those grim thoughts aside as she knew she couldn't afford to walk in fear. Faltering even for a second could lead to her death. She prayed to herself with every step she took as she went deeper into the camp.

The further they got, the fewer tents she began to see. They walked all along the walls of the mountain which had a large opening too perfectly shaped to be natural. The guards went right into it and even though she didn't want to, she followed closely behind. The walls were adorned with torches. The heat hit her face every time she passed one. The subtle flickering of the flames reminded her of the small breeze outside that she was already missing. Deeper into the cave they walked past smooth and jagged rocks alike. On the inside were carvings of faces. They didn't depict any human faces. Judging from the markings they were representatives of gods, not unlike the ones the Xians worshipped. For a moment she thought this place had been built and used by the Xians, but something about the carvings and the characters written made her feel otherwise. As they approached an opening, she felt her heart racing. Sweat began to form at her brow. Nausea and dizziness threatened to arise but she fought against them. This episode would have to wait.' Just a little longer,' she told herself.

Upon entering the chamber her eyes widened. This was not some common cave rooted in the mountain. Above her was a large carving of a Jaguar posed to attack, its mouth open and face fierce. Beautiful and frightening, the brown jaguar had black spots made of stone placed throughout its body mimicking that of a jaguar.

Directly under its massive form was a table where the soothsayer's staff already lay propped up by golden hooks. A chicken sat in a cage next to it unbothered by the different blades laid out before it. The table formed a basin in the center. She already had an awful feeling about what was meant to fill it. Beneath the table was an etched-out picture of a type of bird holding a round object in its mouth.

So focused on the things ahead of her she barely noticed Katsuo seated further up against the wall atop a throne of bone and fur. There were two guards on either side of him, dressed completely in red. Lining the walls were men, soldiers, and other officials of some sort. They were also dressed in variations of red but also had black as well. There were servants present, kneeling and waiting to be ordered about. Though there wasn't a large number of people, there was enough to raise her anxiety significantly. She was brought to kneel before Katsuo who did not move from his position. He was too far for her to see his face clearly, the shadows dancing across his face obstructing her view. The soothsayer had not appeared yet.

A man walked out in front of her in all black save for the red headband.

"The soothsayer approaches!" He shouted making Serenity jump. A jingling sound behind her almost drew her eyes but she decided not to move from her position. In her peripheral, she saw a glimpse of a red robe with lines of black moving past her. She could hear chanting as he passed and the jingling grew louder with the melodic chant. The robe's train slid past her for longer than she anticipated, going on and on for seconds until two servants came, holding its end as they walked by.

He went behind the table. She could see his entire ensemble now. The red robe was stamped in black lines resembling cracks. His head held a single red band. In his hand, he held finger cymbals that he kept shaking to emphasize his chanting. He raised his hand toward the cage and two servants rushed over to bring out the chicken. Being moved brought life back into the animal and it began to buck and fight against them, but it was too small.

Serenity didn't dare watch knowing she could not stomach it. She could still hear his chanting and the clanging of bells along with the cries of the terrified animal. As his chanting ramped up, she squeezed her eyes shut and fisted her hands at her sides fighting the urge to cover her ears. The chicken's distressed noises turn to terrible shrieking which was quickly silenced with a sickening slice followed by awful dripping. The jingling and chanting remained but the chicken was silent.

Serenity opened her eyes but did not look up. The etching of the bird in front of her was no longer a simple showing of artwork. It now began to turn red as the blood of the chicken slowly flowed through it, repulsing her. She did her best to stop herself from gagging, shutting her eyes once more on the violent scene before her. The soothsayer's chanting had stopped and she saw him moving about closer to her. He stood atop the etching, his eyes clouded over, staff still in hand. He hit his staff hard on the floor right on the bird's head.

"Once you have Xian the other nations will follow you willingly," he spoke out. "Their allegiance will come at Xian's fall." Smack! He hit the staff again. "When you break the overstaying king they will break as well. He will break at the loss of that which he holds dear." Smack! "The trust of his people, the ability to protect them, and," He geared up for another hit. "A woman, a woman that he treasures most of all-," Serenity felt like passing out. "This woman-," Smack! Crack!

# CHAPTER 48

The room was now deathly quiet as no one
knew what to do or how to react. On the etched
drawing, the head of the soothsayer's staff lay in the
blood. Lord Sho still held the body of the staff and
at its neck was now only jagged wood. Lord Sho
was completely frozen, face pale. The clouded look
in his eyes was completely gone. Serenity could see
Katsuo, who had jumped up the second the crack
sounded. He was standing away from his throne. He
also looked too shocked for words. Serenity was
suddenly in her dream.

*She sat in front of a bleeding bird as it
placed the emerald in her hand. She took it and
stood walking over to the Jaguar with serpent-like
green eyes.*

*Its early aggression was now gone, it
accepted the jewel from her hand and attempted to
swallow only to begin choking. It fell over, weak.*

Back from her dream Serenity stood as she had in the dream and walked past the soothsayer who still had yet to move. She grabbed one of the clean knives on the table and took a breath before slicing her arm deeply. The pain was a lot but she held on to her tears. Instead of letting the blood mix with the slain chicken's, she walked up to the confused Katsuo. She let the blood run to the ground in front of his feet and looked him right in his eyes, which reflected all of his confusion.

"Two hundred miles from here in the West, a prize awaits you. If you take it, it will cripple the region and be under your control. Obtaining it will lose you little but gain you an opportunity for a great victory, a victory Xian cannot ignore. Take the path west of the smallest river and you will succeed. Any other path leads to heavy loss." She could feel the blood continuously rolling down as she spoke but even as the weakness came her nausea began to pass and her temperature cooled. "You have eight days to claim it. If you hesitate as you did all those years ago on the mountainside, your campaign will falter and your men will suffer." There was a shimmer of pain in his eyes at her words. He wavered slowly, breaking their intense gaze as he looked to the side with a sniffle and a head shake.

Finished with her show Serenity breathed easier and released the tension throughout her body. But once she relaxed the effects of the blood loss came upon her in waves and her stance wavered. The light dimmed over a disturbed Katsuo's face and she felt the floor leave her before everything went dark.


Serenity was cold and her forehead was wet. She reached to wipe it and found a damp cloth in her hands. "Don't move," a familiar voice ordered. She slowly opened her eyes to see Ami, who sat above her removing the cloth from her hand and placing it back on her head. Her throat felt dry and her head ached a little. A tingle in her arm slowly brought her back to what had happened. She turned her head slightly to see her bandaged arm with green herbs seeping from beneath it. She figured that probably accounted for the numbness she was feeling in her arm. "You slept all day. I tried to make sure you drank," he said. She noticed how damp her pillow and shirt felt from his sweet attempts.

"Thank you," she said hoarsely. He quickly grabbed a cup and brought it to her. She drank the water down slowly refreshing her throat and pushing back the pain in her head simultaneously. The nausea was gone, which was a relief. Any other symptoms she'd been feeling appeared to have faded as well. Though she was still weak, she knew it was due to the loss of blood rather than the poison.

She hoped her theatrical "bloodletting" would give her a few more weeks before the poison raged once more. The idea came to her just before she had been summoned for the challenge. She had not been sure she could go through with it at first but seeing what she was up against gave her the courage to use the opportunity to give herself as much time as possible to do what she needed to do. She looked up at Ami who was cleaning her bandage. The image of the broken staff entered her mind along with the shocked faces that followed.

"The staff broke," she said gauging the teen's reaction, but there was none, no surprise and no interest. He grabbed a bowl and held a spoon with a nice-smelling broth in front of her face.

"You shouldn't hurt yourself like this. Not for him," he said. She accepted the food, feeling the warmth go all the way to her stomach.

"It's not for him," she said.

"You shouldn't do it for anyone," he snapped softly in a bitter tone. "Why risk your life for those who would turn on you if you give him the chance?" He fed her another sip.

"Sometimes risking yourself ends up saving others who would do the same for someone else and so on and so on." Ami shook his head.

"Not always," he said sullenly. She raised her brow.

"A risk can make people see things differently, feel things differently, and even do things they never considered before," she said pointedly, unblinking. She knew when he understood her meaning because a light red tint came across his cheeks. He pretended to ignore her and continued his feeding. "Thank you, Ami," she said making it clear she was thanking him not for the food but for what he had done for her. He avoided her gaze and continued feeding her.

"Is what you told him true?" He asked, breaking the silence.

"What's more important is that he believes it," she said avoiding the question. She secretly wished it wasn't true. She did not want to aid Katsuo in any way. It made her more physically ill than the poison and pregnancy combined, but it was necessary, at least she had to believe it was. Her dreams had one central plot that could not be ignored. Gaining Katsuo's trust was crucial to Xian's survival and his downfall.

# CHAPTER 49

The cold wind repeatedly slapped Jung-Soo in the face forcing him to keep his eyes open despite the discomfort. The elevated height brought decreased temperatures and they had not even reached the central mountains yet. They circled the lower peaks looking for signs of trespass but found none. So, they went in deeper looking for evidence of life. If the enemy had gone through, they had hidden their tracks well.

Footsteps had Jung-Soo reaching for his sword only to stop when he saw it was Hae-In and a couple of his men. They had been searching the mountains facing west. "We found their way up." Jung-Soo perked up at the information but the grim look on Hae-In's face gave him pause. "The layout of this place, the sophistication of it all," he said. "From the tracks, we did find, I don't believe this is just a camp. It looks more like their home." Jung-Soo's frown deepened.

"What do you mean?"

"There's no way they just arrived a year ago. Structures like this had to have been around for generations. Not just that, they aren't functioning as an invading force. It's a city. I doubt we'd make it a day in there."

'What was this?' Jung-Soo pondered. How could they not have known about this? Yes, the treacherous conditions of the north made it undesirable to settlers but had they really been here all along? Is that why their invasion had been so silent? To Katsuo, was it not an invasion of enemy territory but his own? There was more going on here but now wasn't the time to figure it all out. If it was as dangerous as reported they could not risk themselves in a suicidal endeavor. Without the aid of Kang-Dae's men, they had no chance of siege. Trying to go in on their own would be unwise, especially not knowing the full layout of the place. The cold feeling of defeat threatened to creep up on him. What could they do? The source of all their problems was so close but impossible to reach. Even with a full army assault, it would be foolish given the uncertainty of what they'd be walking into. Their best bet was to get Katsuo's army to come out and face them on their land. Jung-Soo shut his eyes as he made a decision.

"Let's go," he told them after a moment. They quietly and quickly retraced their footsteps back to their temporary camp. With the new information he was given, his uncertainty and frustration grew into anger, anger he had no outlet for. But that anger quickly switched to dread at the sight of an overanxious and waiting Rielle.

For the first time in his life, Jung-Soo did the cowardly thing and avoided her. He threw himself into giving orders for the men to pack up and prepare to return south. She continued to stand around within his field of vision much longer than he expected or wanted so he started finding other things to do on the other side of camp trying desperately to avoid the unavoidable.

He mistakenly thought he earned his reprieve when he took a chance to look up and saw she was no longer standing there. Assuming she went inside the tent he went back to packing up the horses. He tried to reach for a bag and was met with a pair of dark brown and angry eyes. Jung-Soo swallowed, and focused his eyes anywhere but on her. He could feel her looking at him expectantly.

"Get your things together, we're leaving," was all he could muster before trying to grab the bag again. She smacked it out of his hands. From the silence around them, he could tell they were drawing an audience. Jung-Soo sighed. Silently, he walked across the camp towards the tent and Rielle was practically at his heels the whole way. He had barely entered inside when the verbal assault began.

"What the hell is going on?!" He finally faced all that 5'9 fury. But with all the rage coming off of her she could have been a giant.

"We have to return south and regroup," he said speaking quicker than normal, hating the words but needing to get them out. "It would be foolish to continue to pursue Katsuo into his land. We will meet with the king, get the reinforcements, and force Katsuo out," he spoke not sure if he believed any of it was going to be possible. Rielle must have believed it either because she pushed him as hard as she could, not enough to knock him over, but enough for him to stumble. He did not react outwardly, but inside he felt guilty for breaking his promise to her.

"Wasn't the whole point of coming here to get Serenity and take him out? What about her? She's in there somewhere."

"There are too few of us for such a task and too many unknowns. We gain nothing if we all die here," he explained trying to get her to understand.

"Nothing? Your queen is there. Serenity is there! The enemy is there! Everything is over there and you're just going to go the other way. Coward!" She shouted, pushing him once more.

Those words angered him more than the push and his patience and previous guilt quickly deflated. No longer in the mood to entertain the raging woman he went to walk around her to leave but she quickly blocked his path. "Fine, if you're too scared, I'll go on my own."

He let out a scoff. "Yes, I am sure you'll blend in remarkably well. Shall I give you a uniform to aid you?" Sarcasm coming from him was new to her given the way her nostrils flared and eyes narrowed but the memory of her calling him a coward still floated around in his mind making him less sympathetic to her mood.

"Maybe you should since I'm the only one here with the guts to do anything," she snapped.

"You are mistaking bravery for stupidity. In which case you would be correct, you are the only one with that special asset."

"Go to hell, coward!" she spat stomping around him. She grabbed what he assumed were her things and stuffed them in a small bag.

"You are not going, "he gritted out, losing more and more of his patience. She ignored him as she continued packing.

"Just forget about me, like you did her," she said harshly jamming the last of her items with such force he was surprised her hand didn't go through the bag. She tied it and stomped around him toward the exit or she would have, had he not grabbed her arm. "I'm going to give you five seconds to let go of my arm before I take yours."

If Jung-Soo wasn't so furious, he would have laughed at the threat. "Enough. This will not help her; it will only get you caught or killed."

"Either way, it's none of your business anymore, now let me go," she snapped trying to remove her arm from his grip but he refused to release her.

"Stop this and think. We do not have time for this and I will not waste valuable time and men on you." Something passed in her eyes. Sadness? Hurt? He couldn't be sure but it was so impactful his grip did weaken out of guilt even though he wasn't sure what he'd done to put such a look on her face.

"Let. Go." He almost did only because of that look in her eyes, but still would not allow her to go on a fool's errand.

"It's more complicated than you think. If you get caught, you could compromise my men, our mission, and Xian."

"I wouldn't tell them anything," she told him rolling her eyes as she adjusted the bag on her shoulders.

"You would not have a choice." A flicker of fear passed over her face which also bothered him for some reason.

Fed up with him she shoved him with her other arm. When that didn't work she tried punching him in the shoulder, which hurt a bit but not enough to let her go. When she looked to be going to hit him in the face, he caught her with his free hand. She struggled again. He brought her arms down. He threw his head back just when her head almost connected with his chin. He was momentarily shocked that she had actually tried to headbutt him but not as much as when she tried again. Once again, he avoided the blow and let go of her arms long enough to turn her around and secure her from behind.

"Get off me!" She growled trying to break his hold on her but he was not about to let her go. He was holding her tight, so tight he could feel the warmth of her through his clothes. Even the smell of the scent of her hair and skin penetrated his nose. Her heart was pounding so hard he could feel it on his chest through her back.

"Calm yourself." The words only spurred her on more, prompting him to tighten his hold and her body against his. She was smaller in his arms it seemed. It bothered him how much he noticed how she felt soft and strong at the same time. Or that the scent of her hair reminded him of sweet fruit and how despite the anger and protest of her movements and body he still admired her fight. He needed to stop the madness. He spun her around to face him but held her securely by her forearms. He stared into her angry eyes wanting to get her to understand once and for all what was at stake. Fear, rage, pain, disappointment, he saw it all in her eyes. Needing to remove himself he stormed out of the tent.

"Tae-Soo!" he called out. The soldier rushed over. "Get two men to watch over her. Make sure she goes nowhere," he ordered. The man looked a bit surprised but quickly agreed. He fought the urge to go back in and make sure she stayed put himself. With a sigh, he shifted his focus to preparing for their move.

Rielle shouted in frustration the second Jung-Soo left. 'Would not waste valuable time and men on you.' That statement, those words had set something off inside her.

'You're very articulate.'

'You're pretty for a dark-skinned girl.'

'Let me holla' at your friend.' That last one was spoken to her a lot usually after they pretended to be interested in her all night. She had never been the desirable one, the wanted one. Why would that change here? But it didn't matter in this case.

Serenity was more important. She would get to her herself; she just needed the chance. No doubt 'General Ass' would keep an eye on her until they left. Maybe she could sneak away in transit.

'Stop. Be smart,' her reasonable side spoke up. As much as he had infuriated her, she knew it came from a place of wisdom. There was little she could do other than get captured. It was why she depended so heavily on Jung-Soo and his men but their decision to retreat kept Serenity in a dangerous place and she hated it. She hated all of this. She never should have allowed Serenity to come. Rielle felt she should have forced her to stay home and tied her up if necessary. Anything would have been better than this.

# CHAPTER 50

Sitting at the table, Serenity watched Katsuo eat. Her weak stomach wouldn't even consider the meat before her. She busied herself with pushing around her rice. She had once again been invited to dine with the conqueror once she had recovered from her self-inflicted injury.

"You were quite impressive," he told her.

She gave a tiny, forced smile. "Thank you," she said softly.

"You have a level of power not seen before," Katsuo continued. Serenity forced herself to eat another bite of food, determined to finish enough so that she could leave. "It is almost unbelievable." The way his tone shifted put Serenity on edge. She took the chance to look up at him. Despite his words of praise, the look in his eyes was straight accusation. She looked back to her food not wanting to engage in whatever he was about to put forth.

"This land we are on right now belonged to our ancestors. They resided here for quite a while under Xian rule before venturing out to see what else there was. We found a home, made it our own, and created our own Kingdom. We were content. It was a foolish dream to think we would be left alone."

His tone grew darker the longer he spoke. "I did not tell you who we had to take our land back from did I?" Serenity shook her head not liking where the conversation was going. "Not much is known about the Assani here in Xian. My people have a unique relationship with them that gives us a bit more knowledge. You say you have no idea where you come from, yet you speak the language of the Assani." With this said, he casually took out a dagger and placed it on the table before leaning back in his chair. She had not even realized how much she had been going in and out of English until he pointed it out.

Serenity swallowed and nervously eyed the dagger on the table. "I've never set foot in that land," she told him truthfully.

"Yet, you speak their language perfectly," he accused. "How?"

"There are some in Xian who speak the olden tongue," she responded repeating the very words Kang-Dae had spoken to her when she had first arrived in Xian. "I did not know this was the language of the Assani."

"There are few in Xian that knows what the language of the Assani is."

"How do you know?" She asked him. Katsuo smirked but remained silent. "I am not from Assani." She asserted again.

"What you told me the other night, the other things you've spoken of, that is not information easily gotten. Not from someone who lives in this land and only this land. The little boy you spoke of, how did you know about him?"

"I saw him in my dream," she told him.

He stared at her like he did not believe her. "Lord Sho assured me that vision like yours is impossible. It is more likely you are an Assani spy sent to disrupt my conquest, give me false information to lead my men to our destruction."

"I'm not," Serenity tried to convince him. He gave a sinister smirk that chilled her to the bone.

"Then where did you come from? How did you get here?" Serenity didn't know what to say. There was no way he would believe her true origins. She did not want him to know about her affiliation with Kang-Dae. Her hesitance must have told him everything he needed to know.

"Maybe a good night's sleep will refresh your memory," he taunted. "Have her taken to the dark."

She was roughly pulled up from her seat by the two guards and taken out. She thought of begging or pleading her case but had nothing to say. They walked her down the mountain towards a cave. Once inside, they were led only by the lantern light as it was impossible to see anything without it. The further they walked the more she noticed the changes on the walls, from jagged and random rock to smooth stone. They walked her deeper and deeper until they came to a large door. They opened the door and pushed her inside. The last thing she saw was the last bit of light from the lantern before the door closed and she was left in utter darkness.

Panic slowly rose in her, lost in the silence and the darkness. She stood frozen not knowing what to do. She reached her hands out hoping to find her way back to the door, the wall, or something to hold on to. When she finally made contact with the wall, she jerked her hand back with a hiss. There was something sharp lining the walls. Hand hurting, sight gone, and no hope of anyone coming to let her out, she slowly sank to her knees and sat down on the hard ground in despair. She fought hard not to cry, not wanting to show that weakness and that fear even though there was no one around to see it. She still felt like she would be letting them know that they had won if she allowed herself to cry the way she wanted to. She slowly laid down making sure she didn't hurt herself on anything. She lay on her arm and closed her eyes.

# CHAPTER 51

*Serenity opened her eyes and gasped. Laying his head gently on her very pregnant belly was a smiling Kang-Dae. The sunlight beamed in through the balcony window hitting him with bright and beautiful light. The light made him glow, making him look like an angel, an angel she desperately needed.*

*"Hello my beautiful neeco," he greeted. Tears immediately sprang from her eyes. He gently wiped them before they fell. "Do not cry."*

*"I'm never going to see you again," she cried.*

*"You will," he said, still smiling.*

*"How? He won't let me go. He's going to kill me. I know it." He crawled up her body and took her into his arms. She immediately shrank into his embrace.*

*"I'm scared."*

*He cupped her belly. "I can't wait to meet them," he said completely disregarding her words.*

*"Kang-Dae," she started.*

*He kissed her lovingly. "Look down," he told her. Confused, she did as he asked and a sound caught in her throat. In her arms was a tiny newborn baby sleeping soundly, wrapped in a blue and red blanket. Serenity was immediately calmed, finding joy in staring down at the tiny face.*

*"You've seen this. You've seen us. So, it is not a matter of if we will be together again, but when. This is what you hold onto in those terrifying moments. Because no matter what, we will find our way back to each other." Kang-Dae swore. The tears of despair gave way to tears of relief and joy. She kissed her baby's head and did the same to Kang-Dae.*

It could have been hours or days that Serenity found herself trapped in that dark hole; she would never be sure. She slept most of the time grateful for her pregnancy fatigue. With her sleep came more dreams. Dreams that made her next move clear.

When the door finally opened and the light hit her sensitive eyes, she was less afraid when the men came for her. She was still woozy and weak from lack of food and water so the guards had to carry her to Katsuo's tent. They lay her right in front of his throne. She didn't move or attempt to right herself in front of him, too weak to do anything. She did slightly move her head to see the conqueror staring down at her with eyes that seemed a little regretful. She also caught a glimpse of Sho staring off to the side looking very displeased.

She heard someone call out to get her water or set a fire. She was too out of it to translate properly. She must've passed out for a few seconds because she was suddenly being pulled up to sit and a cup was being pressed to her lips. She drank it slowly before taking hold of the cup herself and gulped it down, almost spitting some up because she was drinking too fast. She coughed heavily but continued drinking until she was done. When the cup was empty, she all but slammed it down. Feeling a little bit clearer, Serenity wiped her mouth and took a couple of deep calming breaths.

"How many did you lose?" She asked. The question had the desired effect. Katsuo's eyes widened ever so slightly and Sho's head snapped to her.

"How-," the soothsayer began.

"You wouldn't have brought me out unless you had a reason to," she said softly.

"You just assumed?" Katsuo asked, not quite believing her.

She looked at him. "No. Of course not. Your losses were made clear to me after...a good night's sleep," she spoke unable to keep her anger out of her voice. After being forced into a worse version of solitary confinement she was going to enjoy making the ones who put her sweat.

"Did it?" the soothsayer scoffed unbelievingly which only angered her more.

She cut her eyes at him. "672. That's how many you lost." Sho fell silent, looking off to the side. "Since you took sent your men east of the river instead of west, they ran right into a large group of Xians. Your men fled back to their lines but they were followed. Now the road you once secured is back under Xian's control. And two of your larger forces are unable to return," she continued. Inwardly, she rejoiced at Xian's victory.

"How do we get it back," Katsuo asked.

"No men you send men will be able to," she said honestly. "That time has passed. Now you must venture south yourself to regain your loses." She met Katsuo's eyes. "Victory is only certain when two kings meet on the battlefield." She studied him carefully to see if he would believe her or not. His away from hers. He had an expression of contemplation.

Katsuo called for one of his guards. "Have her returned to a tent and properly fed," he told them. She supposed it was too much for him to apologize but she didn't care about his apologies or his regret. Regardless of how things had turned out, she was glad he didn't believe her and now Xian had more of a fighting chance.

# CHAPTER 52

Serenity pulled at the veil covering her face gently so she could breathe a bit better. The head covering, along with her new outfit was a gift from Katsuo. He'd told Iko it was to keep prying eyes from seeing her. Serenity knew it was so his men would not see an "Assani" getting special treatment. The disdain for the Assani people ran throughout his entire army it seemed. She didn't care though. The fewer people saw her, the less chance of her possibly being recognized.

She rode on her horse, another gift from Katsuo, not far behind Katsuo's carriage. She had been happy that she did not have to ride with him. They had set off that morning. Katsuo took her warnings seriously now and they were headed south. Katsuo told her he had another place to settle in and make their plans. He didn't disclose where this place was or how he had secured it but the important thing was Serenity was being taken closer to Kang-Dae.

They had only been traveling half a day and Rielle was crabby the entire time. She walked with the back of the party. The one named Hae-In was the only one willing to keep her company. His English was basically nonexistent but that didn't stop him from trying to engage with her which she appreciated. She didn't know how she was going to make this long journey back with nothing but her thoughts for company. How she longed for her phone or even a couple of books.

There were moments of levity. Sometimes she would get so bored she'd find herself humming without realizing it. And after a few minutes of humming the same melody, Hae-In would join in adding his own unique harmony. She was aware he was probably just doing it to cheer her up and though nothing could remove the dark worry she harbored for Serenity, it was nice to have a moment to smile.

She had not seen Jung-Soo at all since they left. She knew he was at the head of the line. After their argument the night before he had not returned nor spoken a word to her. With the benefit of a horrible night's sleep, she came to realize that her anger against him was not warranted. She knew he wanted to save Serenity as much as she did but he did have a whole kingdom to worry about. She should not blame him for that.

A whistle in the sky made her think that it was a bird passing, but the way everyone stopped in their tracks said otherwise. Hae-In held his hand up, gesturing for her to stop and be quiet. Someone from in the crowd whistled a responding tune. Rielle for a moment found it amusing that she and Serenity had used the same tactic to find each other right before they were separated.

From the trees, a man she recognized as one of Jung-Soo's companions came running. He went straight toward the front where she imagined he was going to speak with Jung-Soo. The nosy part of her wanted to walk over to see what was going on.

After a few minutes of waiting in silence, something was shouted out in Xianian and the men began to walk into the forest. She looked to Hae-In questioningly, but he looked as lost as she was. Nevertheless, the two followed suit.

Once they were clear from the road, the men gathered together around Jung-Soo who stood with the scout. He began speaking to them in their language. He appeared to be informing them of something big, judging from the looks on the men's faces. After he was finished, they all responded with a unified grunt and began to unpack their things like they were setting up camp once more. Completely confused Rielle decided to get answers from the source.

She walked up to Jung-Soo before he could get away. "What's going on?" she asked him.

"Katsuo and his army are leaving the mountains and traveling this way."

"What? Why?" she asked, surprised by the news.

"We can't be sure but it is clear he is on the move. This will be our best chance to infiltrate," Jung-Soo informed her.

"Infiltrate? You want to join his army? I thought you said it was too dangerous," she reminded him.

"With as many men as he has, it will be easier to join in the march without suspicion. Without the cover of the mountains, they are more vulnerable and the further south they go, the more advantage we have," he tried to explain. However, Rielle was still focused on the fact that they would be traveling with the people who would want to kill them. It would be one thing to sneak in and sneak out but having to walk alongside them for who knows how long made Rielle nervous.

"I will not allow anything to happen to you," Jung-Soo told her suddenly.

"You can only do so much," she countered, trying to be realistic.

"I will keep you safe," he promised her. Rielle thought real hard trying to decide if she believed him. After a moment she nodded and agreed. Even though she was about to encounter an even more dire situation it was probably a blessing in disguise. They had another opportunity to find Serenity.

# CHAPTER 53

"Do not draw attention to yourself. Stay quiet. Do not look anyone in the eyes," Jung-Soo's warning whispered in her mind as Rielle walked behind the men. She had to give them credit. The Xian men blended in perfectly. With the matching armor, it was impossible for anyone to distinguish them from the others. If she didn't recognize their faces she would not be able to tell the difference. She was very thankful for them as she felt infinitely safer among them while being surrounded by so many enemies.

The group headed to an unoccupied space to set up their camp. Rielle took on the role of servant and immediately got to work on packing and looking as subservient as possible. She went to lift one of the packs but underestimated its weight and ended up dropping it to the ground. Tae-Soo was quick to rush over and help but she waved him off with her eyes. He was reluctant to do so but quickly realized the danger of being too nice.

"Pick it up," he said, or at least she assumed he had said with as much bite as he could muster. She nodded and gathered up the fallen materials.

Rielle busied herself with different menial tasks. As deep in the camp as they were, they still were surrounded by soldiers and she'd already gotten more than a few curious and hateful looks, not unlike the one she had gotten when she'd been captured with Serenity.

Tae-Soo and Hae-In were good at keeping her protected without looking as if they were protecting her. She appreciated their efforts, having gotten off to a rocky start in their relationship. She was deeply grateful for their forgiveness and professionalism. She had yet to see Jung-Soo anywhere. He had gone off on his own just as they had merged into the army. None of the others seemed worried or concerned with his absence so she assumed it was planned. Rielle headed around the recently pitched tents with a bucket to get some water from their supply. There was some regular hustle and bustle about the camp. Rielle noticed a troop going past their settlement. She was determined to ignore them and to keep to herself as much as possible.

A harsh shout in Xianian made her look up. In the distance, she could see one guard trying to push an older woman to get her to keep moving. As sad as the sight as it was that wasn't what had caught Rielle's attention. The woman appeared to have been staring right at her. Rielle began to get nervous. A young teen helped the stumbling woman to keep her moving forward but he also caught a glimpse of Rielle and froze just for a moment before pulling the older woman forward. Rielle was momentarily perplexed at their reaction. Being stared at was not a new thing in this place but it was the way that they were staring at her that gave her pause. They weren't staring at her like they had never seen someone of her color before. They were staring at her as if they almost recognized her or maybe someone who looked like her. A sliver of hope rose in her at the idea that maybe they had seen Serenity. Not only that, but maybe they knew where Rielle could find her.

Before she could think better of it, Rielle went to follow them hoping to get answers. She followed behind them and the soldiers herding them for a couple of minutes waiting for a chance to catch the two alone. As the group turned the corner past some recently pitched tents Rielle went to follow but was immediately grabbed by her forearm. Her first instinct was to snatch her arm away but she froze when she looked into the familiar but angry eyes of one of the guards who had once held her captive with Serenity.

The man had a nasty smirk on his face looking her up and down. He said something to her that she didn't understand and ended it with that same term "Assani" she'd heard quite a bit in her captivity.

"Geunyeoleul noh-a jwo," Hae-In's voice sounded behind her. Rielle silently thanked God for his arrival.

It had taken him a couple of minutes to notice that the woman, Rielle, was no longer among them or in his line of sight. Immediately alarmed, Hae-In went to Tae-Soo to see if he had seen her. When Tae-Soo admitted he had not, both men began to panic knowing if the general knew they had lost her there would be hell to pay. The two immediately went searching for her without trying to draw too much attention to themselves. Trying to frantically search for someone without looking frantic was a challenge. It was pure luck that Hae-In happened upon Rielle just as she had been caught by one of Katsuo's soldiers. He rushed up to them, hoping to deescalate the situation without causing too much of a ruckus.

"Let her go," he told the man.

The soldier looked up at him, unfazed, not bothering to heed Hae-In's command. "Are you responsible for catching this thing?" the soldier sneered.

"She belongs to our men. Release her," he ordered.

"It was my man who captured her first," the soldier asserted. "She belongs to us."

Getting annoyed and not liking the way he held on to Rielle. He knew the woman was already scared and did not want her in the man's possession any longer. "It seems as if you could not hold on to her and now she belongs to us. Release her. Now," Hae-In commanded once again.

"You seem a bit attached. Has she been good to you? She was not nearly as nice to me. Have they tamed you dog?!" the man spat into Rielle's ear making her flinch. Hae-In took a step forward ready to remove her forcibly from his hold. Tae-Soo appeared next to the soldier and grabbed his shoulder in a friendly manner. The action dropped the soldier's guard for just long enough for Hae-In to collect Rielle.

"I believe we all have work to do," Tae-Soo said. "We do not want our superiors to find us at odds."

Hae-In and the soldier stared at one another, unblinking. It was Tae-Soo who got between the two. He took Rielle by the arm. "Let's go," he told Hae-In leading her away. Hae-In lingered for a bit, just as the soldier did, before following behind.

# CHAPTER 54

Lighting the candle by her bed Serenity prepared for sunset. She awkwardly walked over to her cot, saddle sore from all the riding she'd been doing. The journey had been uneventful so far, only mind-numbingly boring. She kept herself distracted with thoughts of Kang-Dae, and what they would do when they were together again. Those thoughts would sometimes take a dark turn when she'd wonder if he would understand the things she'd done to get back to him. That had become one of her newest fears. Just because she had accepted that her actions were a necessary means to an end did not mean he would agree. Would he blame her? Denounce her? Part of her knew he loved her too much to do that, but that nagging part of her that said otherwise was persistent.

"My lady?" Iko's vice called out from outside the tent. Happy to have someone to talk to, Serenity didn't hesitate to call out for her to enter. Iko had come without Ami, which was not strange, just a bit disappointing as she had been worried about the boy as well. She hadn't known if the two would be brought on the journey or left behind.

"Hi!" Serenity greeted happily. Iko smiled, coming in with a small bag and a kettle. Ignoring her soreness, Serenity went to take the items from the woman and put them on the table. Iko attempted to scold Serenity for "doing her job" but Serenity ignored her and helped her to sit. The woman handed her the bag.

"I've gathered more ginger for you," Iko told her. Grateful, Serenity accepted the bag, thanking her.

"How's Ami?" Serenity asked.

"He is fine," Iko responded. "He's with the other children tending the horses."

Serenity was glad to hear he was okay but also saddened knowing that he and other young people like him were being used.

Serenity poured them both some tea. The moment made her recall all the times her mother-in-law had done the same for her. Serenity wondered how she was doing. Iko had the same kind spirit as the queen dowager. Maybe that was why Serenity was so fond of her.

"He cares for you, you know," Iko told her.

Serenity smiled. "He has his own way of showing it," she joked.

Iko let out a laugh. "I hope you do not take his past words to heart. Ami has always had a natural distrust of those with gifts like yours."

Serenity found this interesting. She had assumed he had disliked her because he thought she was Assani like the others had. Had it been his fear of those who dabbled in the supernatural he hated? Had he mistaken her for someone like the soothsayer? Where had this distrust come from? Had he encountered another seer before? Thinking back on his willingness to cross the soothsayer for her, Serenity wondered if the act had been personal for the young boy.

"He was always such a caring child. From the moment he was brought to me, he always tried to take care of me as if it were his duty."

"Brought to you?" Serenity asked.

"Ami was an orphan. He was found wandering around the docks by our village when he was very young.

That may have accounted for his guarded nature. Serenity imagined Ami had quite the story, but she doubted the teen would confide in her.

"Is that where the soldiers found you, in your village?" asked Serenity.

Iko sadly nodded. "They took all of us women and children. The men," she trailed off and Serenity didn't need to hear any more.

The two continued to drink in silence for a bit before Iko spoke.

"My lady, may I ask," she began and then shut her mouth abruptly.

"Ask," Serenity encouraged.

"When you were brought here, were you alone?" Iko inquired. Serenity found the question odd but answered to see where it would lead.

"Not at first, no. I was caught with someone, but they managed to get away."

"Your sister?" she asked. Serenity cocked her head. That was a random guess she thought to herself.

"Sister?" Serenity asked trying to get clarification.

"It's just- I saw a woman. You both looked to be from the same land. I just assumed," Iko told her.

'Rielle?' Serenity thought. "Was she taller than me? Darker?" Serenity inquired. The woman nodded.

"Where did you see her?" she asked frantically.

Sensing her worry the woman quickly sputtered out, "among some soldiers in the camp. It was not far from here. She didn't seem like she had been harmed."

'Oh god, Rielle must have been captured.' Who knows what she had gone through? Serenity felt sick.

"The next time you see her, can you bring her to me?"

# CHAPTER 55

Rielle sat in the middle of their little camp washing clothes. She hadn't planned on immersing herself in the role of their servant so well, but the truth was she was dead bored, and doing these menial tasks kept her from going stir-crazy. She stayed in the tent as long as she could but sometimes she needed to get out and walk around. As she scrubbed one of the shirts with Hae-In standing at her side she wondered once again where Jung-Soo had gone off to. He was always gone when she awoke and never around when she went to sleep. Looking around the camp she paused seeing a familiar face.

The woman she had tried to follow before was back again and staring at her. This time there were no guards around her and she seemed to be waving Rielle over. Hae-In was not paying much attention to her and was staring off in the opposite direction. Since it wasn't very far, she decided there was no harm in going to see what the woman wanted.

She left the clothes and went over. The same young boy was also with her, but he seemed reluctant.

The woman spoke to her in Xian, gesturing frantically. Rielle felt bad that she had no idea what she was saying. Rielle shook her head. "I'm sorry I don't understand," she told the woman.

The boy suddenly stepped forward. "She wants you to come with her," he told her in English. Rielle was taken back shocked that the boy spoke her language. It appeared to be a surprise to the older woman as well as she stared down at him in shock. "She says your sister is waiting for you," he told her.

'Sister?' Realizing her hunch had been right the first time and that the two had been in contact with Serenity Rielle felt elated. She nodded agreeing to go with them, but just as she took a step forward, a hand landed on her shoulder pulling her back. She looked back to see Hae-In standing above her with a disapproving look on his face. Rielle tried to explain but due to the language barrier, it was practically impossible. "I have to go with them," she told him gesturing to the two. Hae-In shook his head.

He opened his mouth and released one word. She recognized the word as relating to Jung-Soo. She knew Jung-Soo had put her in Hae-In's care and he would not let her go off without Jung-Soo's say so.

"I will find you again," she told the woman through the boy. Her heart heavy, she watched as the two walked off. Rielle stomped back over to her spot kicking at the bucket, no longer in the mood to wash.

# CHAPTER 56

Rielle was back in Jung-Soo's tent. The day was over and he still had not returned so she had been unable to tell him about the encounter with the older woman and the boy. Exhausted, she lay down on the cot but she had been determined to stay up to confront Jung-Soo when he came back.

Unfortunately for her, she had fallen asleep almost as soon as her eyes were closed. After an indeterminate amount of time, she was awakened by sounds from across the tent. Alarmed, her eyes shot open but she was instantly calmed by the sight of Jung-Soo who was in the middle of removing his armor. His back was to her, so he had no idea she was no longer asleep. The polite thing to do would probably be to let him know she was awake but Rielle decided she was much too tired. She debated whether to go ahead and tell him about what happened but given how late it was and how slowly he moved she decided it could wait until the morning as they both appeared to be exhausted. She went to close her eyes again but would find herself taking multiple peeks. He was now in just a white shirt. It hung loosely, now free from all the other layers he'd removed.

The shirt suddenly came off faster than she could blink. The scars drew her eyes first. There were not many of them, but given the size of them, she could imagine how much pain he had suffered. She also couldn't help noticing how big he was. She had always assumed it was the armor that had given the illusion of his muscular physique, but clearly, she had been wrong. He went over to where the wash bin was. Jung-Soo used the washcloth sitting beside it to clean his neck and chest first.

Deciding she'd played 'Peeping Tom" long enough, she shut her eyes and pretended to sleep. She managed to keep her eyes closed for a whopping thirty seconds before a small grunt had her opening them once more. He was trying to reach his back but was having difficulty. Remembering how she had stabbed him and therefore was the cause of his struggle, she felt guilty again.

Jung-Soo put down the cloth after his third attempt to reach his back. The pain in his shoulder prevented him from doing so. Normally the ache was light, but given his activities all day it seemed he may have overworked the injury and was currently paying for it. He had spent the day walking the camp trying to get as much information as he could while also surveying for any signs of Serenity. But with the camp's massive size, it was difficult to cover it all. He couldn't go in as deep as he liked as he had to keep from drawing attention to himself. His current status, or the status of the one's armor he had stolen, kept him from being questioned by others. It did not keep him from being bothered by low-ranking officers wanting confirmation on instructions or his permission to do certain activities. He was able to stave off most of them, telling them to go to their own commander.

The biggest challenge was having to remain uninvolved when seeing so many Xian citizens in bondage. It was maddening. A lot of them were children, which made it almost impossible not to react. Was this the fate of all the young ones they had taken? He remembered the Duke's words about how they had kept the children to control the men. How many of their soldiers had stood down for the sake of their children allowing Katsuo to gain more control of the land?

The feeling of cool wetness on his back took him out of his thoughts. He turned to see Rielle standing behind him. She kept her eyes down, focused only on his back. Jung-Soo didn't speak, mostly because he didn't know what to say. Silently, she washed his back and he just let her. Her swipes were gentle but every once in a while, her thumb would brush against his skin and a small shiver would go through him. Jung-Soo tensed and sat up straighter not liking his body's reaction. If she noticed his discomfort, she didn't say anything. She was done after a few seconds. She placed the cloth down by the basin and turned to go back to her cot.

"Thank you," he said to her in his low voice.

She gave him a soft "mm-hmm" and climbed into her bed.

"Has anyone approached you?" He asked. It was a harmless question he figured, just to make sure they were not under scrutiny from others. He was definitely not attempting to engage in regular conversation with her out of desire.

"There's a woman here who I think knows where Serenity is," she told him. Jung-Soo's ears perked up. "She wants to take me to her."

"That may not be wise," he warned her.

"I saw her earlier. She looked at me like she may have known me or someone who looked like me. I think she must have seen her."

Jung-Soo did not want to get his hopes up or put so much faith in a stranger. "We need to stay alert. We do not know who they take their orders from and if they can be trusted."

"I know, but we can at least check it out," she reasoned. "This is the only lead we got. If she's telling the truth, we can't afford not to check it out. It may be our only chance to find her."

Jung-Soo knew she was right but he still didn't like the idea of letting her go off with these strangers. "Wait for her to come to you and take-," he began to say before she cut him off.

"I'll have Hae-In with me." Amused at her ability to know exactly what he was going to say he let the matter go. He should have said no. The risk seemed too great in his opinion. As he went over to his cot and laid down, he almost told her he'd changed his mind but decided to let it be. He did not want to deal with her fury. 'What was wrong with him?' Why was he willing to allow such risk just because she had asked? Frustrated with himself he blew out the candle and went to sleep refusing to give his thoughts any more of his attention.

# CHAPTER 57

The older woman led her to one of the larger tents in the camp with Hae-In trailing behind. They both carried large buckets of water. The woman had given one to her to keep up appearances. Hae-In hung back as they approached a tent. There was a soldier standing guard. Rielle was surprised. She had not known exactly what conditions she was going to find Serenity in, but she did not expect this. The older woman spoke, bowing to the guard on duty. He checked Rielle out suspiciously before turning his eyes back towards the woman. With her heartbeat rising, Rielle tried to keep herself calm. The two were finally allowed in. Once inside, the older woman went straight toward the tub with her water.

Rielle, however, stood frozen finally laying eyes on her friend. Serenity looked at her with watery eyes. Without a word, she ran to her and Rielle did the same, after dropping the bucket. The two embraced, hugging as if they had not seen each other in years. Rielle wanted to cry but she didn't want to alarm the guard out front.

"Are you okay?" she heard Serenity whisper into her ear. She was not okay, far from it, but she nodded regardless because at that moment she felt like she was.

After a while, Rielle slowly pulled away and looked over her friend trying to determine any signs of illness or injury. "Are you hurt? How have you been? Are you having any symptoms?" She fired questions at her one after the other.

Serenity shook her head. "I'm alright," she told her.

"What about you? Are you-did they?" Serenity began to ask.

Rielle shook her head knowing Serenity was worried that she had been captured once more. "No, I came back with a friend," she told her.

"A friend?" Serenity asked.

"Jung-Soo," Rielle informed her. Serenity's eyes widened.

"Jung-Soo? He's here. You found him?"

"He found me," Rielle admitted. "It's a long story. He's not far from here. When we get a chance, we'll get you out of here."

A look passed over Serenity's face that confused Rielle. "What is it?" Rielle asked.

"I can't leave, not now," Serenity said hesitantly.

Rielle took a step back. "What?"

Serenity let out of breath. "I can't leave here."

"Yes, you can. That was the whole point of this!" Rielle exclaimed, becoming frustrated. Serenity hushed her when her voice had gotten loud. Rielle took a breath to calm herself.

"I know, I know you risked so much to come here. But I can't leave with you. There's something I need to do here, something important that I think will help end all of this," Serenity claimed.

"You think?" Rielle questioned disbelievingly.

"I believe it. There's a reason I'm here. There's a reason, out of all the places I could have ended up I ended up here. This is something that I have to do. Something that only I can do. And I can only do it while I'm with Katsuo. If I don't, Xian won't stand a chance."

"I doubt you will be the deciding factor in this war," Rielle argued. "You're just one person. There are whole armies out there that will decide who wins, not you."

"I don't think so. I've seen it, Rielle. I've seen what happens if I don't do this and what could happen if I do."

"Did you forget about your baby? Are you really going to risk yourself and it staying here?

What about Kang-Dae? How do you think he would feel knowing that you're here?" Rielle argued.

"I think he'd understand more than anyone why I have to stay. It's the same reason he had to come back here. He believed he needed to be here to make a difference and I know that I need to be here to do the same. I know it's hard to believe and you have every reason to think I'm just crazy. But it doesn't change the fact that I have a purpose here and I can't just leave," she claimed.

"And Kang-Dae? You're just going to pass up this opportunity to go back to him." Rielle countered.

Serenity got a wistful look in her eye that only confused Rielle more. A small, but soft smile appeared on Serenity's face. "It's because I want to see him again that I have to do this. If not, whatever time we would have together would be cut short and none of it would matter anyway. I want to meet him again the right way, the way that guarantees we won't have to be apart again and we can be together with our child without worrying about any of this."

"What am I supposed to tell Jung-Soo?"

"Tell him to go to Kang-Dae and keep fighting their way. I'm going to fight here, in my way. Go, be safe. I promise it's going to work out."

"You can't know that," said Rielle.

"But I believe it." Serenity took Rielle's hand. "Go back home. Tell my family I'm okay."

"I'm not just going to leave you again," Rielle told her.

"Yes, you are. This isn't your fight or your home. You've done more than enough and I don't want anything else to happen to you."

Rielle slowly shook her head, not believing that this was happening. "I love you," Serenity said, embracing her once again. Rielle held onto her not wanting to let go.

When they pulled away, she was crying again. "Oh," Rielle exclaimed remembering something. She pulled out the remaining pills she brought with her and placed them in Serenity's hand.

Serenity smiled with gratitude. "Thank you," she told her. "You should go before they get suspicious. Tell Jung-Soo," Serenity paused. "Tell him I know what I'm doing and not to worry." Though the message was for Jung-Soo, Rielle knew it was for her as well. The two hugged once more and Rielle left, her heart feeling heavier than when she came in.

# CHAPTER 58

Rielle agonized the entire walk back to camp over how she would explain things to Jung-Soo. She didn't know what Serenity was thinking. She wasn't going to be able to change this man's mind. You'd think someone who had known him for longer than she had certainly would know that there was nothing she could say that would get this man to abandon his mission.

Rielle continued walking silently behind Hae-In as they returned to their camp. They were cutting through the woods and she recognized one of the trees they passed and knew they weren't far. A voice called out making Hae-In stop, so she did the same. Two soldiers were walking towards them. Rielle immediately cast her eyes down as they spoke amongst themselves. They chatted for only a few seconds before Hae-In looked at her and signaled her with his head to tell her to go on. Nervous to go by herself but not wanting to disobey in front of the others she took his cue and left, making the journey between the trees on her own.

It wasn't a quiet night, the murmurings and chatting of numerous soldiers filled the sky. She moved as fast as she could. The snap of a twig had her stopping. She looked around but saw no one and nothing out of the ordinary. Still, she did her best to pick up her pace knowing she wasn't too far from the camp and Jung-Soo. She could see the light of the campfire in the distance. Just as she was starting towards it, a rough arm grabbed at her, forcing her to stop. Before she could let out a scream, a hand was wrapped around her mouth. A familiar voice sneered into her ear something she couldn't understand. The smell of wine hit her nostrils. She was roughly pushed up against the tree and was horrified to see the same soldier who had confronted her a couple of days earlier. Instinct kicked in, and she shot her leg out kicking him right in the groin. He hissed and doubled over in pain. She tried to run off but he recovered enough to grab at her and tackle her to the ground.

Her vision blurred and her teeth clashed on impact. Her hair was ruthlessly grabbed from behind pulling her head up. The man growled insults at her in his language before slamming her face back into the dirt. He roughly forced her onto her back. She saw the shimmer of the blade as it moved toward her throat. Rielle was frozen in shock truly believing that this was how she was going to die. She hated to think that this awful and hateful man would be the last thing she'd see.

Something sprayed across her face forcing her to close her eyes. There was a sudden weight on her. She could feel her shirt dampen as something wet seeped through. The weight was pulled off of her and she hesitated to open her eyes.

"Rielle." She looked up to see Jung-Soo standing above her, a bloody sword in hand. She looked over to her side and saw the dead soldier laying lifelessly next to her. Rielle couldn't bring herself to move, still frozen, barely comprehending what had just occurred. Jung-Soo gently helped her up, but when she remained unresponsive he scooped her up into his arms to take her way.

Jung-Soo carried the traumatized Rielle all the way back to camp. The second Hae-In had returned without her he'd gone looking. He had been scared that he would not find her or worse that he would and it would be too late. It was pure luck that he stumbled upon her. Seeing the man attacking her took all reason and logic from his mind. Where he normally would have taken a second to evaluate the best course of action to keep their identities secret, he had just attacked. In his opinion, he put the dog down too soon, but he didn't want Rielle to endure the vile man's presence any longer. It was clear after he'd done the deed that she was not in a good place mentally. He carried her all the way back to camp. He ordered the first soldiers he saw to go and bury the body he left behind. He continued on to the tent ignoring the questioning eyes of his men.

He sat her down and immediately went for the washcloth on the table. He cleaned her face first as it was sticky with dirt and her attacker's blood. Still in shock, she barely flinched. She just stared off into space not speaking. It bothered him to see her so broken. Once her face was clean, he grabbed one of his shirts. He was about to ask her to change but she was not in a state to hear him. He slowly removed her top, stopping numerous times to give her a chance to stop him but she didn't move. The man's blood had soaked through the top layer but luckily had not reached her undershirt. He wiped what little blood had touched her skin before helping her into his shirt. Even then, she still did not respond. More worried now than ever he bent down to look her in her eyes.

"Rielle?" He called out to her hoping to get her attention. It took her so long to look at him, he was sure she was never going to. She didn't say a word. She just stared at him as her eyes welled up and the tears began to fall. Soon her body shook as she began to sob. Not knowing what else to do, he hugged her to him as she cried. He had no soothing words to tell her, no gentle encouragements. She knew as well as he did that she very easily could have been killed that night. And what was worse was that he imagined she knew it could happen again. So, he let her cry and cry willing to hold her all night if necessary.

Rielle cried for hours, unable to stop. Every time she thought she was done, she'd see flashes of her attacker and start again. Through it all, Jung-Soo stayed with her, not leaving her for a second. When she could no longer cry, she finally calmed. In the silence, there were only the sounds of her breathing and sniffs.

"She's here I saw her." She spoke. Now that she could think clearly, she wanted to forget what happened. Remembering her earlier conversation with Serenity she decided now was the time to inform Jung-Soo of Serenity's decision. After what she had just been through, she no longer feared his reaction.

There was some relief on his face but he was obviously still concerned for Rielle. "Has she been harmed in any way?" He asked.

She shook her head. "They're taking care of her," she said.

"Are there many men posted around her?" Rielle looked down knowing this would not go well. "It is best for us to get her during the night. I should be able to sneak her out without alerting anyone, "Jung-Soo continued.

Rielle took a breath. "She's not going to come with us," she finally said. Rielle didn't look up, she couldn't, but from the silence and the way he tensed, she knew he had heard her. "She said she needed to stay. I think she had a dream, and she believes that the best way for you guys to win is for her to stay with Katsuo," she rushed out the last bit.

After an agonizingly long and silent minute, she looked up at him. That stoic expression of his was there but she must have spent a bit too much time with him because she could read what was beneath it. He was pissed. He shot up from the cot.

"If I could have convinced her to come, I would have, but you know her. She really believes that this is the best thing for her to do and neither you or I can convince her otherwise. So, unless you want to drag her out kicking and screaming and have an army coming down on your head we just have to do what she says and hope that she's not wrong."

Jung-Soo stood still, not moving for such a long time that Rielle felt like he had glitched. "Jung-Soo?" She called him. He turned to walk out of the tent and Rielle knew he was going to go after her himself.

She grabbed onto his arm to stop him. It surprised her when he did pause. "You know as well as I do that you're not going to get her to leave. If she says that this is the only way we have to believe her."

"Why?" The question threw her off. "Why must we just accept that she is doing the right thing? She's not infallible. She could be wrong," he pointed out.

"You don't really believe that," she said still holding on to his arm. "If you try to take her by force, you risk not only your life but hers too. They don't know who she is and that is her best weapon right now. Don't give them any more reason not to trust her." He tried to pull away and she pulled on his arm once more. "Please."

"You could leave her here?" he asked Rielle, not maliciously but desperately as if he were trying to understand and make sense of what she was asking him to do.

"If I trust her and believe in her, I have to."

"I should just slit his throat myself and put an end to all of this," he spoke out loud.

"If I thought it would work, I'd tell you to go for it but I think we have to trust Serenity when she says that this is the only way."

"What would she have me do? Leave her here?" he asked.

"She said that you should go and join Kang-Dae and head south. She says he will need you."

"This is foolish," he said more to himself than to her. She nodded in sympathetic understanding.

"Maybe that's why it will work," she surmised. He scoffed at her but she didn't take offense to it. "What are we going to do?" she asked carefully.

He took a moment to answer. "We'll continue on with them until we know their destination.  Then we'll allow ourselves to fall behind and break off from the party. We'll take the southwest road and hopefully, we'll make it to the king in time." Rielle nodded her understanding and gently led him back into the tent so they both could try to get some rest.

# CHAPTER 59

Kang-Dae and the majority of his men lay in wait for General Hui and his troop to make it back. To draw the enemy to them, the general and his men went off to make themselves an unavoidable target. They marched with horses and multiple carts of food and weapons down the road in a conspicuous manner. Once they drew their attention, they would lead them back toward Kang-Dae under the guise of a retreat. The knot in his gut was building, but it had nothing to do with the upcoming battle. The idea that their entire resistance could have been ended at the hands of these soldiers because of his decision wouldn't leave him. It was a miracle that they had been spared such an end. He didn't feel his desire to save the people was wrong. He would never regret dying for them, as it was his duty, but if it cost Xian its freedom, would the cost have been worth it? No, it wouldn't. He knew that somehow, in this chaotic time, the right thing wasn't what would help them. His dream with Serenity entered his mind. 'What is good isn't always what is needed,' she had said. With the memory came a slow realization. To get what he needed, he had to let go of what he wanted. What was his current desire?

Shouts from up ahead stole his attention. Kahil's archers came into view first. They had formed a strong line, already releasing a slew of arrows as the other returning soldiers fled behind them. The rest of Kahil's men, along with the captain himself, were fighting back the oncoming force.

"Attack!" Kang-Dae shouted, and the horn bellowed.

The men came at the enemy on all sides, surrounding them in a thick barricade of soldiers and shields. The men's faces all took on varying degrees of realization and fear as they pushed in.

"Take them all!" Kang-Dae ordered.

Just like that, one by one, the men fell by way of arrows, swords, and staffs. No one was spared. The ground was littered with blood and

bodies. There were more men than they expected –
definitely more than the survivor had spoken of. It
was enough to take all of them out had they not
succeeded in drawing them into an ambush. His
guilt built up once more. Kang-Dae ordered the
bodies quickly burned. A deed he'd never do under
other circumstances, believing in giving the enemy
the proper burial, but they didn't have the time, and
he didn't have the sympathy. They were fortunate
not to lose but a few men, a feat that would not have
occurred if fate had not been on their side. He was
doing what he thought was right, but it could have
cost him everything.

"Bring General Sun to me," he ordered the
man closest to him.

Later, the reluctant general came before him
with resentful submission.

"I want you and your men to join Fort
Chungi."

The general looked taken back. "Me, my
king?" He asked incredulously.

"The enemy spreads us too thin. We need to draw them out, but we can't do so and protect our borders as well. You and your men will go on and give the fort assistance for a last stand if needed."

The general looked confused but agreed. Yu walked up.

"My king?" Yu questioned.

"We've left our home too open. We need to defend it and keep the enemy from gaining more ground. We will continue on north and meet with general Jung-Soo to draw the bastards out," he said.

Yu hid his confusion in indifference and nodded. Kang-Dae hoped he was doing the right thing – no not the right thing, what was necessary. Right was no longer sustainable to win this war.

# CHAPTER 60

Once they arrived at their destination
Serenity was surprised at how beautiful the estate
looked. It was not as big as the palace, but it was
just as extravagant, if not more so. The owner had
wealth or did before Katsuo had seized it. She still
had no idea where she was. She wished she had
Rielle's sense of direction to at least know if they
had gone southwest or southeast. It wouldn't tell her
much but it would tell her something. Serenity
shifted uncomfortably on her horse. Her bottom was
both numb and sore. She made sure her veil stayed
put. Even if she didn't know where in Xian she was
there was an even greater possibility of someone
figuring out who she was this far South. As the
army slowly caught up to them, they were made to
hang back and set up mostly outside the gates. Only
a small number of the soldiers were allowed inside.
Absolutely none of the captives appeared to have
been granted access either.

Serenity was led further in still following behind Katsuo's carriage and his guard. Serenity looked around fruitlessly for Iko and Ami. She had not seen either of them in the last couple of days of their journey. She hoped they both were alright.

A line of servants waited for them at what Serenity assumed was the main house. There were a few women dressed more elegantly in the middle of the line. Was one of them Katsou's future queen? Serenity was too far away, so she couldn't see their faces but she did notice the dresses that they wore were the types of dresses the noble women would wear around the palace. Were the people of this household Xianians who had switched allegiances? Katsuo stepped out and the line of people began to kneel.

All the finely dressed women bowed at the waist, with the exception of the one in the middle wearing the dark blue and gold dress. She only bowed her head. It was an elegant move but something about it unnerved Serenity. A growing feeling of dread had begun to fill her the moment she arrived. Katsuo touched the face of the woman in blue and they exchanged some words before going inside.

Captain Masao helped Serenity down from her horse with a friendly smile. The captain had been assigned as her personal guard. Unlike the others, he treated her kindly. Sometimes, Serenity had to remind herself that he was the enemy to try and keep herself from liking him too much.

A servant approached them. "I will take you to your accommodations," the servant spoke quietly and nervously. Serenity followed her while Masao stayed close. They were led to a different wing of the estate a couple of buildings away from the main house. Serenity didn't mind one bit as she only wished she could be even further from him. Her room was nice, slightly bigger than the tent she had stayed in during their journey. She was happy to see she had a large window with a nice view of the grounds.

"I will have your food brought up," the servant informed her.

"Is there any chance I can get some honey tea?" Serenity asked.

"As you wish." Serenity had felt the same dizziness a few days ago on the journey. She hoped her ailment was not trying to make an appearance and she prayed the honey would slow it before she had to resort to spilling more of her blood.

"Do you need anything?" Masao asked from the other side of the door.

"I'm fine. I'm just going to rest," she told him. He nodded and shut the door. Left alone she began to explore the room.

The room itself looked minimally decorated but upon closer inspection, she realized they had not finished putting everything up. There were spots on the wall where things were missing. Whatever had been hanging on the walls had been there long enough to leave an impression on them. There were a couple of boxes in the corner with different paintings and items. She picked up one of the smaller paintings. She held up the painting in her hand and walked around the room until she found an impression that matched the painting's size perfectly. It seemed the people of this household had only just recently moved back in. Why had they left? Who was this woman who had caught the heart of Katsuo?

Feeling overwhelmed, Serenity went to lie down. She touched the fabric of the sheets on the bed and admired its softness. Dead tired and unable to resist, she lay down removing her veil so she could rest comfortably.

Serenity must have nodded off at some point as she was suddenly awakened by a knock at the door. The servant from before entered with two others carrying trays of food and a pitcher. They set everything up quickly but not one of them even glanced in her direction. They all wore matching solemn expressions and all of their movements reeked of anxiousness and fear. They were done so fast that she almost questioned whether they ever came in. Only the one servant from earlier had stayed behind. Serenity's stomach growled at the sight of the fresh fruit as she had not had any in what felt like ages. The thought brought a frown to her face.

"Is there anything wrong mistress?" the servant asked.

"No, it's just been a while since I had any fruit. It looks good," Serenity explained.

"Senoia has been blessed thanks to King Katsuo's mercy," the servant praised in an almost robotic manner. "If that is all miss," the servant said before rushing out of the room.

"Senoia?" Serenity repeated. They were in Senoia? That meant she was further south than she thought. Though she had never made the trip to Senoia before, she knew it was only a few days' ride from the lake which meant she was that much closer to the capital and maybe Kang-Dae. That thought filled her with some hope before another thought overtook it. Senoia was not just a city close to the capital. It was also the homestead of the Gi family. The same family that Yoon, the man who'd plotted her death, was the late patriarch of. She was in his familial land. "No, please no,' she whispered aloud to herself as her thoughts grew more disturbing. This home was big, luxurious and obviously belonged to a wealthy family with political ties. 'It couldn't be,' she denied to herself. Kang-Dae had told her the Gi home had been abandoned when he sent men to find the rest of the family after her disappearance. She looked back to the empty spaces on the walls.

The colors of the servants' uniforms had also been the same colors Yoon would wear so proudly. 'Her beauty is unmatched and her loyalty has been tested,' Katsuo's words whispered in her mind. It had been a weird statement she thought until now. Now it all began to make terrible sense.

Katsuo's queen-to-be was not just a Xian, she was the daughter of her worst enemy. Lady Gi herself, Jae-Hwa.

# CHAPTER 61

"Lady Gi," her servant Lie-Wei called. Jae-Hwa took her eyes off her husband-to-be as the young woman approached. All guests have been accommodated," she reported. Jae-Hwa was about to thank and dismiss her when Katsuo spoke.

"Is it a Xian custom to address your lady before your king?" Tension heavy silence filled the room. Jae-Hwa turned her focus to the teacup in front of her, picked it up, and took a sip. Lie-Wei dropped to her knees letting her head hit the floor.

"A-apologies my king," she stuttered. "This servant deserves death for her insolence."

"Then who would wait on my future queen?" Katsuo said with a little smile. Jae-Hwa smiled back and placed her hand in his.

"You shall receive 10 flogs for your offense. Leave here at once," Jae-Hwa ordered.

"Thank you, my king. Thank you, my lady," Lie-Wei sobbed before two men pulled her to her feet and escorted her out to dole out her punishment.

Katsuo raised Jae-Hwa's hand to kiss it. "You are too lenient, my lady."

"Finding another servant already familiar with this palace is cumbersome," she told him. He gave a slight nod of understanding.

"How has it been, being back? I trust you had no trouble?" he inquired.

Jae-Hwa shook her head. "The men you sent to collect us were very diligent. I was well cared for."

"Are you glad to be back in your home?" Katsuo asked.

She smiled warmly at him. "I am. I am very thankful you have given it back to me."

"I could not allow my queen's birthright to be taken from her. Of course, once I take the Xian throne, your new home will be the palace." A shiver went through her at his words. She bowed her head gracefully to him. "Thank you, my king."

# CHAPTER 62

Rielle could barely keep Jung-Soo in her sight as she walked directly behind him. The oversized helmet she wore completely obscured her peripheral vision and every time she moved the metal helmet shifted disrupting her sight constantly. Her feet burned and throbbed from being on them all day in an effort to keep up with the great army.

After the incident, Jung-Soo had given Rielle spare armor so that she could disguise herself as a soldier. They both had wanted to avoid another unpleasant situation like the one before, by making those around them think she was one of them. The way this particular helmet was made it completely blocked her face from view. Following their plan, they stuck with the army long enough to determine their destination. They had been slowly falling further and further behind. Seeing as the army was about to set up camp indefinitely, they knew they didn't have much time to enact their escape. As they were close enough, Jung-Soo decided it was safe for them to make camp without drawing unnecessary attention to themselves. Jung-Soo figured Katsuo's soldiers would just think they were planning to make their way to the estate the next day as it was getting late.

As soon as the tent was up Rielle sprinted inside expelling a great breath of relief. Jung-Soo was at the entrance trying to close it. She didn't dare remove her helmet until he gave her the okay. Once he did, she slowly removed it wincing as it pulled at her locks. "Ow!" she hissed as it got stuck. Jung-Soo was suddenly beside her quickly unsnagging it and taking the helmet from her.

She was about to thank him but he had already walked away to the other side to remove his own armor. It had been like this for days. He had not spoken more than two words to her other than to give her an order. Knowing Serenity was within reach but not being able to bring her home, was taking a toll on him. Though Rielle understood how he felt she was annoyed that he was taking his frustration out on everyone, including her. Even without knowing the language she could sense his harsh tones and lack of patience by how he ordered his men about. She felt sorry for the one called Tae-Soo he seemed to suffer the brunt of his wrath more than anyone. Rielle would have liked to steer clear of Jung-Soo but he now formed the habit of never letting her out of his sight. She figured it was his way of doing something for Serenity since he could not bring her home. On one hand, she was grateful, but another part wondered if he would have been so insistent if she wasn't important to Serenity. She shook thoughts like that away. What did it matter? The important thing was to get to their destination alive.

Rielle wasn't in the mood or the mental space to even pretend to have the energy to deal with him so she went over to her cot to begin removing the pounds of armor she was wearing.

Voices outside the tent hit Rielle's ear. Heart pounding as unfamiliar voices spoke clearly from right outside, she fumbled with her helmet trying to get it back on as quickly as she could but her locs kept getting in the way. Jung-Soo pushed her toward the back of the tent.

"Stay quiet," he whispered. He rushed outside. Rielle, still panicking, continued trying to get her helmet on. After several more attempts she succeeded and the voices outside quieted.

The first thing Jung-Soo saw upon exiting the tent were two of Katsuo's soldiers engaged in conversations with two of his men.

"You all need to be gone by dawn," the man was telling them.

"What is going on?" Jung-Soo asked.

"We had reports of enemy troops in the surrounding area," the left soldier spoke.

"We need you and another group to go out and check it."

"Perhaps someone else should go. We have only just-," Jung-Soo began to give an excuse.

"No backtalk!" the left one snapped. Jung-Soo's jaw clenched but he held his tongue. Unfortunately, he was currently wearing low-ranking armor, so he was not in a place to argue with them. He had changed in hopes of not drawing the attention of the other soldiers as many of the high-ranking officers were towards the front of the party.

"Pack it up and move out. If you find nothing you can return."

Jung-Soo stopped trying to argue. Maybe he could use this to his advantage. They were being permitted to split off from the group, which is what they wanted to do anyway.

"Yes Sir."

"Is this all of you?" One asked while entering the tent. Jung-Soo's heart seized and he quickly followed behind him with his hand on his dagger ready to take him out if necessary.

"Hey, you!"

Jung-Soo entered the tent. Rielle sat on her knees in full armor facing the back. "You're not exempt. Get out here, you have a mission." Releasing a sigh of relief, Jung-Soo relaxed his hand. Rielle slowly stood and bowed in submission keeping her head down. The guard left and Jung-Soo gave her a look before returning outside. He watched as the two soldiers left.

"What do we do?" one of his men asked.

"Inform the others." Rielle came out of the tent and Jung-Soo's eyes rested on her. "We're heading out."

# CHAPTER 63

Although Serenity was not a hundred percent sure her frightening assumption was correct, she refused to leave her room. Veil or no veil, she would not risk ever being in that woman's presence. Even if they had parted on amicable terms the last time they saw each other, Jae-Hwa's father had been killed due to his part in Serenity's attempted murder. She doubted the woman held any pleasant feelings for her. It appeared she had completely turned her fury toward her own country.

Serenity didn't know if she should feel enraged or guilty. The last time they spoke it seemed like Jae-Hwa was taking steps to do better for herself and become more independent outside of her father's demands. She must have abandoned the idea for vengeance. Serenity wouldn't put it past her. She had been complicit in plenty of evil deeds in her previous attempts to become queen. If she felt justified, Serenity could see Jae-Hwa turning her ambitions back on to seek revenge.

Serenity shook her head of the thoughts. Right now, the only thing she needed to focus on was making sure her identity stayed secret.

"Dream walker?" the captain called out from the other side of the door. The voice startled her and she found herself reaching for her veil.

"Yes?"

"The king wishes for you to join him and his lady for dinner."

'Oh, come on,' she groaned to herself. Maybe she could refuse, but given her previous two refusals to leave the room she doubted Katsuo's patience with her would continue. "I will be there," she said, her heart pounding just from the thought of having to go.

The clothes Jae-Hwa sent were almost as conservative as the ones Katsuo had forced her to wear on the journey here, but shockingly they were without the veils. She decided to innovate and make it work. Taking one of the veils from another outfit of the same color, and a sash from another outfit, she unfolded the sash and let it sit atop her head binding it with ribbon from the curtains on her bed. She cut a piece of the sheer netting from the window and draped it over her head as well. The darkness of it covered her skin color and face simultaneously.

Masao didn't bat an eye at her appearance once she stepped out, so she knew she didn't look too out of place. He walked her out where they met more guards who all walked her toward the main house. Throat dry, palms sweating inside the delicate glove she wore, she kept picturing the worst-case scenarios in her mind. Every one of them ended in her excruciating death.

The dining hall was empty when she entered save for a few servants setting the table. Not knowing what to do or where to go she stood frozen on the spot.

The captain came to her side. "You'll be sitting there," he told her gesturing to the pillow opposite the low bench at the head of the table. She nodded in gratitude to him. She went over to the gold pillow but did not sit. As she waited the minutes ticked by. Slowly a couple more people arrived in the room they too did not sit but stood by the table. The men were clearly Lords, Xian lords. No one moved or even shifted their feet probably out of the same fear she was feeling.

"The king arrives!" the announcer shouted. The doors opened and around the corner came Katsuo and the woman herself.

'God help me.' Wearing matching colors, the couple fell in perfect step as they approached the table. Once the two took their seats Serenity and the others did the same.

"Dream walker, allow me to introduce your future queen and my future wife, Lady Gi of Senoia." Serenity got to her knees to give a little bow.

"Your majesty," she said in a soft low voice praying Jae-Hwa wouldn't recognize it.

"You may sit," Jae-Hwa told her.

Serenity slowly moved to her seat sitting on the pillow with her legs to the side. As the servants put out different dishes she kept her head down.

"I've told her all about you and the power you yield. I wanted my beautiful lady to meet the person who would win us this war," Katsuo spoke.

"It is nice to meet you," Jae-Hwa spoke in her sickeningly delicate voice. It filled Serenity with stifling anger. Serenity nodded politely. She tried busying herself with food hoping it would keep them from asking too many questions.

For the most part, the men and women talked amongst themselves but Serenity refused to relax.

The men spoke of pointless things, so pointless she was sure that they had been forbidden from speaking about the war or any upcoming plans. Did Katsuo not completely trust them? Why should he? If they could betray Xian, why wouldn't they betray him?

No one addressed her or even looked her way. It took a moment for her to realize it wasn't because they were overlooking her. They were all going to great lengths to not even glance in her direction. Katsuo must have let them know that even now no one was meant to lay eyes on her.

"How do you find my home? Is it to your liking?" Jae-Hwa asked her. Throat dry, Serenity had to answer without sounding nervous but also without sounding like herself.

"Very beautiful my lady." She couldn't tell through the veil but she just knew that fake smile was plastered on her face.

"That is good to hear. My king informed me of your upbringing." Serenity stifled a cough.

"I hope you will see better parts of the land and know more brightness."

'I ought to snatch you up by your hair.' Serenity thought.

"Thank you, my lady, that is very kind of you to say," Serenity said.

"I had only just returned myself and have forgotten its beauty," continued Jae-Hwa.

"Yes, my poor lady had been unjustly forced from her home after the unjustified murder of her father. It is a crime I will see the Xian king face when I depose him," Katsuo announced.

'That lying heifer.' Serenity sipped on her water, fist clenching at her side. The men chortled and shouted out their agreements raising their cups in the air. She looked at them all, committing each face to memory. She would remember every single one. When it was all said and done, whether she succeeded in retaking the country she would make sure they faced the consequences of their betrayal. The dinner went on agonizingly longer than she wanted but thankfully it came to end and the men were dismissed. She anxiously awaited her dismissal as well.

"Come Dream walker," Katsuo beckoned. Serenity swallowed hard as she forced herself to her feet. No matter how hard she tried she couldn't make her feet move any faster than a snail's pace as she made the trek across the room. She stopped short ten feet away and kneeled hoping that doing so would keep him from asking her to come closer.

He didn't ask, instead, he came over to her. He slowly pulled the netting off. Serenity was finding it difficult to breathe. She focused all her strength on not running. She kept her eyes down and prayed the veil was enough to mask her face. She didn't dare look up. He took her arm in his hand, turning it so her healing but scarred cut was shown.

"Does it still hurt?" She shook her head quickly. "I've told my lady about your sacrifice for me and our cause. I've asked that she send the best healer she has to minimize any negative consequences."

"That is not necessary," she tried to tell him.

"It is no trouble. You are important to my king, therefore you are important to me," Jae-Hwa spoke.

"Thank you," Serenity managed to get out without gritting her teeth. Katsuo's fingers softly touched the edge of the puckered healing skin. She suppressed a shudder from his touch. He was behaving oddly. He never cared about her wellbeing before. Was he putting on a show for his fiancé?

Katsuo released her and told her to stand. "Go rest," he told her. She bowed, turned on her heels, and headed towards the door. She could hear Jae-Hwa speak to Katsuo in a low voice keeping her from hearing exactly what was said. Anxiety at an all time, high she exited the room. On the walk back she considered making an escape. Even if Jae-Hwa hadn't recognized her, how long could she keep this up? Maybe she should have left when Rielle asked her to.

# CHAPTER 64

Jung-Soo took the lead as his men scouted the area. Even with the majority of his focus on the task at hand, he would still periodically check on Rielle who was in the back with Hae-In and Tae-Soo, keeping her protected. The other group of soldiers that had been told to accompany them, were on the other side of the village doing their search. The inhabitants were in their homes hiding from them all. He gave his command and his men dispersed, searching the individual homes and establishments. Rielle looked around lost but Hae-In gently prodded her to come with him.

The search did not take long for any of them because they were not actively trying to find anyone. Their attempts were just a show for the other soldiers. If there were Xian men around Jung-Soo prayed it would be them that found them and not Katsuo's men. When they finished, no one reported anything out of the ordinary.

"Let's go back," he ordered.

"Come out now!" The shout echoed throughout the village. A knot of dread formed in Jung-Soo's stomach. He, followed by his men, headed over to the other side of the village. The other soldiers were posted outside what looked to be a tavern. Their bows and swords were drawn. An arrow flew out from the window hitting one of the soldiers in the stomach. The soldiers released their arrows into the building but only a few made it through the windows. When the arrows stopped it was quiet. The captain signaled for his men to wait as he slowly approached the tavern, being sure to avoid the open windows.

Something about the scene did not sit right with Jung-Soo. It made no sense to attack unless death was the goal. Perhaps the men inside had other motives. Maybe their goal had been to draw the soldier's attention. Just as soon as Jung-Soo completed the thought, his eyes shifted to the back of the tavern and he could see several men fleeing toward the woods. Perhaps they would make it, he hoped.

"Stop him!"

Jung-Soo's hopes appeared to be dashed but he noticed the soldier who shouted wasn't looking at the fleeing men but at a single one that was now running through the village towards Jung-Soo's men, toward Rielle.

His men were smart, they knew what was at stake so they would make believable attempts to capture the man but Rielle was no soldier. She would not want to stop someone who she knew would face death if caught.

"Stop him!" the soldier shouted again. If Rielle allowed the man to go past her, her identity would be questioned and her life would be in jeopardy. The bow was in Jung-Soo's hands before he could even finish the thought and he released the arrow at the fleeing man just before he got to Rielle.

Rielle was crying beneath her helmet. The tears poured and she couldn't stop them. There was blood on her, blood from the dead man at her feet. When the man rushed toward her, she froze. She didn't know what to do. Grabbing her sword didn't even cross her mind. Rielle was just going to let him pass but before she could even do that, he was dead. In the distance, she vaguely registered Jung-Soo, who was standing with his bow out. Hae-In moved in front of her. He discreetly pushed a dagger into her hand. Later, she would realize it was to give the illusion to the other soldiers that she was going make a move to stop the man. She looked down at the poor soul, silently wondering why he wore plain clothing and carried no weapon on him other than a very old and regular looking knife.

"He's not a soldier," she whispered to herself. The men spoke around her in their language making it easy for her to tune them out but unfortunately giving her nothing to focus on but the dead body at her feet.

They stayed in the village another couple of hours, being forced to continue searching just to be sure there weren't any more rebellious villagers around. The poor people were rounded up, fearfully hugging and clinging to one another as their homes were searched and the soldiers intimidated and threatened them to make their point. They used the body of the dead man to press the idea that it was useless to fight against them. At least that was what Rielle managed to gather from the context.

Eventually, they were given permission to return to camp, but Rielle had no desire to return anywhere but home. She just wanted to go home. She looked down at the armor, seeing the blood on it. She wiped at it frantically needing to get it off. It was almost as though she could feel it through the thick armor. A gentle hand stopped her. She looked up to see Jung-Soo.

They walked back to camp together. He led her into the tent. She felt her bindings being undone on her left. Seconds later, her breastplate was hanging on the side. She went to reach for the binding on the other side but was once again thwarted by gentle hands stopping her. The binding came undone and the plate fell to the ground. Next, the padding at her knees was removed followed by the ones on her arms. Left only in a shirt and pants, she felt lighter in more ways than one. After looking into the strong but concerned eyes of Jung-Soo, she felt more weight lift off her.

"You are alright. You will be safe. I will keep you safe," he spoke his declaration confidently. He said it in such a way she felt she had to believe him.

"You killed him to save me, didn't you?" she asked because she couldn't not ask.

"I killed him to save us all." He was reassuring her, she could tell. The tears came back but he wiped them before they could fall.

"He wasn't even a soldier," she cried. Jung-Soo shook his head.

"No, he wasn't. But he gave his life so soldiers could get away," he told her. Hoping that knowing that the man had not died in vain would help ease her guilt.

"Sleep," he told her. She slowly nodded and went to her cot. Laying her head down and pulling the covers over her, she turned toward the walls of the tent. She could hear Jung-Soo moving about removing his armor. As she lay there praying for dreamless sleep she fought the overwhelming fear that today would not be the last time she had to witness such acts.

# CHAPTER 65

The healer Jae-Hwa had sent to her was a very old man with shaking hands and missing teeth but he had kind eyes. He handled her tender cut carefully and gently. She was surprised when the ache she would normally feel when using that arm was practically nonexistent.

She was nervous as he examined her arm. He started taking her pulse with a smile. At first, Serenity didn't think anything of it until his smile slightly dropped and he seemed unsure. His lips pursed as he looked to go into deeper concentration.

Could he tell she was pregnant through her pulse? Thinking fast she began coughing profusely. The healer released her arm and went to pour her water. The old man offered her a cup. She took it graciously. She asked about how bad her scar would be to distract him further. He chatted with her for a few minutes before rebandaging her arm and leaving her a small tonic to combat infection.

She wondered if the tonic would do anything for her current illness. She only had a few antibiotics left and had resorted to splitting them in half to extend their usage. Not the most effective plan but it was the best she could do. She did not want to have to cut herself again.

Once the healer left Serenity's body sagged with relief. Needing some air, she went over to the window to stare out of it. Feeling warm she removed her veil and scarf. The wind hitting her face felt amazing. The room was starting to feel like a prison within a prison. She still refused to leave unless she had absolutely no choice.

The view of the courtyard was comforting. She was surprised by the lack of soldiers inside the grounds. Was it arrogance or Katsuo's paranoia? There were no shortages of servants, however, which tracked. Katsuo always had an abundance of unwilling servants. However, instead of the unwilling captives he liked to use, the estate was filled with servants of the Gi family.

Serenity leaned against the side of the window just breathing in the fresh air. She listened to the chirps of the birds and the songs of the breeze. She rested her hands on her belly in a comforting gesture as she did on occasion when she was alone. The reassurance that her baby was still there and still safe gave her hope. As long as she had hope she had the ability to make it through all of this.

*She was being led outside through dark hallways. She couldn't see anything around her only her feet beneath her. The hand leading her held onto hers tightly almost painfully as if they were unwilling to let her go. They walked along until they stepped through a door leading them outside. The darkness did not dissipate much but she could make out the dark skies above. As she looked to her left, she saw she was standing outside a stone building with a railing along the edges. The strong walls had no type of decoration or color leading her to believe this was a practical place built for necessity only. She looked at the hand in hers letting her eyes move up the strong arm to the man's back. Dressed in black and red he stood looking over the railing, his face hidden from her view. She hesitated to step further. For some reason, she feared what she would see on the other side. The hand brought her closer and she felt her feet move forward. Approaching the edge, she held her breath but released a horrified scream a second later. The bodies piled up along the walls were stacked like awful bricks layered one under the other. The dead consisted of both Xian and Katsuo's soldiers alike. The hand in hers loosened. She turned her gaze to it and recoiled as blood seeped between her hand and theirs. The blood was flowing from him onto hers. Staring up into the proud grateful eyes of Katsuo she wanted to scream again.*

*"This is our victory," he said raising their blood-soaked hands to place a kiss on hers.*

*"And your defeat!" Serenity gasped at the sudden appearance of Kang-Dae who was standing*

*on the bodies he scaled with his sword drawn.*
*Before Katsuo could react the sword was plunged*
*right into his heart.*

Serenity awoke to her stomach rolling. She had barely made it to her pot before expelling the contents of her stomach. Shaking and fatigued, she sat by the pot, feeling the breeze from the open window hitting her wet cheeks. She wiped at them knowing she had been crying once more in her sleep. As the memories of her dream played over in her head, she felt the tears return.

"Please God," she whispered to herself but knew she'd received no reprieve. No matter how she looked at the dream or tried to twist it so it didn't mean what she knew it meant, she could not change it. As much as she had already done to gain Katsuo's trust it was not enough. The message was clear. Katsuo's downfall was contingent on her betrayal. But she couldn't do it, how could she? She clutched at her belly. This was her home, her people. She couldn't be responsible for such a thing. But could she live with the consequences of her choices? If this was the only way to ensure Xian's victory, how could she not do it? How many more lives would be lost because she couldn't bring herself to do it? She thought back to her other dream and how new and great everything had become after the walls had come down. She held that dream in her mind and her heart. There was a victory at the end of this, she had to believe it. It was the only way to move forward.

# CHAPTER 66

A day later, Serenity was right where she didn't want to be. Kneeling before Katsuo, Jae-Hwa, and the Soothsayer. She had to steel herself to do what she knew had to. Beneath the veil, she was sweating heavily but she made herself speak confidently. "The vision that Lord Sho had was correct," she began. The words caused the soothsayer to huff. "If you break the trust the people have in the king people, it will lead to his downfall. But without knowing what you need to strike, you can do nothing."

"And you know what it is we need to strike?" Katsuo inquired.

"I do, my king," she forced out. "There is a place in the south near the capital that holds the hopes of the Xian people. If you strike it, you will bring the Xian king to you. Once you do, you will meet him on the battlefield and there will be a great victory." She finished.

The room was quiet and Serenity could hear nothing but the pounding of her own heart.

Katsuo looked at Jae-Hwa. "Do you know of such a place?" he asked her. Jae-Hwa's eyes did not leave Serenity's kneeling form.

"I believe so my king. It is Xian's greatest stronghold. It has never fallen nor faced a defeat."

"To venture further south would be unwise," Lord Sho spoke.

"Do you not have faith in your own vision?" Serenity challenged. The soothsayer's nostrils flared and his cheeks grew red.

"How dare you?!"

"That is enough Sho," Katsuo quieted him. "My men to the south are limited. How will we be able to achieve such a feat?" Katsuo asked.

"Call all the men you can, everyone who can get here in time," she told him. "If you call to them now, they will not meet much resistance on their way. The Xian soldiers have begun to gather, leaving many ways open for them. Once you've gathered enough there will be an opportunity that will allow you to take the place with ease," she claimed.

"And if I choose not to take this opportunity?" he asked.

"You will have missed a chance for you to put an end to this war," she warned him.

Katsuo regarded her words carefully. He looked to Jae-Hwa who looked back at him. The two seemed to exchange silent words before he turned back to Serenity.

"We will consider your words," he told her. Katsuo looked to Lord Sho. "Find out how many of our men are in the region."

Lord Sho frowned. "It will be done, my king."

"Thank you for your service dream walker," said Katsuo. With a nod and a bow, Serenity left the room to be guided back to hers by the captain.

As soon as she was behind closed doors, she snatched the veil off and collapsed to her knees, and cried. She cried out to God for confirmation that she was doing the right thing. She cried out for her child, hoping that she would not be born in a war-torn land. She cried out for her husband who she prayed would survive. She cried out for Xian, praying that she had not caused its doom.

# CHAPTER 67

Rielle walked beside Jung-Soo as the troop continued to travel South. Once day broke, they did what they had intended and removed themselves from the army. They'd only been on the road a couple of days but the further they got from Serenity the longer Rielle felt like she'd been traveling.

She pulled at the armor at her neck that was starting to chafe her. She would have complained but she was grateful she no longer had to endure the helmet. Once they'd been clear of the main army Jung-Soo had allowed her to lose at least some of the disguise. As for the rest of the armor, he would not hear of it claiming it was extra protection that she shouldn't turn her nose up at. Now that they were away from Katsuo's army their pace had increased. Jung-Soo was eager to meet up with Kang-Dae and would not lose any more time if he could help it.

A small canteen was suddenly placed in front of her face. She looked over to see Jung-Soo holding it out towards her. "Drink," was all he said. Had he noticed her fatigue? Was she breathing heavily? That was embarrassing, she thought but couldn't understand why she was worried about that. Of course, she was tired. She wasn't used to these conditions. Her legs were constantly sore, she was always hungry and every moment they stopped she felt like sleeping for a week. She wished she could ride on a horse but Jung-Soo claimed it would slow them down as their main job was to carry the carts of supplies they had with them.

She accepted the canteen and took a swig before returning it to him. "Thank you," she told him and as always, her thanks was not acknowledged. "Would it kill you to-," he cut her off with a loud shush. Her first instinct was to fuss at him but remembering where she was, she quickly understood that something was wrong. She wanted to ask what it was but was afraid of making a sound. It was only now she noticed that everyone had paused, so whatever it was, they'd all noticed except for her. Jung-Soo grabbed a hold of Rielle's wrists and pushed her behind him. Before she could question what exactly was happening there was movement in the trees. All the men pulled out their various weapons in preparation. Coming out of the forest was a group of Katsuo's soldiers being led by a general she had seen in camp.

Jung-Soo didn't tell his men to attack yet, he doubted that this group was the only one around. He shouted out the command for his men to go back-to-back to cover all of their surroundings.

"We've been looking for you for quite a while. You hid yourselves well amongst us," the general spoke. Jung-Soo didn't respond. There was no point in talking. "If you surrender now, your men can live to serve our great king."

From behind, one of his men shouted out letting Jung-Soo know that they were now surrounded. He called out to Hae-In who was near him. Hae-In understood immediately and took a protective stance around Rielle. "Tae-Soo!" Jung-Soo called out. A tiny whistle filled the sky and came to an end once an arrow embedded itself into the neck of the man standing to the right of the general.

Taking advantage of the stunned general and his men, Jung-Soo attacked the man head on and his men did the same. The general was able to get his sword out in time to block Jung-Soo's blade just before it hit him. He pushed back against Jung-Soo. Jung-Soo spun out of the way while swinging his sword high to try and catch the general in the back of the head but he managed to duck.

The sound of the men fighting was all around him. In the back of his mind, he wanted to check to make sure Rielle was being taken care of but knew he couldn't risk dividing his attention at such a crucial moment. The general came swinging at him. Jung-Soo leaned back causing him to miss. A couple more arrows flew by, most likely from Tae-Soo and his hidden men, taking out several other soldiers. The two engaged once more with their swords, neither holding back.

Rielle screamed as a man with a sword came rushing at her. Luckily, Hae-In quickly jumped in and cut the man down. He kept her close taking out one more soldier while trying to get her clear of the skirmish. Rielle felt helpless and she was terrified.

Two fighting men came so close she thought they would knock her over but Hae-In pulled her forward at just the right moment. They ran a few more yards, beyond the fight, before he pushed her against a tree. Hae-In held out his hand silently telling her to stay put. She nodded and he ran back into the fight. Rielle turned to look back to the battle. It was hard for her to distinguish who was who. She could not tell who was winning, as more and more bodies fell. Witnessing such violence, she found herself finding it difficult to breathe. Unable to stomach anymore she turned back, covering her ears and shutting her eyes tight. Even through her hands she could still hear the faint screams and fighting from behind her. She just wanted to be home.

As time went by it got quieter and quieter. Rielle didn't know if that was good or bad and she was almost too afraid to peek. She pulled her hands from her ears and looked around the tree. There was less than half the number of men standing than there were before but she still couldn't tell which side had the upper hand. She finally caught a glimpse of Jung-Soo just as he was pushed to the ground. She audibly gasped and slammed her hand onto the tree to keep herself from jumping out and shouting his name. She watched the general try to slam his big sword right into Jung-Soo. She almost screamed but Jung-Soo was able to roll away just in time and the sword hit the ground instead. She released the breath she had been holding but kept her eyes glued on him.

As Jung-Soo rolled away from the general's sword, he kicked out the man's legs causing him to fall to the ground. Jung-Soo quickly got back onto his feet ready to go in for the kill as the general had now been disarmed. Out of nowhere, someone tackled him into a tree. He found himself unable to breathe for a second. He kneed the attacker in the stomach and hit him in his exposed nose, breaking the bone. Unfortunately, the general had now recovered and retrieved his weapon. Jung-Soo went to confront him once more but paused at a pain in his side. He looked down and was surprised to see a small dagger sticking out. His attacker had done more than just run into him.

Seeing him in his weakened state, the general smirked before coming at him once more. Jung-Soo still managed to block his blows ignoring the pain in his side. Locked together in a hold Jung-Soo struggled to keep his stance when he noticed the general's eyes flickered to his left. Quickly understanding what was about to transpire he used all of his strength to kick the general back before spinning around and blocking the blade of an oncoming soldier. He kicked at the soldier's leg and ran his sword across his torso. The motion caused the knife in his side to move, cutting more of his flesh. The pain made him fall to his knee. Jung-Soo tried to quickly catch his breath when the shadow of the general appeared around him. He looked up to see the man preparing to make his final blow.

An arrow hit the general in the shoulder making him stumble back. Not sparing a moment Jung-Soo shot up and embedded his sword upward through the belly of the general, who gurgled and grunted before Jung-Soo removed his sword and pushed the body away. With that obstacle gone, the pain seemed to increase exponentially and he began to feel the effects of his blood loss. Jung-Soo found himself unable to stand.

"General!" he heard Tae-Soo call out as he ran up to him, bow in hand. He helped Jung-Soo up with difficulty as he could barely walk.

When Tae-Soo started dragging him away from the battle he began to protest. "I cannot leave my men," he rasped. However, in his current condition, he could do nothing but allow Tae-Soo to drag him. He suddenly felt the arms of someone else on his other side holding him up. He looked down to see Rielle's hair. He wanted to command her to get away and hide but it had become difficult to speak. They continued to carry him away from the battle despite his weak protest. They laid him against a tree once they had gotten far enough. Rielle immediately took to his wound. With Tae-Soo's help, they removed his armor so she could get a better look at it. He was struggling to stay conscious up until she pressed her hands onto the wound as hard as she could. The pain jolted him out of his previous stupor. Trying to focus on anything but the pain, he focused on Rielle. Her cheeks were wet but her face was determined and focused. He knew she had been crying and found himself empathizing with her and admiring her at the same time. He imagined all of this was new to her and indeed would take a great toll. But here she was doing her best to save his life even though she barely knew him. In the distance, he could vaguely hear his men shouting in triumph. Realizing they must have overcome the enemy he was able to relax. Not long after, he lost consciousness.

# CHAPTER 68

Serenity was pulled roughly out of her sleep and out of her bed. It was pitch black; she could barely see anything. She was being pulled up by two strong individuals but she couldn't see their faces. Before she could scream out for help her mouth was covered. She heard the distinct sound of something sliding and she was pulled into a hall with dim lighting. She had not ever seen this hallway before and realized she had not been taken out of the front door of her room. She was being taken through some kind of hidden passage that she had not known was there.

She was dragged for a few minutes until they reached an unfamiliar room. Serenity was put into a chair roughly and the hands finally left her. She was shaking as she was fearing the worst. Was Katsuo finally getting rid of her? Had this whole thing been a ruse he used to get what he wanted and now he believed he had no more use for her? Steps behind her made her tense and she was too afraid to look.

When the figure came and sat down before her, her eyes widened and her heart dropped.

Looking just as regal and graceful as ever, Jae-Hwa sat before her triumphantly. She had a slight smile on her face that did not reach her eyes.

"It's good to see you again my queen," she said mockingly.

The tears Serenity had been holding back threatened to spill over. She tried to blink them away but one did escape.

"Hello Jae-Hwa," Serenity greeted, feeling defeated.

"I apologize for this unorthodox meeting but I wanted to have a chance to talk with you without unwanted ears listening in," she told her.

"I understand," said Serenity knowing she had no options.

"I admit I was surprised when I realized who you were. Part of me wished I'd never see you again so I suppose that was my fault. Although rumors of your death might have contributed to my slow response."

"Well rumors aren't really reliable sources of information," Serenity said not knowing what else to do but continue the conversation. After all, her life was literally in Jae-Hwa's hands and she didn't expect she'd be safe for much longer.

"I suppose you're right. It was jarring to see you, especially given how your "death" affected my family," she said, the polite and feminine voice disappearing into one of anger and malice.

"Considering I am only alive *despite* your family's lack of trying, it's not very surprising," retorted Serenity. Yes, she was afraid but Serenity was not going to sit here and act like Yoon had not had every intention of putting her in the ground. If Jae-Hwa wanted to rewrite history to make her father an innocent victim Serenity would shatter those ideations right here now.

Jae-Hwa was silent just staring at Serenity. Serenity nervously played with her hands unable to stop.

"I lost everything because of you," Jae-Hwa claimed.

"If you lost anything it was because of your father and the things that he did, not me."

"He only wanted what was best for me," she said her voice started to break. She managed to garner just a little bit of sympathy from Serenity. As much as she had hated the man, he had still been Jae-Hwa's father.

"He wanted what was best for him. I think you knew that. It was why you decided to leave, remember?" Serenity reminded her.

"I was foolish. If I had listened to my father-," Jae-Hwa began.

"If you had listened to your father, you would have spent a lifetime trying to obtain something that was never going to be yours. Your father filled you with delusions about being queen and turned you into an opportunity, an opportunity for him to gain power. You said it yourself. You had no identity other than the one he forced on you. But you were never going to be queen and no amount of scheming was going to change that."

"You led him to his death!" she accused.

"I wasn't even there when he died," Serenity responded coldly. "but from what I know it was a consequence of his actions. You know better than anyone what he was capable of."

A lone tear fell from Jae-Hwa's eye.

"What are you doing, Jae-Hwa? What do you want? To kill me? If you were going to turn me in you would have done it already," Serenity surmised.

"Maybe I just want to make you suffer."

"And how will you explain that to your future husband?" Serenity prodded.

"He would thank me for removing a traitor," Jae-Hwa said.

"Or will he begin to question whether his trust in you has been misplaced? Especially if I tell him you knew about me and kept it to yourself. Given that you are Xianian, I imagine he already has some doubts about your loyalty. This certainly won't help."

"Loyalty?" She laughed. "You lecture me about loyalty while you advise your husband's greatest enemy?"

"What I'm doing is what is necessary for Xian's survival. My husband would understand because he knows me. What does Katsuo know about you?

Jae-Hwa turned her head defiantly. "You do not know anything about our relationship."

"Of course I do. It's the same one you had with your father. Another man using you for their own purpose. Another person telling you who you are and who you should be and you sit there believing every word of it as if you have no thoughts of your own. Didn't you say you wanted to find yourself?

You seem to be back where you started," Serenity said in a disapproving tone.

"Who are you to judge me?"

"I'm just someone trying to keep everything from falling apart," Serenity retorted. "In order to keep doing that, I need to know that you aren't going to do anything stupid."

"And why shouldn't I? You and I both know that with one word from me, your life can end tonight. After all you have stolen from me, why should I risk myself to protect you?"

"Because you, Lady Gi, the real you, cares about this land. You care about the people, your people. I don't think you want it to fall into Katsuo's hands.

"I will be queen," she asserted half-heartedly.

"But you don't want that, you're not sure you ever wanted it." Jae-Hwa's eyes shifted and she swallowed.

"How about this? You don't expose me and I won't expose you. And whatever happens at the end happens and we won't intérfere with one another. That way you get to continue being the loyal wife to be and Xian still has a chance of making it through this," offered Serenity.

"And if you fail?" Jae-Hwa asked.

"If I fail, you get what you always wanted according to you," Serenity told her, throwing her words back in her face.

"Maybe I should just leave you wondering. Have you looking over your shoulder, constantly. Living in the fear that I could destroy you at any moment," Jae-Hwa threatened.

Serenity felt a chill go through her but she kept her cool.

"You can do that Jae-Hwa, but if you do decide to expose me, it won't just be me that suffers, or even you. It will be those around you, those you care about."

Jae-Hwa stared at her coldly. Serenity could see there was more she wanted to say.

"Take her back," Jae-Hwa ordered in Xian. The rough hands were back, pulling Serenity out of the chair and leading her back through the dark hall.

When she was thrown back inside, the two men left the way they came shutting the hidden door behind them. Serenity walked to her bed in a daze unsure of what would happen next. One thing was for sure, Jae-Hwa was right. Waiting to see if she would eventually turn her in would be torture.

# CHAPTER 69

"You can't move him anymore," Jung-Soo could hear Rielle say once he came out of the fog of sleep.

"We have to move. We cannot stay here any longer," a voice that sounded like Hae-In spoke out.

"Listen, he cannot be moved. It could cause too much damage," Rielle continued unable to understand what Hae-In had told her. Jung-Soo opened his eyes to the night sky. He had no idea how long he'd been unconscious. He felt groggy and weak. In his slumber, someone must have fed him something to combat his pain because he could barely feel anything at the moment. He looked to his side to see Rielle, Hae-In, and Tae-Soo in a seemingly unproductive debate as neither side could understand the language of the other.

"Try to move him then, if you want to," she warned the men in an attempt to be threatening. Whatever they gave him must have messed with his ability to censor himself because he let out a chuckle before he could stop it but immediately regretted it when the pain made itself known once more. The noise caught the attention of all three and they came rushing over. Rielle kneeled down next to him; face marred with concern.

"Try not to move," she told him.

"Were you hurt?" Jung-Soo asked, looking over her for any sign of injury. She shook her head.

"How many did we lose?" He asked the other two.

Tae-Soo looked down so it was on Hae-In to answer, "eleven."

Jung-Soo shut his eyes, slammed his fist into the grass, and threw his head back in frustration. "Are there any more of his men following us?"

"We managed to cover our tracks," Tae-Soo spoke.

"We hid the bodies," Hae-In chimed in. "Hopefully they will not be able to pick up our trail."

At least there was that, Jung-Soo thought to himself. "We've lost too much time already," Jung-Soo said attempting to sit up. "We have to move." Rielle immediately stopped him with a hand on his shoulder gently forcing him back down.

"You need to rest," she said to him. "The more you move the more damage you cause. Trying to keep you from getting an infection is hard enough out here, but if you keep being jostled around it could cause some permanent damage."

"There is no time to waste," Jung-Soo reiterated. "If we don't reach the king in time he may find himself walking into a situation he is unprepared for."

"And if you die before you ever get to him?" Rielle questioned. "What then?"

"I am sure you will keep me alive," he said.

"No. You need to rest for at least a few days to make sure it heals properly."

"We cannot afford a few days," he reminded her. She looked down at him with a look that he had come to know as her "frustrated with Jung-Soo" look.

She stood up and began to converse with Hae-In and Tae-Soo. She spoke slowly exaggerating her words and using confusing hand gestures. "He. Moves." She began pointing aggressively at Jung-Soo. "He. Dies." She let her head go limp, and her eyes closed as she faked being dead.

It was so ridiculous Jung-Soo rolled his eyes but he also found it annoyingly amusing. Even though her methods were ridiculous to Jung-Soo it appeared she had done her job in translating her words to the two men. They both looked at Jung-Soo with matching expressions of worry. Not liking the looks on their faces Jung-Soo was about to remind them that they were to follow his orders.

"General as you said, we cannot afford to slow our pace. It may be best for you to stay behind long enough to recover." Hae-In suggested. Jung-Soo could barely believe what he was hearing. They had never gone against him before. His eyes shifted to Rielle silently blaming her for this new development.

"I will not be left behind like some useless cart," he told them.

"It's the best idea," Tae-Soo spoke up. "We have to move as quickly as possible now. You are not able to do so. We need you strong and capable. The best thing for you to do is heal so that you may fight when the time comes."

"Are you choosing to go against my orders?" Jung-Soo slowly asked. He watched the unsure expressions come across each of their faces and they both looked at each other for a couple of seconds before seeming to make a decision amongst themselves.

"We will accept full reprimand once this war is over," spoke Hae-In.

If Jung-Soo could move, he would have punched him already. Even though Rielle couldn't possibly understand exactly what was being said she seemed to get the gist that she had gotten her way. She gave him a small smile which should have infuriated him instead he was mildly pleased that she was pleased. Of course, that smile only lasted a few seconds once he told her he was sending her off with his men.

# CHAPTER 70

Kang-Dae grunted as he threw another body into the ditch. They had been cleaning up the evidence of their previous battle for hours now. This had been their 4th attack in the last week. The more he tried to get north to join Jung-Soo the more the attacks came. He did not know where they were coming from. It seemed like they were all making their way south all at once. It also appeared as if they were drawn to his men wherever they went, which did not make sense. At first, he thought they were following the many different troops from around Xian as they were making their way to join Kang-Dae and his men. but that didn't appear to be the case, as the attacks were always sporadic and unpredictable. Luckily, they were still deep enough in land that they knew very well, which gave them an advantage every time.

He had not heard from Jung-Soo in days which worried him even more. Had he already made it to Katsuo? Would Jung-Soo have attacked without him? No, Kang-Dae thought to himself. Jung-Soo wouldn't be rash. He would know it would be better to wait. But the longer it took Kang-Dae to get to him the more he worried Jung-Soo would take it upon himself to try and take Katsuo out.

Jung-Soo's silence coupled with the fact that they had been dealing with Katsuo's men in droves made Kang-Dae begin to wonder if Katsuo was making his move. With all these men heading South was he gathering his forces somewhere closer to Kang-Dae's home? While Kang-Dae was preparing to meet him where he was, had Katsuo decided to do the same thing? If that was the case then there was a chance Katsuo was no longer where they thought. Kang-Dae cursed at the thought. Were they back to not having a clue as to where he could be?

Kang-Dae gathered all the generals and captains together to talk.

"Does anyone else feel as if there is something happening back home that we are unaware of?" Asked Shum.

"It is not just you," said Kahil.

"All these men we're facing, they weren't just waiting here for us," Hui speculated.

Kang-Dae shook his head. "No, they aren't, they're heading somewhere, somewhere opposite of where we're going."

"What do we do? Our last intel tells us that Katsuo is in the mountains." Captain Li spoke.

"Our last intel was days ago. It is possible things have changed," remarked Kahil.

"Do we return home?" asked Shum.

"But what if he is still there and we miss our opportunity?" asked Captain Park.

"If he has decided to move south, we've left the capital vulnerable," countered Shum.

"We can't know that the capital is his target," the young Captain Bin spoke up.

"What else could it be?" challenged Yu.

Perhaps it was all a distraction, Kang-Dae thought.

*Kang-Dae stared at Serenity, from across the table, as she pondered her next move. Her forehead crinkled and she chewed on her bottom lip as she was deep in thought. Kang-Dae supposed he should be considering what his next move on the board would be but his eyes kept getting drawn to her. She was in one of her simpler dresses, made for warmer weather, so her upper arms and parts of her chest were exposed. Her hair was up showcasing her delicate neck. Thoughts of how it would feel to kiss it began to enter his mind.*

*Almost as if reading his thoughts, she drew her finger down her throat before she slid it back up to rest on her chin. She wet her lips and he swallowed hard. What was he doing again?*

*"It's your turn," she said suddenly. He hadn't even noticed she made a move. Kang-Dae had been too distracted by her. He looked up at her and noticed she had a knowing smile on her face. Had she done it on purpose? When he looked at the board, he saw that she had trapped him in an unwinnable position. His focus had not been on the game at all but on her, it seemed she took that to her advantage.*

*"Aren't you quite the strategist?" he joked with her. She gave him a sweet smile.*

Kang-Dae recalled that last match he had with Serenity the night before she had set off to return home on her own. That day had been full of distractions and misleads from her. She had even sent him off on a wild goose chase so she could accomplish her goal. Maybe that was what was happening right now. Perhaps Katsuo knew that a huge part of Kang-Dae's army was no longer south and was using these attacks to keep Kang-Dae busy, while he went after a greater prize.

"We need to go back," Kang-Dae announced.

"But my king we're not even sure-,"

"These attacks are not attacks but distractions. An attempt to make us think we are on the right path and keep us from discovering his true goal," Kang-Dae revealed.

"How can you know for sure?" Yu asked.

The truth was he couldn't. Kang-Dae had no actual proof that what he was feeling was right but something in him was trying to warn him that his home was in danger. Perhaps it was the same force that gave him the dreams that had been trying to guide his way.

"Pack up, we turn back tonight."

# CHAPTER 71

"You're hurt," Rielle argued. The men around them were moving about preparing to continue south. They were hidden deeper in the woods, close enough to the river but far enough from the main road that they shouldn't be happened upon. Jung-Soo would stay in this area along with, Tae-Soo, while Hae-In led the others back south. The plan was to rest and recoup for the next couple of days before joining them. Rielle was not on board with this plan.

"You have done all that you can do. I will not be alone. The fewer people with me the better chance we have of not being noticed."

"I can stay with you. It's better if I do. If something goes wrong with your wound, and you end up getting an infection, who will look after you? Him? He won't know what to do," she said pointing at the clueless Tae-Soo.

"I assure you as soldiers we have much more experience in dealing with stab wounds than you think," he remarked dryly.

"And if you get an infection? What then?"

"I'd imagine if that were to happen your presence would not change anything as we are ill-equipped to deal with such a thing out in the wilderness anyway. At this point you are just arguing for the opportunity to be the one to watch me die," he quipped.

She let out a scoff. "That's not funny. I know what to keep an eye out for."

"As do we, I promise," Jung-Soo told her.

"You're really just going to stay here, the two of you? What if they find you? No," she shook her head. "I'm not leaving you here on your own out here," she said in an attempt to give a final word.

"I am already in a compromised position. If something were to happen and we were to be found, what could you do? You have no combative skills. We would only put ourselves in more danger trying to keep you alive." Harsh as the words may have been, he knew they had to be for her to understand. Given her frown and the way she looked away, he knew his words had had the intended effect. "Go back with the men, get to our king. Let him know about Serenity."

After a long pause, she gave a small nod and walked off. Jung-Soo's eyes followed her the entire time. When he looked back, Tae-Soo was staring curiously at him. Jung-Soo gave him a hard stare and the soldier quickly went to busy himself with something else. Jung-Soo knew this was the best thing for her. She needn't be concerned with him. She would be much safer with the others.

# CHAPTER 72

Jae-Hwa quietly shuffled out from under a sleeping Katsuo. She grabbed her robe and went out onto the balcony to stand in the fresh night air. It was late, but a few soldiers were walking the grounds. If she closed her eyes she could pretend that her home was what it used to be before she had been shipped off to the palace, before she lost her father, and before she met Katsuo.

She had been fleeing to one of her cousins' homes. She never stayed in one place too long knowing they were being pursued following the death of her father. The last time she saw him he told her not to return home unless he had sent for her. She should have known what he had been planning. Maybe she could have stopped him. Then he'd still be alive.

Her fifth cousin, who stayed further north, had invited her to live with them for as long as she needed. They claimed that the king's men would not find her as Katsuo's men had settled in the area.

She had been surprised to know that her cousin had been one of the Lords who'd chosen to surrender to the invader.

She thought back to her conversation with Serenity. A part of Jae-Hwa did put the blame for her father's death at her feet but there was another part of her that remembered who her father was and the type of person he had tried to compel her to be. He was not above sacrificing anyone or anything to get what he wanted, even her happiness.

When she got word of his death, she had been devastated but more so because she had lost the only other parent she had left. Secretly, she blamed him. Blamed him for leaving her alone, blamed him for losing her home, blamed him for convincing her she was going to be someone she wasn't. He had never truly seen her as anything but the "future queen". She blamed Serenity for all she lost that night because she would never have the opportunity to blame her father.

That fateful day when she met Katsuo, she had just wanted to save what was left of her family and household. She surrendered herself to keep them alive. Then she did what she had been raised to do, be the perfect lady. Soon after, she was told she would be the perfect queen, once again. And once again, she had begun to believe it was her destiny and that she had been mistaken to think otherwise. How else could she have been given such an opportunity twice?

However, as soon as Jae-Hwa realized who Katsuo's dream walker was those thoughts came crashing down, and she remembered how things had ended the last time she tried to walk such a path. She had left not only because her father's plans for her would never be obtained but because she saw how their actions could have impacted the country and the people. And here she was about to do it all again.

It had honestly just been about survival and keeping her friends and family safe but now she had to make a choice. If she chose to continue on this path, she would have to throw herself completely behind Katsuo and pray for the downfall of Kang-Dae, Serenity, and everything Xian stood for. On the other hand, she could allow herself to put her trust in the person who had been a catalyst for the destruction of everything she'd ever known.

# CHAPTER 73

The spread before them was extravagant even for Katsuo. There were only a few people at the table and they could never consume everything that was sitting in front of them. Even though Serenity's focus tried to be on the food she could see both Katsuo and Jae-Hwa at the head of the table. He was being extra attentive to her and she appeared to be enjoying it. It only made her nausea worse. She meant what she told Jae-Hwa before, she would bring her down with her but she truly hoped it would not come to that.

As some of the guests spoke amongst themselves Serenity pushed her food around, only taking tiny bites knowing she would not be able to keep it down. Once she had finished the last of her pills her symptoms returned at full force. After being suppressed for so long it seemed the poison was now attacking her body with everything it had. No amount of honey ginger was helping. Serenity's hand shook slightly as she reached for her cup. She quickly put it back down hoping nobody noticed.

Suddenly Katsuo stood cup in hand. "Tonight is about more than coming together as men with the common goal of unity. Tonight, we celebrate the further completion of my legacy in this land." He looked over at Jae-Hwa. "My queen-to-be is with child."

The room immediately erupted with cheers and congratulations. Serenity felt her hope take a nosedive. As she looked at Jae-Hwa who smiled up at Katsuo lovingly while cradling her still small stomach Serenity knew now that Jae-Hwa had the upper hand. Having his child gave her way more sway with Katsuo. He would be more likely to take her side now in anything no matter what Serenity told him. It appeared Jae-Hwa had made her choice. Serenity's vision started to darken a little. She shut her eyes and took several deep breaths hoping to stave off what she felt was coming. In the background, she heard Katsuo still speaking but could no longer focus on the words. Vaguely, she heard him call for a toast but she could barely open her eyes let alone lift the goblet. She hoped that if she stayed still long enough, they would ignore her and not notice the state she was in.

"Are you alright?" She was able to hear the question coming from Jae-Hwa. How could she be, she wanted to scream. She prepared herself to put on a fake smile but as soon as she opened her eyes the room spun and she felt herself falling from her chair and then she felt nothing.

Serenity awoke in her room all alone. It was darker outside so she knew a bit of time had passed. Opening her eyes, the pain in her head intensified and she quickly shut them back again. She rolled over on her side hoping to stifle the pain a bit with the pillow pressed against her temple. She slowly opened her eyes once more and smelt the scent of something bitter. On the table it looked like there was incense burning, filling the room with the aroma. There was also a small bottle on the table, reminiscent of the one the healer had brought when he had first been sent to her. Had he been here? If he had examined her, the chances of her pregnancy still being a secret were slim. Serenity began to panic. Did Katsuo know? She jumped out of bed ignoring the pain and rushed to the door. She placed her hand on the knob but was too fearful to turn it, afraid it would be locked, confirming her worst fears. Instead, she took a step back and released a shuddering breath. What would she do now? There was no way Jae-Hwa wouldn't use this to her advantage. Knowing she'd been lying for so long there will be no coming back from this. Maybe she'd be better off trying to escape. She tried to come up with various explanations she could use to try and explain herself, but apart from immaculate conception which she didn't think Katsuo would buy, she came up with nothing.

Serenity went back to bed and lay down waiting for the inevitable. Hours passed but no one came, not a soldier to escort her to a horrible dungeon or even a servant. Eventually, the morning came but Serenity was still left to an unknown fate.

# CHAPTER 74

Serenity was sitting at the window staring at the moon. No one had to come by to punish her or take her away. Waiting for the unknown was the absolute worst thing she'd ever experienced. At least that's what she tried to tell herself to dispel the fear of what could and probably would happen when someone did come for her. She jumped at the sound of a door opening. When she saw it was not the front door but the hidden one, she didn't know how to feel. From the secret entrance in the corner of the room, the same guards from the night Jae-Hwa first confronted her emerged. They stood by waiting not saying a word. Serenity stood and proceeded to go with the men ready to speak with Lady Gi. They took her through the long tunnel back to that room.

Jae-Hwa sat in the same chair waiting for her. Serenity sat down on her own, not waiting to be forced or asked. Jae-Hwa started pouring tea. She placed the cup in front of Serenity, but Serenity was not going to touch it.

"How did you sleep?" Jae-Hwa asked. After having to wait on whether or not she was going to be dragged off and thrown in the prison or just straight up killed for the past 24 hours Serenity was not in the mood for this.

"What is it that you want?" Serenity demanded. Jae-Hwa just took a sip of her tea.

"I haven't told him yet if that is what you are worried about." Serenity tried to keep her cool and not show her momentary panic.

"Told him what exactly?" Jae-Hwa gave her a sympathetic look.

"My healer says you're not that far along. I could provide you with some tonics to nourish you while you're here," she offered casually. Serenity wanted to throw up and if Jae-Hwa kept pressing her, she was going to vomit all over her. "I know you have no reason to trust me," Jae-Hwa started, "but I do not wish any harm upon your child."

Serenity let out a humorless chuckle, not believing a word she said.

"I understand the desire to protect one's child even before it comes into the world," Jae-Hwa continued.

"I'm sure you do," Serenity said. "Now that you're having his child, you'll do anything to protect it and yourself."

A hint of a smile crossed Jae-Hwa's lips. She looked down at her stomach. "I suppose you are right," she said. "Now it's just a matter of knowing what the right course of action for us is."

Serenity felt the tickle in her throat as a coughing fit was underway. She closed her eyes and cleared her throat hoping to avoid it. The tea in front of her was starting to look promising but remembering the source of it, she decided to grit her teeth and fight through it. Jae-Hwa must have noticed her eyeing the cup. "Please have some." Serenity looked at her as though she were crazy.

"Would it do me any good to poison you now?" Jae-Hwa asked. "All I would need to do is wait for the poison already in your system to take you." Serenity went cold. So, she knew that as well. Maybe that was why she didn't bother telling Katsuo the truth. If Jae-Hwa waited her out long enough there would be no need, and Serenity would be out of her hair forever.

The stress of the conversation was not having a great effect on her body. Unable to hold back anymore she released a string of coughs almost as if her body knew there was no point in hiding anymore. Jae-Hwa once again offered her tea. Whether out of distrust or pure spite Serenity continued to refuse. Jae-Hwa almost looked remorseful watching her so distressed which made no sense to Serenity.

However, it seemed her mistrust was warranted because not a second later Jae-Hwa gave word to the man behind her. His strong hands were now on her shoulders holding her down. Another pair of hands came to take the teacup in front of her.

And a third pair of hands attempted to pry her mouth open. She fought against them as hard as she could and even managed to bite the finger of one. The man let out a small shout. Serenity's nose was suddenly pinched, preventing her from breathing. Serenity pressed her lips shut as she continued struggling against them but the more she struggled the less air she had and eventually she had to take a breath. As soon as she did, the cup was there and the tea was being poured into her mouth. Before she could even try to spit it out, her mouth was forcibly closed and her head was pushed back. Serenity tried to keep from swallowing but it was a fruitless battle.

Once they were sure she had swallowed, the hands released her and the men went back into position behind her. Serenity looked at Jae-Hwa in disbelief, tears swimming in her eyes. "Why are you doing this?"

Strangely enough, Jae-Hwa looked sympathetic. "I told you, I do not wish your child harm. This was the only way to save it."

Confusion swept over Serenity. "What does that mean?"

"You are very lucky you came here," Jae-Hwa began. "There is nowhere else in all of Xian where you will find the antidote to our jinjiu poisoning."

It took Serenity a moment to register what it was Jae-Hwa was trying to say. She stared down at the now empty cup. "Was that-," she began to ask, scared to get her hopes up.

Jae-Hwa nodded. "It is."

"Why?" Serenity asked still completely confused.

"It is like I said, I do not wish your child harmed by my family's deeds. Who knows what punishment we will face in the afterlife for causing such a thing."

Serenity wasn't sure she was buying that excuse but the hopeful and happy part of her didn't care why as long as it meant she was no longer dying.

"You could have just told me," Serenity grumbled.

Jae-Hwa arched her brow. "Would you have believed me?" she asked. They both knew the answer to that. Serenity found herself smiling with Jae-Hwa. "No," she answered honestly with a tiny laugh. "Can I have some regular water now?" Serenity asked.

Jae-Hwa nodded. "of course." A fresh pitcher was brought out along with cups.

"What's the end game here Jae-Hwa?" Serenity asked after pouring her water, still trying to figure out her angle in all this.

Jae-Hwa wrinkled her nose in confusion. "End game?" she repeated the words not understanding them.

"You're about to have what you want, at least, what you say you want," Serenity reminded her. "Saving me and my child doesn't get you any closer to that. You know I'll do everything in my power to keep Katsuo off the throne." Serenity told her honestly.

Jae-Hwa did not answer her. Serenity wondered if she even knew what she wanted. "I am a lady of the Gi household, and I will do what is best for those under my care," she finally said which they both knew was a non-answer but it was probably the only one she would give.

# CHAPTER 75

Kang-Dae and his men have been traveling day and night. They only slept when they took short breaks and then got back on the road and continued south. They were trying now to avoid any more fights so that they would waste no more time. He sent scouts ahead to different routes so they could report which way would be clear for them to go.

The men were tired, he knew because he was tired too but they pushed on. Supplies were dwindling. Getting back south was no longer just about cutting off Katsuo's attack but not starving out here in the wilderness. With all the movements of all the different soldiers and people, the number of game in the area was extremely limited. Kang-Dae began to fear that the entire forest had been overhunted.

A lone soldier came running up to them. Kang-Dae was glad to see it was only Ji.

"The southwest road was clear," Ji reported. The soldier had volunteered to be a scout as he claimed to be more comfortable alone following the loss of his entire troop so Kang-Dae allowed it. His other scouts reported men on the southern, and southeastern roads. Now, with Ji's report, their path was clear, so they veered west.

Their new tactic had been working well for them as they had not run into any of Katsuo's soldiers. Despite that good fortune, something was pressing on Kang-Dae. That same feeling that had come over him to make him decide to return south was back once more pressing on him. He was having a difficult time trying to understand what it was urging him to do. They seemed to be on the right path and the way had been cleared, so what was it?

# CHAPTER 76

Serenity had been feeling off all day. Now that she was cured, she knew it was not due to sickness. She tried to chalk it up to cabin fever. Being stuck in the same room for hours on end day after day had to have been taking a toll on her. But even with that, it felt like something else, something brewing that she couldn't quite put her finger on. With everything that was going on it was hard to pinpoint exactly what it was she should be worried about. A knock at the door and the entrance of Jae-Hwa's servant Lie-Wei, relieved her as she was feeling hungry.

As always, the handmaid did not engage with her. She always sat the dishes down and allowed the others to bring in the water and tea before scurrying out. It was because of this routine that Serenity was momentarily vexed when the woman paused while setting down her spoon. Lie-Wei looked her briefly in the eye before letting her gaze shift to the small bowl of black beans on the side, then back to Serenity. The woman did not say a word. After only a second, she left the room with the others.

As soon as she was gone Serenity reached for the bowl. She picked it up and something small fell back onto the table. As she looked closely at it she realized it was a tightly rolled piece of paper. She quickly unraveled it revealing tiny writing. 'Katsuo is plotting Kang-Dae's assassination. It is already in motion.' Serenity's heart stopped and she rushed toward the door pounding on it to get the captain's attention. The doors quickly opened before he could ask her what was wrong, she demanded to see Katsuo immediately.

On the walk there, Serenity's earlier panic had died down just enough for her to consider how she would proceed. She couldn't let Katsuo know she had been warned about his intentions. And she couldn't let on her true motives for him not to go through with it. One wrong word she would be exposed. Still, she didn't stop because she could not allow Kang-Dae to be harmed. If she could stop it from her end she would.

While passing through the gardens she heard Jae-Hwa calling out to the guard and her.

"Hello," she greeted with a smile. Captain Masao bowed to her but Serenity remained unmoving, doing her best to keep her emotions in check. Jae-Hwa quickly glanced at Serenity before she spoke to Masao. "I'd be happy to escort her the rest of the way. Why don't you go to the kitchens and get something to eat? I had the cooks prepare something special just for you to thank you for your diligent service." The captain bowed once again and thanked her before walking off.

Once he was gone the smile quickly dropped from Jae-Hwa's face. She didn't speak but she turned toward the main house and began walking and Serenity followed her. "When I told you of his plans, I did not expect you would be foolish enough to just confront him," she scolded with a whisper.

"Did you think I would just sit back and do nothing?" Serenity asked in the same tone.

"I thought you would be smart enough to figure out a way without compromising yourself or me."

"I don't have the time for that. Kang-Dae doesn't have the time for it."

"I thought you were smarter than this. I suppose that's my mistake," she quipped. Serenity didn't care, Jae-Hwa could throw all the shade she wanted it didn't stop her from wanting to do whatever it took to save her husband's life.

"What's *your* plan? What exactly do you want to come of this? I mean, you're close to getting everything you ever wanted why not just let it happen? Or was this your plan to scare me into exposing myself so you can finally get rid of me?" she asked, her voice rising as she became more and more frantic.

"Calm yourself," Jae-Hwa said.

"Calm myself? I'm trapped in this place with the man who's actively seeking to kill my husband and my only ally is the woman whose father tried to kill me. Every day I'm worried and scared that I'm going to be caught and my baby-," she trailed off unable to finish her voice cracking under the emotion. She wiped at the tear that threatened to fall. Jae-Hwa stopped walking and Serenity did the same.

"Rushing into this does not solve any of those problems. Stop and think. Katsuo is no fool but he can be pushed in certain ways. You just have to have the right," she paused for a moment trying to find the right word.

"Leverage?" Serenity finished for her.

Jae-Hwa gave a slight nod. "Yes, leverage. If you find the right one you can steer him in the right way."

"What leverage do I have? He doesn't care about anything other than taking over."

Jae-Hwa looked away momentarily following that comment. It almost made Serenity feel a bit guilty but at the same time she did not want to attribute any kind of sentimental feelings to that man and she was not in the mood to placate whatever complicated feelings Jae-Hwa had for him. "It's not taking over that he cares for the most, it is his legacy." Serenity didn't know what to do with the information. What could she say or do that would impact his legacy in his mind?

"The seed has already been planted. You just need to make it grow," continued Jae-Hwa.

"Please don't speak to me in riddles right now I do not have the time," Serenity mumbled.

"Have you not already told him the secret to his victory?" Jae-Hwa reminded her.

"A lot of good that did," she muttered.

"You need to strengthen his belief in you. Give him a reason to fear going against your word."

"I don't have anything to back it up," Serenity retorted.

"That may have to come later. For now, you need to stop him." Serenity sighed. It was strange to be given advice from such an interesting source. But if Jae-Hwa had wanted to kill her, she could have done so in a dozen different ways. So Serenity allowed herself to take the advice to heart.

# CHAPTER 77

The two women came to the main house. Inside they found Katsuo with Lord Sho and another in the main hall. The man standing in front of the two was not someone Serenity had seen before. His skin was very tan like he'd spent a lot of time in the sun. He was quite thin with long legs. He was not dressed as a soldier. He wore no armor and his clothes were loose-fitting. His hair was wet with sweat and his cheeks red. He looked as if he had just run a great distance. Was he a messenger?

Katsuo's face lit up when he noticed Jae-Hwa and Serenity. He dismissed the man but allowed Lord Sho to stay.

"What great deed have I done to warrant a visit from my beautiful wife-to-be?" Katsuo asked. Jae-Hwa left Serenity and went to Katsuo. He took her by the hands and kissed her cheek. Jae-Hwa blushed and smiled.

It was stuff like this that had Serenity going back and forward on Jae-Hwa's motives. If she truly was willing to shift her allegiance, she deserved an award for her continued act as the doting fiancé because she was killing it.

"I was in the gardens and I noticed the dream walker coming to see you and decided to join her," Jae-Hwa told him.

"Is that so?" he turned his gaze to Serenity. "Is there something you wish to tell me?" he asked her.

"I-I," she cleared her throat and gathered herself. "I had a vision of confirmation," she told him.

"Confirmation?" repeated Katsuo.

"Yes. I know now that your victory will surely come when you meet the Xian king on the battlefield." Katsuo shared a look with the soothsayer but Serenity continued. "I saw you both standing on a grand stage surrounded by thousands. The more people who came to witness the event, the more you shined. Eventually, you became so bright the Xian king could no longer look at you and you were able to defeat him."

Katsuo looked like he was picturing the vision in his head and he liked what he saw. "That sounds like something that would be great to behold."

"The battlefield is not just a battlefield, it is a stage, a stage to showcase your great victory to the land so that you may take your place in the people's hearts as their true king," she lied.

Lord Sho spoke up and asked, "what is the point of having two different dreams to say the same thing? Perhaps your dreams are telling you there are multiple ways to achieve victory."

Serenity glared at the man before adding, "I also had a warning dream."

Katsuo's face darkened and she could see his jaw clench.

"A warning?" he said in a low voice.

Serenity nodded." Along with the first dream came a second one, to warn you of what would happen if the dream was not heeded," she spoke hoping to express the severity of the situation with her tone.

"And what happened in this dream?" he asked.

Serenity thought quickly. 'His legacy, remember his legacy' she reminded herself of Jae-Hwa's words.

"There was a giant statue at the center of the world. On it, there were thousands and thousands of names of thousands and thousands of great men. There were two ways to reach the statue. There were red stairs and there was a gold rope. You saw the rope and decided not to use it, wanting to take the stairs because it was easier. But every step you took only took you further and further from the statue. Eventually, you were so far from it you couldn't even see it anymore and then you could no longer find it." The words poured out. She had had the dream some time ago but at the time opted to keep it to herself. She could see it all happening in her head as she spoke like a movie.

Katsuo's face seemed to have lost any shred of amusement. "What exactly does it mean?" he questioned her. At his side, Jae-Hwa was stroking his hand as if she were trying to soothe the beast.

"I believe it means that if you attempt to bypass your fate by trying to avoid a challenge, you will not be remembered, and your name will disappear in history forever," the false interpretation came out easily. In actuality, the dream had shown her the consequences of Katsuo's many misdeeds. What she left out was that the stairs he chose to climb also had names, hundreds of names of those he harmed and brought misery to. Every time he stepped on those names, on those people, in order to achieve his goal, it cost him. The rope represented the path he should have taken.

"Avoid a challenge? You think I would avoid anything?" Katsuo accused. "What is it you think that I fear?"

"I only have the dreams and give the interpretation. The rest is for you to figure out," she told him.

"I have a different interpretation," Lord Sho spoke.

All eyes turned to him. "I believe that by avoiding the rope you found a way to set yourself apart from even the greatest men. You will do what no one else can. You were purposely pulled from what others had done to pave your own way," he finished with a sly smile.

Is he using his own fake interpretation to cast doubt on my fake interpretation? Serenity thought to herself angrily. Now Serenity had witnessed firsthand, how this man had managed to wrongly convince Katsuo of his great purpose.

"Well, you have given me a lot to consider," said Katsuo. "Thank you for your words."

Serenity quickly glanced at Jae-Hwa who kept her eyes on Katsuo. Frustrated and feeling like she had not accomplished her goal she left the room.

# CHAPTER 78

Jung-Soo ran quickly through the trees wanting to cover as much ground as possible while there was still light. Tae-Soo was trailing behind him breathing heavily.

"General, could we slow down just a bit? We have to be careful of your injury," he said attempting to manipulate him by reminding Jung-Soo of his injury but he knew Tae-Soo's motives were less about Jung-Soo's well-being and more about his inability to keep up.

"I feel fine," he had to practically shout back as the distance between them had grown that much.

"Remember what Rielle said about not pushing yourself. We already left sooner than we should have."

Yes, Jung-Soo recalled Rielle's warnings but he had been immobile for far too long and needed to get back to his men and back to Kang-Dae. He figured at his current pace he will be able to catch up to them before long.

"General please, Rielle said we had to rest at least four times a day. She gave us instructions."

Jung-Soo felt the corner of his mouth twitch. "How will she know how many times we rest?" he asked. "Will you tell her?"

His question was met with silence. Jung-Soo almost wanted to laugh. He stopped and turned to look at Tae-Soo "You do remember that I am your commander, not her?"

"I know that general," Tae-Soo assured him, holding on to a tree, trying to catch his breath. "It's just-,"

"What?" Jung-Soo prompted.

"She was very adamant," he said carefully. "Also, I do not believe she would tell you to do something if it wasn't necessary for your healing. She clearly li-," Tae-Soo immediately stopped talking noticing the shift and Jung-Soo's demeanor.

Tae-Soo gave a nervous smile. "Never mind, general. Let's keep going," Tae-Soo said quickly. Jung-Soo gave the soldier a hard stare before turning around and continuing their trek deciding to increase his previous pace.

# CHAPTER 79

There was very loud talking going on outside. It was beginning to annoy Serenity as she was trying to pray for guidance on how to move forward, and pray for Kang-Dae's safety. She went towards the window to shut it hoping it would drown out some of the noise.

"The men are already starting to drink," she heard a voice say from outside. She looked out and saw a couple of soldiers walking across the courtyard.

"Not just the men," the other soldier spoke. "The king, his future queen, and the nobles are already celebrating in the main hall. They're claiming the Xian king will be dead by morning."

Serenity backed away from the window in shock. He had done it. He'd gone through with it. Serenity felt like she was dying. This couldn't be real. She had to stop this, she had to stop him, or at the very least make sure it was Katsuo who didn't see the next sunrise.

Serenity entered into a very jovial atmosphere. The men were laughing and toasting amongst themselves. Katsuo sat in the center of it all with Jae-Hwa at his side, a grand smile on his face that both repulsed and angered Serenity greatly.

"Ah! Dream walker," he called out the moment he noticed her. "Come." he beckoned. She slowly moved toward him, her anger building up. "Soon you will see me take my place in history. If you put more faith in me, I will show you what it truly means to shine," he boasted. The knife she'd hidden was burning a hole in her sleeve. If she could just get close enough, one strike was all she needed. She had made peace with the fact that she would not escape but if she could remove the cancer once and for all then Xian would still have a chance.

The closer she got to him the more at peace she was with the decision. Maybe it wasn't peace, maybe it was blind rage that comforted her with the idea that she would bring her would-be husband's killer to justice. Just a few more steps, she told herself. Her focus was solely on Katsuo, so much so, she didn't notice Jae-Hwa's stare as she moved forward. Nor did she see Jae-Hwa stand as she began to lower her sleeve so the knife could slide out easily into her hand. A cry broke out in the room which silenced everything. Everyone looked to see Jae-Hwa clutching her stomach, eyes closed in obvious pain.

"My king," she whispered. "The child," was all she managed to say before another cry escaped her lips.

"Get the healer in here!" Katsuo shouted. Multiple men ran out at once. Serenity stood frozen watching her. The fury she was feeling before shifted into concern. That concern turned to action when she saw droplets of blood hit the ground. Serenity ran up the steps past Katsuo ignoring everything and everyone. She grabbed onto Jae-Hwa's hand. She didn't know if her concern was a form of gratitude for what Jae-Hwa had done for her or just sympathy as an expectant mother herself but she wanted to help her. Jae-Hwa held on to her hand, squeezing it for comfort. The healer came after a while and Jae-Hwa was taken back away. Serenity had been barred from going with her and sent back to her quarters.

Not able to do much else, Serenity prayed for Jae-Hwa and her baby. Despite who the father was she didn't wish ill upon either mother or child. Minutes turned into hours. A full day had passed and she had heard no news from anyone. Serenity didn't know whether the captain had not been informed or if he had been told to keep what happened to himself but he was tight-lipped as well. Serenity could do nothing but wait, wait for news of Jae-Hwa and news of her husband's fate.

# CHAPTER 80

Ji moved quickly in the night between the trees. It had taken a while for him to find an opening to get away but when he did, he didn't waste a moment. He found a spot just far enough from the Xian king's camp but still close enough for his plan to work. He began to set up a small pyre. He had to move fast before the fire caught their attention. His fellow brothers should be nearby. He had been dropping things, carving markings on trees throughout the journey for them to follow. By order of his King, he had been given permission to enact the plan to kill the Xian king.

It had not been easy living amongst the enemy. When his captain informed him, he would be left behind following their fight with the Xians. He'd been skeptical. Still, he did as he was told. He disguised himself as a Xian soldier and waited to be found so he could keep an eye on the enemy. The fact that it was the Xian king himself that had come across him made Ji believe it was his fate to take part in his death.

Unfortunately, his first attempt to lead him into an ambush had been thwarted when more of the Xian army had shown up. He'd lost many brothers that day and it had been hard for him to stay silent and not turn his sword against them but he bided his time and waited. He had only been able to save one soldier and get him away before anybody noticed. Ji had told the man to alert the king of where he was and who he was with so that they could keep track of him until it was time to strike. After that, he'd stayed in contact with his king through means of a messenger. He'd leave notes for the runner every time they moved on. Hiding it in the spent remains of the previous night's campfire

Ji lit the pyre and prepared to sneak back into camp so he could pretend he had been sleeping all along. Soon all the nearby forces he'd been secretly leading to the Xians would see the fire. It would expose the Xians' position, and let his brothers know it was time to strike. He imagined there were at least several forces nearby at this point. It would not take long for them to rain down on them. By the end of the night, the Xian king would be dead and King Katsuo would be the land's new ruler. He was so honored to be a part of his king's rise.

An arrow hit the ground right by his foot startling him. Ji looked around and his heart dropped to see a man wielding a bow coming out of the darkness along with the Xian king himself and a dozen others. Ji fell to his knees. "My king, I had come upon this fire and was coming to warn you. There's a spy amongst you," he rambled out desperately.

"Is that so?" the one called Kahil remarked sarcastically.

"I swear my King, I just found it." Ji figured if he could keep them distracted long enough his brothers would arrive soon.

Kang-Dae stared down at the treacherous man. How he wanted to just run him through and be done with it but he could still prove to be useful. "How many men are you expecting?" Kang-Dae asked.

"I'm not expecting anyone, my king, I swear," he lied.

Kahil took a step forward clearly as impatient as Kang-Dae was but Kang-Dae held up his hand stopping him from going any further. "if you wish to live past the night, you will tell us what we want to know," Kang-Dae threatened.

The man put his head to the ground submissively. Kang-Dae rolled his eyes and he could hear Kahil's irritated groan. "My king please," Kahil started. "just let me end this."

At this point, Ji must have finally come to the realization that none of his lies were working and his demeanor changed. He sat up looking at all of them defiantly.

"Do what you wish to me, it is you who will not live past the morning," the snake claimed.

"Is that so?" Kang-Dae inquired with absolutely no concern.

"My brothers will be here soon to wipe you all out and my king will take his rightful place on the Xian throne," the man bragged.

"How exactly are they going to find us? As you can see, we put out your little fire?" Kahil goaded. The man began to chuckle before full-out laughing.

"Yes, you did very well putting out *this* fire." he congratulated them insincerely. "I'm sure the other ones I've lit have done their job well," he taunted.

Kang-Dae came up to him and bent down to his level. "I'm sure they would have," he told him. "If we hadn't found them already and put them out."

The smirk quickly dropped from Ji's face. "You lie!" he growled.

"Do I?" At that moment two of his men came forward dumping pieces of charred wood at the man's knees. "I've had my suspicions about you since you tried to lead my men into that ambush. When you offered to be a scout, I had you followed to see what you would do," revealed Kang-Dae. "You were smart, giving me true reports so you could catch us off guard with a false one. But you see, now that we are aware of your people's duplicitous methods, we will not allow ourselves to fall to them ever again," Kang-Dae swore.

Kang-Dae got in the man's face. "I will ask you once more and then you will speak no more. How many are out there?" The man defiantly pressed his lips together and looked away.

"I suppose it doesn't matter. Now that we know exactly how to lure them out we can meet them wherever we want, whenever want," boasted Kang-Dae.

Ji's face paled and Kang-Dae just smiled. Standing up, he turned and walked back towards the camp. "Kahil," was all he said. One short scream and a thud later, he knew the man was no more.

# CHAPTER 81

Serenity had been staring out the window when the door burst open and Katsuo came staggering inside with wild eyes. He looked as though he were drunk. His clothes were in disarray. His hair was loose, falling over his bloodshot eyes.

"Undo it," he told her. Serenity stared blankly not knowing what he was talking about. He kicked the table across the room and stumbled over to her. Serenity backed away quickly as far as she could until she became blocked by the wall. Katsuo was on her quickly, with his hand around her throat squeezing to give just enough pressure to make her gasp. "Bring it back," he cried. "bring my child back."

Terrified and confused Serenity shook her head as best she could. "I don't-, I don't know what you're talking about."

"It was your words that caused this. Undo it. Bring it back."

"I didn't cause anything," she gasped out. His grip tightened and Serenity pulled at his wrist.

"You will do what I say," he threatened. There was a smell of wine on his breath. Staring into his wild eyes, Serenity could now see all of the sadness, pain, and anger swirling within them.

Jae-Hwa must have miscarried and in his grief, he attributed the cause to her words of warning.

"If there was a price for your actions you chose to pay it," she said boldly. With a roar, he threw her to the ground.

"My king!" Lie-Wei came flying in, throwing herself at his feet. "My lady wishes to see the dream walker," she said quickly.

Katsuo stood above them, breathing heavily. The manic look in his eyes was still present. "Please my king, she is waiting."

Katsuo rubbed his hair out of his face. "Fine," the trio took the long and awkward journey to Jae-Hwa. The first thing Serenity noticed when seeing her was how pale she looked. Jae-Hwa looked weak as she lay under a pile of blankets, propped up by pillows.

"Thank you, Lei-Mei," Jae-Hwa said dismissing the servants. Katsuo went to her side attempting to hold her hand but she pulled it away. Serenity enjoyed the look of disappointment on his face. "I wish to speak with her alone," said Jae-Hwa.

Katsuo shook his head. "I will not allow that. She-," he started but Jae-Hwa quickly interrupted.

"What has she done? What has she done but given you exactly what you needed to ensure our child will be born a prince? Her words did not cause this," she said reiterating everything Serenity had tried to tell him before. The guilty look on Katsuo's face perhaps would have tugged at Serenity's heart a couple of days ago but at that moment she felt no pity for him. After a moment Katsuo staggered out leaving the two alone.

Serenity approached the bed slowly. "How are you feeling?" She asked genuinely concerned.

Jae-Hwa stared down at the blankets. "I will survive as I always do," she answered.

"I'm sorry," Serenity said though the words felt inadequate in such a situation.

"You do not need to apologize; you need to seize this opportunity."

Serenity was taken back. "Opportunity?"

"He will listen now. That anger of his will fade and he will come back to you begging for your visions." Serenity could hardly believe what she was hearing. Was she really thinking about that in the midst of what she was going through?

"You don't need to worry about that right now," Serenity tried to assure her.

"Listen to me. They failed. Kang-Dae lives." Serenity's hands flew to her mouth.

"He's alive?" she asked, praying she'd heard Jae-Hwa right.

"Not only that, but Katsuo, has lost many men. When he comes to you, this will be the time to get him to do the thing he would not have done otherwise. It's your chance, our chance to be rid of him for good."

Serenity felt so elated and also so confused. Jae-Hwa was not acting like someone who'd suffered a great loss. Instead, she spoke like a mastermind who'd put the perfect plan in motion. "Jae-Hwa, what did you do?"

The tiniest ghost of a smile came upon Jae-Hwa's lips and Serenity felt a bit of a chill. "I took back my fate from the hands of another."

"What about-," Serenity paused, the words 'the baby' failing to come out.

"Do not worry about me. I have taken care of everything including my need to seek rest with relatives in the east. I'll be able to rest under the watchful eye of my healer and people." It suddenly occurred to Serenity that it had been Jae-Hwa's healer who had come to check on her that night she had collapsed. The same healer who had kept Serenity's condition and poisoning to himself under orders from Jae-Hwa. What other things would he have done under her specific orders? Just how much of this had been Jae-Hwa's plan? Did she really lose the baby? If she did, had it been intentional? Serenity stared down at Jae-Hwa like she was seeing her for the first time. She almost wanted to ask Jae-Hwa if she had even been pregnant in the first place but that seemed too ridiculous. She would have had to have planned to betray Katsuo before she'd found out Serenity was pregnant. Surely, she hadn't been planning this since then, had she? Serenity decided not to ask. Jae-Hwa had done more than enough. If she wanted to keep her secrets Serenity would let her.

"Are you sure about this?" Serenity found herself asking. "There's no guarantee that we can win this. This is your best chance to finally be the queen."

Jae-Hwa looked up wistfully as if she was considering it. "It did sound nice once upon a time but now it just rings hollow in the wake of the cost. I am Xianian and will die as such just like my mother. I will not allow my country to fall to ruin for my ambitions."

Touched by her words and her determination Serenity did something she never thought she'd do. She bowed to her. "Thank you, Lady Gi."

"Save our country, my queen."

# CHAPTER 82

Just as Jae-Hwa predicted Serenity was called before Katsuo a couple of days later. The room was empty. No lords, no nobles, no Sho. Katsuo chose to sit at the foot of his throne. In a box in front of her were what looked like piles of silk dresses along with gold and jewelry. Serenity ignored the box and stared at him.

"It was wrong of me to accuse you of causing-," his voice broke off. He cleared his throat and began again. "Please accept this gift as a token." He would not ever actually apologize, Serenity realized. This was the best he could do to make amends.

"Thank you," she said not caring about any of it.

"My lady will be leaving soon. She will be safe and well cared for. In the meantime. I need to destroy the Xian king, now more than ever. How can I do it?"

"I have already told you the path to victory," she reminded him, enjoying the new level of power she had over him.

"Where will this battle need to take place?"

"At Xian's greatest stronghold."

"What do I need to do?" he asked, looking like a lost child begging for guidance.

She told him exactly where he needed to go and the time frame in which he needed to do it. She only hoped it wasn't too late.

"Are you sure?" He asked.

"This is how you end the war."

He nodded, accepting her words. He stood and walked over to her placing her hand on her shoulder. "Thank you dream walker," he said thoughtfully. So thoughtfully she might have felt just a twinge of guilt knowing she was leading him to his end but that was quickly stamped out by the overwhelming hope that not only would she see Kang-Dae again but they would take back this country together. Within two days they were back on the roads traveling toward Fort Chungi.

# CHAPTER 83

Serenity had been made to stay behind as Katsuo and his men went through with their plan. She was a nervous wreck the entire time. It was an odd and complicated feeling both wanting him to fail and succeed. Her dream had told her that there were Xian soldiers on the way to the fort. She knew if Katsuo could intercept them, he could switch them out for his men and infiltrate the fort allowing his men to gain access and overtake the fortress.

Serenity knew how important Fort Chungi was to the country not just as a military stronghold but as a symbol. Giving Katsuo the keys to taking that away from Xian was more than a leap of faith, it was a completely ridiculous and nonsensical move that could very well bring the downfall of Xian. But Serenity would trust her dreams that this move, though painful, would lead to Xian's victory in the end. She just had no idea how yet.

A commotion sounded outside her tent. Just as she was about to step outside to look, she heard the captain's voice right outside. "I have been ordered to escort you to the fort," he reported. Serenity knew then that they had succeeded and she never felt worse in her life.

The captain took her on horseback through the wilderness along with the other hundreds of soldiers who had been left behind on standby. As they approached the fort Serenity felt her heart tighten at the damage in the aftermath of what looked to be a hard-won battle. There didn't seem to be as many bodies as she expected, not that she was complaining. She wondered if many had retreated once things became pointless.

Just outside the gates of the fort was a triumphant Katsuo. He stood proudly over his new conquest. After the captain helped her down from her horse, she was brought to Katsuo who held his hand out for her. She accepted his hand and he led her inside. There were a number of prisoners kneeling in the dirt. Katsuo had told her that his goal was to unite the strongest under one rule and he would avoid killing as much as possible to add to his strength. The reputation of the fort made him believe that these men were the perfect addition to his army. Serenity knew otherwise. She knew these men were loyal to Xian and would never join Katsuo even on threat of death. Serenity didn't want to look at the faces of the men, knowing they would haunt her. She almost gasped out loud when she saw General Sun as one of the captives. Their eyes met and she became terrified that he would out her right then and there. He stared at her with the same loathing he used to stare at her with.

"You were right. They took us in just like you foresaw. After that, it was just a matter of opening the gates. They had not been prepared for such an attack. Many of the men fled."

Serenity forced a smile despite the horrible guilt she was feeling. "Good work," she told him. "But we still have more to do."

Katsuo nodded his head.

"Of course."

# CHAPTER 84

"Impossible!" Kang-Dae exclaimed.

"We've had multiple reports confirming it my king," General Li spoke dejectedly. The men sat in a circle away from their soldiers.

"How? No one has ever been able to take the fort," Kahil said in disbelief.

Kang-Dae stood not believing this was happening. The fort had stood for generations and now under his rule, it had been lost. He walked over to the nearest tree and leaned his head against it, feeling overwhelmed. They were too late. Katsu managed to outmaneuver him. How had he succeeded?

"The people have begun to flee the capital in fear. We've gotten word some Lords have decided to give Katsuo the support of their men to gain favor," General Hui revealed.

The somber mood increased amongst the men.

"What do we do now? Katsuo has infiltrated the heart of us. How can we defeat him now?" asked Shum.

"We will take it back," vowed Kang-Dae rejoining them.

"Take it back? Chungi is our most impenetrable fortress. How would we even begin to take it back?" exclaimed Hui.

"Katsuo managed to," Yu reminded them.

"My king!" one of the soldiers came running up to them.

"There is someone here with a message from Katsuo."

Sun reached the camp after several days of running through the wilderness. It had been exactly where he'd been told, which meant the enemy was a step ahead. He wanted to get there as soon as possible to warn the king. He drank when it rained and only ate whatever he found along the way. His weapons had been taken, so he had to be careful not to run into any of Katsuo's men.

"Hold!" a guard called out.

"I am General Sun!" he panted out. "I have a message from Katsuo."

Brought before his King, Sun was allowed to sit as he spoke. A healer tended to his various scratches and wounds as he relayed the message. It was an entirely different scene than when he was brought before Katsuo and *her*.

*3 Days earlier*

*"He's a bit old. Are you sure this one will be able to make it?" the invader inquired.*

*"It has to be him. He will let them know what needs to happen." Sun stared up at the duo, specifically the former queen of Xian. The first time he saw her, after his capture, he had been convinced he was seeing things. Everyone knew she was dead and gone. But when she caught sight of him and reacted the way that she did, he knew right*

473

then that it was her. Not only was she alive but she was guiding the enemy. 'Treacherous witch' he cursed her in his head. Lord Yu, had tried to warn the king that she was a danger but he had not listened and now their land was on the verge of collapse because of her.

Katsuo stood in front of him. "You have five days to relay this message to your king. If he does not respond, we kill all the men we have and we move toward the palace."

Sun's eyes narrowed and he grunted beneath his gag trying to curse at the man but being unable to. When the witch came forward, he tried to lunge at her but it was quickly stopped by the man holding him down. "Tell your king that he is to meet with Katsuo here, so negotiations can begin," she spoke, her voice cold.

Sun growled through his gag, "Xian will never negotiate with you. Just kill me and be done with it!" Most of what he said had not been understood, but the tone and attitude had translated *well enough. Katsuo moved forward to grant his request but the witch moved faster and a dagger was placed at his throat and her lips were at his ear.*

*"If you wish to save your land, you must do this," she told him. "He needs to know that this is the only way." Sun's eyes narrowed at her desperate tone. "Tell him we await his arrival." she emphasized the 'we' as if she wanted him to tell the king that she was there. Sun became confused and began questioning her motives. As she stepped back the invader stared down at her with great admiration. The would-be king clearly trusted the woman. But so had his king. His anger refreshed he decided then he would do as he was told, but only to ensure the downfall of both of them.*

After telling his king the message he had been sent to give, Sun waited for the king's response.

"Is there anything else you can tell us? Anything about his men or their positions?" the king asked him.

Sun thought about the witch who now resided with the enemy. It was pressing on him to relay everything he saw and who it was that had given him the message, but he stopped himself. "I'm afraid not my king. I was not able to garner such information."

The king exhaled in frustration. "Very well. Prepare the men," he ordered his generals. "We move out tonight."

"You mean to meet with him, my king?" Sun asked.

"It is time I spoke with the one who wishes to replace me. Once I do, I will burn every last trace of him from this land," the king swore.

# CHAPTER 85

Kang-Dae chose only a few generals to head up with him to the fort. Only a quarter of his army came with him to deter Katsuo from trying to take them all out right then and there. The rest of his men lay in wait back at the camp. As they approached the walls, he was disheartened to see the bodies of some Xian soldiers strewn up by the gates. On the wall stood several Katsuo soldiers staring down at them. Kang-Dae stared back, imagining killing every single one of them.

The gates slowly opened and a small force emerged. Katsuo's guards made a line across the wall. Once they were in place he watched as a man in heavy gold armor emerged. This man was confident, and smug, as he strolled out before them. Kang-Dae did not need to see the crown on his head to know this was Katsuo. A few more people came trailing behind him. A man with a staff, two generals, whose armor paled in comparison to Katsuo's, and another soldier stood in the back, blocking Kang-Dae's view of someone else. He could barely see the shorter unknown person dressed in black. Kang-Dae dismounted from his horse and walked up toward them all. His generals followed suit, but he made sure they stayed a couple of steps behind him. At once, every one of the soldiers posted in front of the wall unleashed their weapons. Kang-Dae did not flinch which made Katsuo smile. Katsuo ordered his men to stand down and their weapons were re-sheathed.

"Katsuo," Kang-Dae spoke. Even standing in front of him, Kang-Dae found it hard to believe this was the real cause of all their trouble. This man had alluded them for so long and now he was right in front of him, within a sword's reach. Images of Kang-Dae removing the nuisance's head filled his mind. It could be over in a second, he thought to himself. Regardless of the pleasant thought, Kang-Dae did not cater to his desires.

"*King* Katsuo, soon to be your king," the nuisance replied.

Kang-Dae gave his own smirk at the man's overconfidence. "I guess we will see," he told the fake king.

"I had hoped you were here to discuss your surrender," Katsu boasted. "We both know that Xian will belong to me in a matter of days."

"Xian will never belong to you," asserted Kang-Dae.

"Oh?" Katsuo looked back at the fort dramatically. "Do I not stand in the heart of your greatest stronghold?" he quipped.

"Only for a moment. Xian has held together for thousands of moments. You are but a sour note in our history that will soon be forgotten," Kang-Dae replied. Finally, Kang-Dae saw Katsuo's smug demeanor drop and his face twist in anger.

"You will never comprehend what I am charged with, the weight of my destiny," Katsou spat.

"I do not care how important you think you are, or why you felt the need to bring this destruction to my land, to my people!" Kang-Dae growled. "In the end, you and everyone who followed you will pay for all you have done in blood," vowed Kang-Dae.

Serenity kept nervously wringing her hands as she watched the exchange from behind the captain. Seeing her husband so close but unable to get to him was torture. She wanted to jump up and down and shout "I'm here!" over and over. She didn't dare, knowing it would start a battle right then and there. Instead, she tried to be more subtle.

She used her hand to write out Xian characters by her thigh, in the same manner, they would do their "sky writing" in the night in their peaceful moments together. She knew there was a slim chance of him seeing the movement but she had to try something. With the captain blocking most of her it was all she could do to try and catch his attention. Unfortunately, Kang-Dae seemed solely focused on Katsuo.

"I am giving you this chance to end this peacefully," Katsuo offered.

"It's not peace you offer, it's subjugation and my people will not have it. If you wish to claim Xian as yours, you will have to take it from me." Serenity was extremely proud of her man for not even considering giving in.

"I will gladly adhere to your conditions," retorted Katsuo.

Serenity knew their conversation was coming to an end and she was quickly losing her window to alert Kang-Dae of her presence. She slowly slid out from behind the captain, trying to get within Kang-Dae's sightline. She resumed her "writing" more vigorously with her finger, moving it about so hard she worried she would cause a sprain.

Kang-Dae smirked at Katsuo and his eyes ran over the back line. Serenity's heart stopped as his eyes moved over her but her hope was immediately deflated as they shifted back to Katsuo.

"Make your peace and be thankful for the fact that though you may never rule in Xian, your bones will reside here for eternity." With that said, Kang-Dae went back to his horse. Serenity wanted to cry. She was so close.

"All of you at this false king's back, have a chance to save yourselves! The next time you see me, I will not be merciful. Eat well, sleep deeply, and dream," his emphasis on the word dream made Serenity perk up. "Dream of a place beyond here. It will be the closest you will get to heaven I'm afraid. Make no mistake I will come for you, *all* of you." His eyes seemed to go past Katsuo at the moment and look straight into hers as he said those last words. Serenity's breath caught. 'Had he noticed?' she wondered. Kang-Dae and his men retreated leaving Serenity alone with the enemy, but this time she had a spark of hope that she would not be left for long.

# CHAPTER 86

Kang-Dae returned to his camp on a mission. He did not stop nor he did not speak to anyone. He stomped through the grounds toward his destination with a deep scowl on his face. He felt Kahil at his back but he did not inform the man what he was doing. Once he arrived at the tent he was looking for, he barged in not bothering to announce himself. Yu sat with Sun at the table. The two were in the middle of a discussion. Kang-Dae said nothing, he just went over to Sun, grabbed him by his shirt, and dragged him out of the tent. Yu shouted after them but Kang-Dae ignored him. He slammed the general to the ground and placed his foot squarely on his chest to hold him there.

"Did you know she was there?" Kang-Dae asked.

"Who are you talking about?" Yu questioned, not understanding what was happening. Sun, on the other hand just stared at him defiantly.

"Did you know?!"

"She's a traitor," he spat. "She is helping the enemy. it was she who sent me here with that message."

"What is going on?" Yu asked, becoming angry.

"Were you hoping we'd attack the place and she'd be killed along with him? Were you planning on allowing her to die with our enemy without speaking a word?" Kang-Dae accused him.

"She is the reason we lost the fort. How do you think he knew when to strike?" Sun snapped.

"You have no idea what she has done for us, do you?" chided Kang-Dae. "She brought the enemy right to us. How many men would we have lost? How long would we have fought trying to get to Katsuo ourselves? She brought him to the heart of our land where we had the advantage, where we can take him out once and for all. But you were too blinded by your hate to see that."

Sun's angry face began to fall, as uncertainty took over. He shook his head. "No, she is a traitor, a witch."

"She just handed the enemy over to us. We now have a chance to end this war for good because of her, and you were going to let her die!" Kang-Dae condemned him, pushing his foot deeper into his chest. Sun grunted in pain. Yu appeared to finally have caught on to what was happening as he became silent. Sun looked over to Yu, probably expecting the man to speak for him, or to agree with his words. When Yu remained silent, Sun looked at the man in disbelief.

When Kang-Dae saw the woman in black at the back of the line playing with her hands in a familiar way his first thought was how Serenity used to do the same when she was nervous. Kang-Dae had not known who the woman was or what she meant to Katsuo. She was covered from head to toe. He dismissed her quickly turning his focus to the invader but that unknown feeling returned. He couldn't see her eyes but he felt them on him. He kept her in his sights as best he could while he spoke. When he saw her gloved-covered hands start moving in a more deliberate way his heart seized. 'It couldn't be' he thought to himself. It took him a minute to catch exactly what she was spelling out.

It wasn't until the fourth attempt that he realized what she was saying.

'I'm here.'

He had to hide his shock. As soon as he turned his back to go to his horse he swallowed deeply, forcing back emotions of fear, anger, and relief. Once Kang-Dae had faced Katsuo again, he gave his warning but he also gave Serenity a message hoping she understood.

A crowd of men had gathered to observe the dire scene in front of them. No one knew what Sun had done but seeing how furious Kang-Dae was, they did not intervene.

"Take him away and lock him up. Once we're done with our enemies I will take care of him," he vowed. Two willing soldiers stepped up and pulled him from the ground to drag him away. To Sun's credit, he did not fight or argue any further, choosing to accept his fate.

Kang-Dae turned his gaze to Yu. His question must have shown on his face because Yu suddenly answered, "I did not know." Kang-Dae stared at him contemplating whether he believed the man or not. His hate for Serenity had been clear from the beginning. It would not even be the first time he tried to have her disposed of. Yu took a breath before going to his knees. It was an act of submission Kang-Dae had never seen from the man.

"I swear on my family's name, I did not know."

Choosing to believe him, Kang-Dae walked off. His most pressing concern at the moment was rescuing his wife.

# CHAPTER 87

Rielle and the others approached the massive encampment of Xian soldiers. The tents spread out far and wide. The number of men Kang-Dae had gave Rielle hope that the country would be able to hold its own against Katsuo. Authoritative shouts rang out ahead of them. A group of guards stood, bows drawn as they shouted at them in Xian. Hae-In stepped out in front holding up his hands while speaking. Whatever he said must have convinced the guards they were not the enemy because they all lowered their bows. The group was then ushered into the camp. Deep within the encampment, the group was brought to a tent. They were kept waiting outside as one of the guards went inside and returned with Kang-Dae. At the sight of him, all the others bent down to kneel while Rielle almost collapsed in relief. When Kang-Dae saw her, he immediately rushed toward her. Rielle hugged him practically sobbing overcome with emotion having finally found him. Kang-Dae returned her hug.

Kang-Dae had not expected to see Rielle when he went to meet the returning troops. "What are you doing here?" he asked once they pulled apart. However, as he asked the question the answer was abundantly clear to him. If Serenity was here, of course, Rielle would have come along. He knew how close the two women were and that Rielle was just as protective over Serenity as he was.

"Serenity. She's with Katsuo. We have to save her," Rielle told him.

"We will," he assured her. Touched by Rielle's loyalty to his wife he took her by the shoulder and led her into the tent. He called Hae-In to follow.

"Where is Jung-Soo?" he asked Hae-In once they were inside. Hae-In winced at the sound of Jung-Soo's name. Kang-Dae could already tell he would not like what Hae-In had to say.

After explaining to Kang-Dae how Jung-Soo had to stay behind to heal from a serious injury, Kang-Dae called for some men to retrieve him and

Tae-Soo. Knowing his friend, he knew Jung-Soo would not have waited long and was probably already on his way.

"Kang-Dae?" Rielle spoke up. Hae-In looked at her in shock at her use of his name. "What about Serenity?"

Kang-Dae ignored the slack-jawed Hae-In and went to Rielle. "She's in the fort. When the time is right, I will retrieve her myself."

Rielle's brow raised. "How?" she asked unsure, despite his confidence.

"The fort has many secrets that are unknown to Katsuo," Kang-Dae answered.

# CHAPTER 88

Kang-Dae, Hae-In, and Kahil snuck through the trees in the dead of night. Their target was hard to spot but they could not risk using any type of torch or lantern to light their way. If they did, the guards or men on patrol would be alerted to their position. Without stealth, the plan would fall apart before they even had an opportunity to enact it. Even with the darkness against them, Kang-Dae charged ahead, following the path in his mind. As they approached their destination, movement just ahead caused them all to freeze. All three men had their weapons at the ready prepared for whatever lay ahead. When Jung-Soo stepped out from behind the tree all three men released matching sounds of relief.

"General, how did you get here?" Hae-In asked. Kang-Dae stared in awe at Jung-Soo. He must've returned not long ago and upon finding out where Kang-Dae was going had come to join them.

"Did you run here?" Kahil asked incredulously. Jung-Soo didn't answer any questions. He just turned and started walking. Kang-Dae just followed behind him, as did the rest. Within minutes they were where they wanted to be. The hidden door in the ground was covered with foliage. After quickly removing it all, it took both Kang-Dae and Jung-Soo to open the heavy hatch. Kahil went down first, followed by Hae-In. Kang-Dae was set to go last but one look from Jung-Soo and he knew his friend would not allow it. With a roll of his eyes, Kang-Dae gestured for Jung-Soo to go ahead. Kang-Dae climbed down the hatch into the darkness. Now that they were inside, Hae-In lit one of the lanterns they had brought with him. Before them was a long stretch of hallway. It went so far, they could not see its end, but Kang-Dae knew exactly where it led.

The men began their journey through the tunnel. Every so often there was a ladder leading upwards. Kang-Dae kept counting in his head how far down they were going and where exactly they needed to stop. What Katsuo did not know about the fort was that not only could it house a great number of soldiers to man the vast fortress it could also house the same amount of soldiers underground. The tunnels also gave the men a secret way of escaping if there was no other choice.

Kang-Dae came to a stop as he looked up at the ladder. He looked over Hae-In and Kahil. "You two go on," he ordered. Both men nodded and went off to carry out their assignment leaving Jung-Soo and him alone. Kang-Dae began climbing up the ladder, with Jung-Soo right behind him. The doorway leading out opened inward. The door sat right behind a built-in wardrobe. Between the cracks of the wardrobe doors, Kang-Dae could see a little bit inside the room. There was soft light from candles giving him some visibility. He could see the bed and hear the snoring of the man sleeping on it. He motioned for Jung-Soo to wait as he stealthily climbed through the wardrobe on his belly. He stood up, took out his dagger, and approached the bed slowly. The snoring grew louder the closer he got to the sleeping figure. He could barely see the face of the man but knew he was older and most likely one of Katsuo's generals. Granting him what Kang-Dae considered a merciful death he slit the man's throat. The man's eyes shot open but he was only able to gurgle and grab at his throat for a few seconds before he was still.

Kang-Dae signaled for Jung-Soo to come out. Kang-Dae went over to the door of the room. Jung-Soo went over to the wall to the left of the door by a seemingly normal small painting. He quietly shifted the painting out of the way to look into the small hole that had been drilled there for Xian soldiers to look out of in case of infiltration. Jung-Soo gave Kang-Dae the signal that it was all clear and the two exited the room. Knowing the kind of man that Katsuo was Kang-Dae figured he would be in the largest room at the center of the fort. The obstacles between them and Katsuo would be numerous. They would run the risk of being caught if they tried to go after him. However, Katsuo was not their target tonight.

The duo went down the hall and made a left toward the other bedrooms built for nobles and visiting Lords. They would begin their search here. The first hall they came to was empty. They took their time using the peepholes to see who was inside. Not finding what they were looking for they moved on.

He peeked around the corner of the hallway. One lone guard was standing by one door. Kang-Dae had a feeling this was exactly where he needed to be. Kang-Dae looked at Jung-Soo and they spoke silently with their eyes and hands as he alerted him to the threat ahead. As Jung-Soo had the most experience being a "soldier of Katsuo", he went first.

Serenity had been unable to sleep for the past couple of nights. Following the confrontation between Kang-Dae and Katsuo, she had not had any dreams to guide her any further. She had begun to fear that she had led Xian to its doom and there was no longer anything she could do. She debated whether or not she should escape herself and take her chances to try and reach Kang-Dae herself.

"What are you doing here?" she heard the muffled voice of the captain ask outside her door. Whoever he was speaking to was too far away for her to hear them clearly. She could barely hear their faint response. It was quiet for a few seconds before she began to hear the sound of a skirmish. Was it an attack? Jumping out of bed she grabbed her dagger and pointed it at the door, preparing herself for whatever may come through. She knew if the average Xian soldier found her they would most likely kill her without a second thought, believing she was just an associate of Katsuo. The shuffling of feet increased and she heard what sounded like a clashing of blades. She put herself by the wall next to the door. If someone came in to take her perhaps, she could sneak around him when they made their way in. There was a soft grunt and something heavy hit the door.

As the door handle moved, she made herself as small as possible, while clutching the dagger to herself. The door swung open and a man in armor stepped through.

Taking a chance, she ran behind him out the door only to be caught immediately by another. She was about to plunge her dagger into her assailant when she froze in shock, as she stared into the smiling face of her husband.

"Hello, Neeco." Tears sprang to her eyes and the dagger fell from her grasp. She threw her arms around him and buried her face in his neck, as he lifted her. "Is it so hard for you to stay out of trouble?" he teased making her laugh.

"Every time I'm in trouble you come and save me. So why would I stop?" She retorted. He tightened his hold as he chuckled. Serenity could hardly believe she was in Kang-Dae's arms after so long.

"We are still surrounded by enemies. Perhaps you could do this later," Jung-Soo dryly suggested. Releasing her hold on Kang-Dae, she went over and hugged Jung-Soo as well. He acted as though he was annoyed at the gesture but he still gave her a halfhearted hug in return before pulling away. "Let's go," Jung-So said.

As she was pulled away, she finally noticed the deceased body of the captain. A pang of sadness hit her, even though she knew it was inevitable it was hard knowing he died trying to "protect her" in his mind. Though a soldier of Katsuo he had always been very nice to her.

After making their way through the halls of the fort and into a room with a hidden door, Kang-Dae guided her down a ladder into what seemed to be a secret tunnel beneath the fort. Amazed that this had been under her feet the whole time, she looked around in awe. The two men took her down the long hallway toward what she hoped was the exit. Waiting at another ladder were two men that Serenity vaguely remembered seeing in the palace a few times.

"Is it done?" Kang-Dae asked the men.

"Yes, my king," they responded in unison.

"In two days we can return," the taller one responded. Curious as to what they were speaking about Serenity decided to ask about it later. The two men went up first, one at a time before she was encouraged to go. Once they were all out and amongst the woods, Serenity felt overwhelming joy at finally being free.

# CHAPTER 89

Serenity's moans hit his ear and his eyes closed in pure ecstasy at the sound. He wrapped his arm around her stomach wanting her as close as possible as they moved together in sync.

After making it back to the camp, Kang-Dae didn't bother with any big announcement of their success. He would save that for later. Sharing his newly returned queen with the world was not at the forefront of his mind. Instead, he dismissed his co-conspirators, who each had knowing smiles as he walked off, taking his wife straight to his tent.

Serenity reached her hand back to grasp Kang-Dae's head as he kissed her neck. She moved back against him matching his thrust with great enthusiasm. He slid his arm from her stomach to her thigh lifting it so they could join themselves even deeper. The change in position made Serenity cry out which almost sent Kang-Dae spiraling, but he held off. He needed this to last as long as possible. The closer she came to completion the louder her moans became. Kang-Dae whispered sweet vows in her ear. Her moans turned into soft mewling noises. He promised never to let her go again. Swearing to her that she was the most important thing in his life. He uttered ridiculous statements about giving her oceans and the sun if she asked, the pleasure overtaking any semblance of sense he had. When she bucked faster against him, he figured she was only seconds away.

Serenity shouted out, "Oh God!" before shaking in his arms. Her insides tightened around him and he was lost within seconds. Releasing a loud grunt Kang-Dae spent himself inside her.

The two did not disengage from each other, still trembling in the afterglow of their pleasure. Neither could move for several minutes as they lay together panting. The scent of their love filled the tent. The two didn't speak. Though there was much to say, at that moment, nothing mattered but them. Kang-Dae lazily kissed her neck again and again as Serenity lightly stroked his arm.

After finally detangling themselves, Serenity rested her head on Kang-Dae's chest. They lay there listening to the sounds of the night.

Serenity suddenly gasped out, "Rielle!" She sat up, frantically. "Kang-Dae, Rielle is out there. I told her to find you."

Kang-Dae brought her back to him.

"It is alright. She is here, in the camp. She's safe."

"Really?" He nodded. Instantly relieved, she allowed herself to lay back down.

"You are lucky to have such a friend," he told her.

Serenity nodded her head. "I know. She wouldn't let me come alone."

"Why come at all?" he finally asked.

"I had to. I saw it. You needed me." Kang-Dae smiled to himself, knowing she was right.

Without Serenity's influence, they would have never been able to force Katsuo out of hiding.

"I did," he affirmed.

"I was so scared. I hated having to help him but," began to explain.

"You did what was necessary, what was needed," he told her. "I understand." Hearing him say the words she had prayed for, she leaned up and kissed his lips softly.

"But how did you get back? Did you find more flowers?" Kang-Dae asked curiously. It hadn't occurred to him until now that she should not have been able to even reach their world without the aid of the violet flower.

Serenity chewed on her bottom lip and her eyes shifted as she thought about whether now was the time to tell him how she had managed to return.

"We did," she said slowly. He appeared skeptical due to her delivery but she just kissed him again.

When Serenity pulled back, she had a mischievous smile on her face. "What is it?" Kang-De asked. She lay down next to him and took his arm in her hand. She lifted his pointer finger and began using it to write out a message. Amused by her antics he played along. He followed his finger with his eyes, as she guided it to write out the characters.

'Love Xian?' the first question asked. He looked at her with a confused smile but answered her nonetheless by writing out yes with his other hand. She began writing again.

'Love Me?' Again, he wrote out yes with a light chuckle. She giggled, clearly having fun. This time she took her time. Carefully spelling out each character.

'Love daughter?' Kang-Dae's heart stopped and his arm dropped as soon as she released it. He looked at her with wide eyes.

"Are you-," she nodded enthusiastically before he could even finish his question. He was on her in an instant, practically tackling her to the cot making her laugh out loud. He pulled back, knowing he probably looked ridiculous as he could not stop smiling.

"A little girl?' he confirmed. She nodded again. He stared down at her bare stomach, imagining the life they created laying inside.

"She protected me" Serenity explained. "I didn't need the flower because she was made from both of us. Two people from two different worlds." Kang-Dae shook his head in awe. Their miracle had created another miracle. He gently lay his palm against her slightly rounded stomach. He felt a tear escape the corner of his eye. Serenity wiped it away, her eyes shining with tears of their own.

"We need to make this land safe for her," she told him. He looked her in her eyes.

"We will."

# CHAPTER 90

Rielle headed toward Kang-Dae's tent. She had waited all night for the king to return, to see if he had been successful in rescuing Serenity or not. No one had ever come and told her anything. Now it was morning and she still didn't know what happened. Frustrated she decided to go search for him herself. Rielle came up to the tent and stopped short seeing Jung-Soo standing guard. She had not known he had made it back. She touched the top of her head, making sure her locs had not fallen out of the bun she secured it in. She walked up to Jung-Soo, her mission to see Kang-Dae momentarily forgotten. "You made it," she said.

"I did," Jung-Soo responded.

"How are you? Are you in-," she started to ask if he had any pain.

"I am fine," he interrupted. He looked at her for a moment before staring back off into the distance.

Rielle nodded. "That's good." She was glad he appeared to have no lingering effects from his injury. She hadn't been able to stop worrying about him since their departure. "Does your wound look okay? Is the coloring good?" she asked, going to reach for his shirt ready to check for herself.

Jung-Soo side-stepped to avoid her before she could reach him.

"Was there something you needed?" Jung-Soo asked suddenly interrupting the awkward moment.

Remembering what she had come for she asked, "did he come back? Did they find her?"

"The mission was successful. She is inside with the king," he told her in a matter-of-fact way.

Rielle was relieved but also frustrated. "Nobody was going to tell me," she huffed going into the tent. Jung-Soo didn't say a word, he just waited.

"Oh crap! Sorry," he heard her stammer from inside the tent before she came rushing back out. Jung-Soo stifled his laugh. She looked at him, with narrowed eyes. "You didn't think to warn me?" Jung-Soo just shook his head. A few minutes later Serenity emerged in one of Kang-Dae's shirts and bottoms, which she must have just thrown on in a hurry.

"Rielle," Serenity said embracing her. Rielle did the same. "Are you okay?" Serenity asked her.

Rielle nodded. "I'm fine. What about you?"

"I'm perfect," she told Rielle.

Rielle pulled back with a chuckle. "I saw," she joked.

Serenity laughed. "Stop," she chided jokingly. Soon Kang-Dae had emerged, shirtless, from the tent as well.

Rielle could barely look him in the eye. "Heeey," she greeted him awkwardly. Kang-Dae looked at her disapprovingly. Rielle gave him an apologetic smile. "Thank you for bringing her back," Rielle said to him.

Kang-Dae allowed himself to smile at her. "Of course."

Serenity took Rielle by the hand and led her into the tent leaving Kang-Dae outside with Jung-Soo.

Jung-Soo looked at the smiling Kang-Dae. Kang-Dae looked at Jung-Soo. "What?" Jung-Soo said nothing, only giving him a small shrug. Whistling a jovial tone Kang-Dae took a walk and Jung-Soo followed.

"Cured? Like completely?" Rielle asked excitedly from inside the tent.

Serenity nodded. "Completely." The two women embraced once more on the cot.

"Thank God," Rielle sighed. "So, what happens now?" she asked.

"We take the fort back and get rid of Katsuo once and for all," Serenity explained.

"How are you all going to do that?" Rielle questioned.

"Apparently, they have a plan. They're going to attack the fort in two days." From what Kang-Da told Serenity about it, it was a doozy. She didn't think Katsuo would expect it.

"Two days?" Rielle repeated. Serenity nodded.

"How do you know they're going to win?" Rielle asked.

"They will. They have to." Serenity said confidently.

# CHAPTER 91

The night before they would go off to war Kang-Dae spent the evening doing what was probably the best thing he would ever want to do on what could have been the last night of his life. He lay in bed with his nude wife talking to the baby inside of her. Serenity giggled as he traced his finger around her belly button in an attempt to tickle the baby. She gently pushed his hand away to stop him while giggling. "What?" he asked smiling up at her.

"She can't feel it but I can," Serenity told him. Kang-Dae just shrugged and went back to his conversation with his child.

"Once you arrive, I'll get you a horse and we'll go all around the capital. Your mother will have to stay behind since she's so afraid of horses."

"Hey! I'll have you know I've gotten pretty good at riding," Serenity claimed.

"Have you?" He asked raising his brow unable to stop the mischievous smirk that came on his face. She looked at him curiously before she closed her eyes with a groan at the realization of where his mind had went.

She thumped him on the head. "Don't be a pervert," she scolded. Kang-Dae just laughed before turning his attention back to his unborn child.

"As soon as you're old enough I will teach you how to handle a sword. And the first man who attempts to court you will have to fight you for the honor," he joked making Serenity chuckle.

"How long until we give her brother?" He asked suddenly.

Serenity looked down at him in disbelief. "Can we have this one first?"

Kang-Dae shrugged. "There is no harm in planning for the future."

Serenity shook her head. "You can do all the planning you want when the babies start coming out of you," she told him.

He ran his fingers down her side. "Have you really seen her?" he asked Serenity, peering into her belly once more. Serenity nodded. "What does she look like?"

A gentle smile came across Serenity's face. "Beautiful."

Kang-Dae placed a soft kiss on her belly before climbing up to align his face with Serenity's. "So just like her mother?" Serenity's smile widened and she brought him down pressing his lips to hers.

The morning of the battle Serenity was helping Kang-Dae into his armor. Kang-Dae never took his eyes off of her as she tightened his breastplate and checked to make sure it was secured. Saving the helmet for last, she held on to it. Kang-Dae caressed her cheek and she covered his hand with hers. He bent down to kiss her. With a sigh, Serenity nodded to him letting him know she was ready to see him off. The two exited the tent together. Outside there was activity all around as all the men prepared for war. Captain Kahil came up to them. He politely greeted Serenity and she did the same. The two warriors began to speak amongst themselves going over last-minute details.

Serenity stood by looking around when something caught her eye. Jung-Soo was exiting one of the tents fully dressed in his armor and helmet. But it was seeing Rielle emerge from that very same tent that had Serenity gobsmacked. Rielle was watching as Jung-Soo walked off her eyes following his every move. 'What happened there?' Serenity wondered to herself. Rielle must have felt Serenity's eyes on her because she suddenly turned to her. Once Rielle realized she had been spotted, her eyes became shifty and she awkwardly turned and ran back into the tent. They would talk about that later, Serenity told herself. Kang-Dae and the captain finished their conversation and the captain left. Kang-Dae held out his hands and Serenity handed him his helmet. He gently grabbed the back of Serenity's neck and leaned down to rest his forehead on hers. The couple stood there, in their own world, eyes closed, just breathing each other in.

"I love you," Serenity told him after a few moments.

"I love you," he responded. After a few more seconds he released her, kissed her on the head, and left.

# CHAPTER 92

Kang-Dae stood on the front line with his men. His whole army was at his back. Now was the time to show full strength. The battle for Xian would be fought here and now. Ahead of them were the gates of the fort. Rows of Katsuo's men, along with Katsuo himself, stood outside the gate. His other soldiers stood lining the walls of the gate, all armed with bows. Kang-Dae was sure there were even more of Katsuo's men inside, waiting. Both armies stood by, waiting, neither making a move toward the other. Kang-Dae looked toward the sun noting its position in the sky. 'It was almost time,' he thought to himself.

On his horse, he trotted out between the two armies. Stopping midway he dismounted and slapped his horse on the rear sending it away. Taking a cue from Kang-Dae, Katsuo came forward as well on his horse and did the same.

"Are you willing to let all your men die today for your pride?" Katsuo taunted.

Kang-Dae smiled. "It is not my men you should worry about."

An angry expression came upon Katsuo's face. "Where is she?" he demanded. "It was you who took her was it not?" Kang-Dae's smile widened. "You will return her to me now or I would go through all your men and take her back myself," Katsuo demanded.

"Return?" Kang-Dae laughed. "As if she belonged to you."

Katsuo frowned. "You wish to use her to win this battle but it matters not. The fate of this war has already been written and it will not change," he boasted.

"Is that what you think? Is that what she told you?"

Katsuo scoffed. "Whatever words you managed to force from her do not matter. I know the truth and when you are gone, I will retrieve her and take my rightful place as this land's king."

Kang-Dae once again looked up at the sky. Seeing the sun right above him, he smiled to himself. He turned his gaze back to Katsuo.

"This land will never be yours. Would you like to know why?" Just as he spoke, one by one the men on the wall begin to fall forward their screams echoing in the sky.

Katsuo looked up, face agape.

"Attack!" shouted Kang-Dae. His men charged forward just as he swung at Katsuo who was able to block the blow with his sword. The battle began to rage around them. More and more of Katsuo's men fell from the wall. The men scrambled for a bit, trying to shoot both inside and outside the walls of the fort. A deep rumbling sounded. Katsuo became distracted, looking toward the sound. Kang-Dae took the opportunity, to slash at the man's shoulder. The man cried out and clutched at the slash. He looked at Kang-Dae with murder in his eyes.

On the wall, a large section had begun to fall apart. The men standing in that section fell to their deaths. Men clad in Xian armor began pouring out of the gates and immediately engaging in the battle.

"What did you do?" snarled Katsuo.

Kang-Dae smirked. "You truly thought you had taken our stronghold from us?" Kang-Dae asked. "that my men had retreated?"

Before going in to rescue Serenity, Kang-Dae had informed Hae-In and Kahil about the secret of the fort. When he and Jung-Soo had gone after Serenity, he sent the other two to meet with General Wen, who was hidden within the tunnels with most of his men. When Kang-Dae heard about the fall of the fort, he hadn't believed it possible because they had been prepared for this exact thing. The fortress was built to defend, but in the event of enemy infiltration, it was also built to come down. The weakest points of the structure were buried deep in the ground, where the tunnels lay. If infiltrated, the men were trained to fight to win, if possible, if not, they would feign retreat, but in actuality, they would go into the tunnels to hide amongst the enemy until the right time to attack. Then they would bring the fort down right on top of their enemy's head. This had been the plan the moment Katsuo sought to occupy the place. It was why he had been so angry Sun had tried to keep Serenity's presence to himself. Had Kang-Dae not known, she would have been caught in it.

"This was never your victory," Kang-Dae told Katsuo. "You just walked into your defeat."

With a yell, Katsuo swung at Kang-Dae. The invader's blade hit his so hard the steel shook, but Kang-Dae managed to hold his ground. "Do you know how I know?" Kang-Dae continued taunting the invader. He pushed Katsuo off. The man stumbled back. "Because your dream walker, has always been *my* seer."

"You lie!" Katsuo fumed. Kang-Dae grinned.

"Look around you!" he shouted. Katsuo charged at him. Kang-Dae blocked his sword and kicked him in his chest sending him to the ground. "This is the end she predicted. But it was never for me." Katsuo got back to his feet and came at Kang-Dae once again. His attack was more ferocious now. His swings were stronger. Kang-Dae continued to meet him, blow for blow. Katsuo swung at his midsection and managed to catch him in the stomach just a bit before he could jump back in time. Kang-Dae hissed. Katsuo took the chance to swing at Kang-Dae's head. Luckily, he managed to block it but the blow was so strong it knocked his sword from his hand. Katsuo didn't waste a second.

Wildly swinging at Kang-Dae, he kept coming. Kang-Dae jumped back and kept veering out of his way over and over. Kang-Dae narrowly avoided a blow to the throat by throwing himself back onto the ground. He landed on his rear but quickly rolled and grabbed his fallen sword before returning to his feet.

"I will be king of all nations. It is my fate!" Katsuo maintained. His eyes were wild, and he looked crazed.

"Then prove it," challenged Kang-Dae taking a stance. He could see the invader clutch his sword tighter, before taking an offensive position. Kang-Dae took a breath. Katsuo ran straight at him, before faking going left. Kang-Dae went right to avoid him just as Katsuo quickly moved in front of him and swung at his arm, catching Kang-Dae in the bicep. The pain was deep but he held on to his sword. Kang-Dae spun left going for Katsuo's side. Katsuo managed to block it. Kang-Dae spun low, going right, and hitting Katsuo right in the knee. Katsuo let out a shout. He limped a few steps back, but Kang-Dae was not about to let him go. This time he charged at him. As Katsuo lifted his sword to block Kang-Dae's blow, Kang-Dae slid to his knees sliding across the ground right past the invader while hitting him in the thigh with his blade on his other uninjured leg.

"Ah!" Katsuo cried out. The man was stumbling now, trying to shift his weight between both injured legs. He knew Kang-Dae had the upper hand. Kang-Dae could see the desperation in Katsuo's eyes.

With a shout, Katsuo rushed at Kang-Dae with his sword in his left hand. Kang-Dae moved to the side and saw a dagger waiting for him in Katsuo's other hand. Kang-Dae caught Katsuo by the wrist, stopping the dagger before it could go into his eye. Katsuo dropped the sword in his other hand and used it to strengthen his hold on the dagger. The blade gained an inch, getting closer to Kang-Dae's pupil. Kang-Dae screamed while pushing the blade to the side with all his strength.

His eye safe, and the path clear, Kang-Dae took the opportunity to slam his head into Katsuo's, a painful but effective strategy. The man stumbled back. Kang-Dae took his sword and swung it at his torso. It got stuck in Katsuo's right side, penetrating the armor.

Wide-eyed, Katsuo spat up blood before dropping to his knees.

Kang-Dae stood above him ready to deal a killing blow. Bang! The area was suddenly filled with smoke. Kang-Dae waved at the smoke, coughing, and sputtering. He could barely see only able to make out shadowy figures. Once the smoke had cleared, he could see Katsuo being led back into the fort by an old man. Kang-Dae ran after them.

A pair of Katsuo's soldiers jumped in front of him. Kang-Dae released a breath before he took both men on.

It felt good to be fighting in Xian armor once more, Jung-Soo thought to himself as he grabbed the lone arrow from the ground and stabbed it into the face of the soldier he'd been tussling with. He got back to his feet and quickly dodged as another soldier attempted to charge at him, sword at the ready. Jung-Soo immediately grabbed the attacker by the wrist shifted it out of the way and ran him through. He kicked the man off his sword and went looking for another fight. He heard a bang in the distance. Jung-Soo caught sight of Kang-Dae just as he was enveloped in smoke. Jung-Soo took off toward him.

Just as two soldiers went to attack Kang-Dae at the same time Jung-Soo ran up, caught one by the waist, and threw him to the ground. Jung-Soo rushed toward the fallen man just as he tried to roll away. The soldier kicked his legs out wildly making Jung-Soo jump back. As the man struggled to get up in his heavy armor Jung-Soo kicked him back down and stabbed him right through the heart.

Removing his sword, he looked back to check on Kang-Dae who had the other soldier in a chokehold. Kang-Dae cut the man's throat and let him fall to the ground. The pair took just a second to catch their breath before being run up on by three more soldiers. The two friends shared a look before rushing at the men. The three soldiers did not last long against them.

# CHAPTER 93

Ami huddled up with Iko along with the other captives in the courtyard of the fort. None of them had been allowed to seek shelter inside. They had only been allowed to stay out in the open, where a stray arrow could strike them at any moment. Ami believed they wanted to use them as decoys in case the enemy made their way in. Ami tried to cover Iko as best he could, wanting to keep her safe. He and the others jumped as another section of the wall came down. More and more pieces of the fort seemed to be crumbling around them. Through the wreckage, Ami could see some of the battle going on outside the gates. He caught a glimpse of the Xian king going against Katsuo. The fight looked brutal.

Ami's eyes shifted to the numerous dead soldiers on the ground. When the Xian soldiers had come running out of the fort in all directions the captives had run to take cover. Luckily for them, it seemed they had no interest in captured civilians.

They went straight to Katsuo's soldiers who had been lying in wait to be called out for battle. Caught by surprise many men fell in the first couple of seconds. The rest fell after a few minutes and those who didn't die just fled. After clearing the courtyard of soldiers, the Xian men went out of the gate to join the battle.

The battle continued, and they could do nothing but wait. Ami looked up and saw what looked to be Katsuo being led inside the fort by the soothsayer. He strained his neck to get a better look just as a slew of Katsuo's men came rushing back through the gates trying to flee from the enemy. Ami and the others attempted to back away as the fight moved inside the courtyard.

A soldier came running and tripped right where Ami and Iko were huddled. A Xian came forward, sword raised, ready to deal a killing blow. The panicked soldier on the ground reached out and grabbed Iko's wrist. Before Ami could stop him, he had pulled her on top of him just as the sword came down stabbing her through the waist. "Aunt Iko!"

Ami shouted. The Xian soldier was shocked at what he had done. He had little time to dwell on it as another soldier came forward and stabbed *him* through the back. Spitting out blood the soldier fell forward and the other soldier ran, being chased off by another Xian.

The cowardly soldier was still scrambling to get from under Iko. Ami grabbed the dead soldier's sword. A rage he'd never felt before was upon him as he stood above the scrambling soldier. The soldier held out his hand and opened his mouth to plead for his life. Ami swung and cut the hand off. The soldier screamed while staring at his new stump. Ami buried the blade in his heart. Tears leaking from his eyes, Ami went to grab Iko. He pulled her into his arms but she had already passed. Ami could do nothing but scream out his anguish.

# CHAPTER 94

From a distance Serenity and Rielle watched the battle unfold. They were far enough away to be out of any danger but close enough to see the outcome of the battle. Another chunk of the wall came tumbling down.

Rielle grasped at Serenity's hand. "They got this right?" Rielle asked needing the reassurance.

Serenity nodded. "They got this," she told her. "My man doesn't go down easy," Serenity said, believing what she was saying. It was like Denise had told her before she came back. She had to trust that Kang-Dae would do everything in his power to make it back to her, and she did. The numbers looked to be dwindling from what they could see. Serenity was glad to see more Xian soldiers standing. Black smoke had begun to rise from inside the gates. Serenity hated to see the destruction of the great fort. She knew how important it had been to Xian. But it was like her dream had shown her. Sometimes you had to let some things be broken down so they can be built back up even greater. They may lose the structure of the fort for now but they would rebuild it, just like the rest of Xian, once this war was over.

Ami walked the chaotic halls. No one paid him any mind, too concerned with escaping to save their own lives. The walls shook and rumbled as more and more sections began to collapse. A man went by with his arm aflame screaming for help as he limped through the halls. Ami did not let the sight deter him.

He came upon a room with an open door. Inside, he could hear someone grunting in pain. Ami entered the room. On the bed was a writhing Katsuo, being tended to by the soothsayer. The wounded king was bleeding profusely from his side. Half his armor had been removed so the older man could attempt to stop the bleeding. The soothsayer noticed him.

"You! Go fetch the healer!" He ordered Ami. Ami did not move, his gaze focused on the man on the bed. The older man shouted at him again, demanding he go and bring back a healer. Still, Ami did not leave. Fed up with his lack of movement, the soothsayer stood and shoved past him. "Out of the way!" He snarled as he went past, most likely in search of help.

Katsuo continued moaning, coughing, and writhing in pain holding a cloth to his injury. Ami slowly walked up to him. He noticed Katsuo's crown had fallen off and was laying above his head on the bed. Ami reached out to take it into his hands. The golden headdress had specks of blood on it. Ami stared into his reflection in the crown.

"Get out!" hissed Katsuo. Ami raised his gaze to him.

"It's smaller than I remember," Ami said softly.

"What?" sneered Katsuo. He shook his head in annoyance. "Just go!" He ordered Ami before checking his wound. Katsuo scoffed at his bleeding side before letting his head fall back to the bed.

"You believed everything he said. Not once did you consider he could be wrong. Now here you are. Did he not see this in his visions?" Katsuo stared up at the teen with a scowl. "When you sent that murderous man after a child, did you believe you had to?" Ami asked.

Katsuo seemed to get even paler at Ami's words. "What are you talking about?" he sputtered.

"Did you believe that a child would try to take your crown? Your own brother?" he asked, emotion coating his words.

"Who are you?" Katsuo asked.

"If the visions were true, why are you laying here like this? Why are you not already king of the world? Why do I stand here before you, alive?"

Katsuo's frown deepened, not understanding Ami's words at first before revelation finally hit him and his eyes widened. "Akimitsu?"

"You had Akimitsu killed, remember?" Ami responded. "You sent that killer to his room to slay him in his bed." Ami felt the tears build up in his eyes. "If not for our mother, he would have succeeded."

"Mother?" Katsuo whispered to himself.

"I never wanted your crown. I never wanted to be king. I was happy to just be with my brother," cried Ami.

Katsuo's eyes began to water with tears of his own. "I had to," he whispered looking away unable to look Ami in the face.

"I was a child! You were my family! You and mother were all I had. I never wanted your throne. I never wanted any of it!"

Katsuo slowly reached his bloody hand out to Ami. "Akimitsu," he called. Ami took a step back. The ground began to rumble again.

"Because of you, I was forced to grow up far from my home. I had to be raised amongst the people you hated, the people you tried to subjugate. Even then, you still would not let me alone. I've been under your nose this entire time forced to serve you and your soldiers, a prisoner, and you didn't even recognize me." Katsuo let out a choked sob. Ami stared at the crown. "You started a war because of words. You killed and hurt so many because of his words, because of his "prophecy". Now you will die here in this land, alone. All this because of the words of one man." Ami stared down at Katsuo. "Do you still believe him?"

Katsuo continued to reach for Ami. Eventually, he reached too far and fell off the bed. Even then, he began trying to crawl toward Ami. "Akimitsu, please," he gasped, coughing up blood.

"*Here*, I am Ami." Ami clutched the crown in his hand. "But maybe I will return to Anoeka. After you die here, maybe I *will* become the next king. Perhaps he had been right about that," Ami taunted. "Or maybe you both played with things you never understood and now you have fallen victim to your ignorance and ambition. Maybe this was how it was always going to end, all because you believed his words over mine." With that said, Ami gave Katsuo one last look as the ground beneath them began to crumble. He shut his eyes, turned his back on his brother, and ran out of the room.

He could hear Katsuo shouting behind him, "Akimitsu!" followed by a loud crash. Ami turned back to see a gaping hole where the room had once stood. He could hear the agonizing screams of Katsuo as the light of the flames below flickered. Wiping his tears, he ran down the hallway to escape the collapsing fortress.

# CHAPTER 95

Kang-Dae watched as the rest of Katsuo's men that had run into the fort to escape them now ran back out to escape the raging fire and collapsing building. Kang-Dae and his men dispatched each one. They wanted to take as many of them out as possible, a consequence of infesting their lands for as long as they had. Even the Xians sent by the lords who had defected were killed, not being shown any mercy. Screams echoed from inside as the men that had been too cowardly to come out and face them were now caught in the destruction.

Kang-Dae knew Katsuo was inside as well. He would wait all night for the man to emerge if he had to. More soldiers came stumbling out along with young men and women, who Kang-De knew were captured Xian civilians. He ordered his men to take care of them and lead them away from the fort to safety. Among a few more running soldiers, who were quickly killed by Kang-Dae's bowmen, a boy exited the fort. He walked slowly, as if in a daze.

One of his soldiers went to guide him but brought him to Kang-Dae when he noticed what was in the boy's hand.

Katsuo's gold crown was in the hands of the young teen. "Boy?" Kang-Dae called out gently. "Is Katsuo still inside?"

The boy slowly looked up. "He's dead," the teen rasped.

"Are you sure?" Jung-Soo asked the boy.

"The floor fell and he burned," the boy spoke flatly, emotionless. Seeing that the boy had been deeply affected by the day, Kang-Dae had him taken with the other civilians.

Jung-Soo and Kang-Dae looked at each other reeling from what they had heard. "Do you think it's true?" Jung-Soo asked him. Kang-Dae stared into the fort that was now completely ablaze.

"Most likely. Once the fire burns out, we will make sure."

In the meantime, his men had already begun cheering amongst themselves at the great victory. Kang-Dae shut his eyes and released a breath feeling like their fight had finally come to an end.

Long after the sun had set, Kang-Dae and his men returned from the ruins of the fort. Their excitement and joy manifested in loud cheers and songs. As soon as Serenity spotted him, she flew into his arms, not caring about the sweat, dust, or blood that covered him. He wrapped his arms around her, not caring about any of his aches or injuries, content to hold her forever.

"Is it over? Is he dead?" she asked as she pulled back.

"Yes," he told her. Once things had calmed Kang-Dae sent men to retrieve the invader's body. They later reported they found a burnt body beneath a pile of rubble in the same golden armor Katsuo had been wearing. Serenity looked as though a great weight had been lifted off her shoulders. Kang-Dae felt the same way.

As the men around became rowdier with enthusiasm, some tried to get Kang-Dae to join in the merriment. Kang-Dae was about to pass, content to celebrate with his wife but once Serenity noticed his bleeding injuries, she forced him over to see the healers.

At the healer's tent, she made him sit as she helped clean and bandage his wounds. To his surprise, Rielle was also in the tent. It seemed she had decided to lend her services out for his injured men. But what was even more surprising was that she was currently tending to Jung-Soo. Kang-Dae's mouth fell open at seeing how gentle she was being and how Jung-Soo was allowing it. He looked to be using a great deal of effort to keep from staring at the female healer. Serenity noticed where his gaze had landed. She gave him a look that told him she had no idea what was going on either.

After being tended to, they all went out to join in the celebrations.

# CHAPTER 96

They all were back in the capital after a few days. When they returned it was like a parade. The people cheered in the streets welcoming them home. Now that Serenity had been officially "resurrected", word had gotten around that she had been vital in finally putting an end to Katsuo's invasion and the people cheered for the return of their queen as well.

Upon returning to the palace Serenity mentally took pictures of everyone's faces when they saw her, especially her mother-in-law who had immediately broken out in tears. The two had embraced like they'd been apart for years. In her arms Serenity felt as though she were hugging her own mother. Amoli had come to her tears flowing freely. Serenity held her for so long Kang-Dae had to make her let go.

The most surprising reaction had been Satori's, who had actually bowed and welcomed her back sincerely. She never would have expected that.

That night they had a grand dinner with all their loved ones and friends. Serenity had even forced Jung-Soo to join. They all ate together, talked, and enjoyed each other's company like a family. Serenity felt so blessed to know she had a family in this land as well.

Halfway into the dinner, Kang-Dae took it upon himself to stand and make an announcement.

"The Kingdom will soon have a new Princess," he revealed joyously.

The room erupted in cheers. Unlike when she had been in this very situation with Katsup and Jae-Hwa, where she felt sick and trapped, now she was filled with joy. Everyone came up one at a time to congratulate her. The moment was so special she promised herself that before she gave birth, she would return home and share the news with her family as well.

Around the room, everyone joked and laughed but when Serenity's eyes landed on Ami, she felt her heart sadden.

When the young boy had been brought back to camp he looked utterly broken. As soon as she asked about Iko, he fell apart in her arms. She held him as he cried, letting him unleash his sorrow as long as he wished.

"Let us toast to the new Princess!" Amir chirped in from his seat with Amoli beaming up at him. 'I have clearly missed a lot,' Serenity thought.

"To the new princess!" the room declared.

"Are you sure you don't want me to come with you?" Serenity asked Rielle for the 10th time. "I told you I'll be fine," Rielle said.

"It feels wrong not to see you off," Serenity said with a pout.

"You just got back. I think Kang-Dae would have an aneurysm if you set foot near that lake right now." Rielle explained.

Knowing Rielle wasn't wrong, it still didn't sit well with Serenity, letting Rielle return home on her own.

"Do you have to go back so soon?" Serenity asked.

"I need me some internet, girl," Rielle joked.

Serenity laughed. "Right," Serenity said.

"I just need to be back home," Rielle said, her voice taking on a more serious tone. Rielle had been very tight-lipped about what all she'd gone through when they were apart. Serenity knew some of it had been bad. As much as she loved Xian, she recognized that Rielle's experiences had been very different and didn't blame the woman for wanting to leave.

"Why won't you let Jung-Soo take you?" she asked. If Serenity didn't go, she would feel a lot better knowing Jung-Soo was with Rielle.

"That man has had enough of me," Rielle joked but something in her voice told Serenity there was more to it. Rielle still had not disclosed what had happened between the two on the night before the battle. She would barely disclose what happened between them while they were traveling together.

"I trust Hae-In and Tae-Soo. They'll get me there alright," she assured Serenity.

"Okay," Serenity gave in.

The next day they were at the gates of the palace. Rielle had everything she needed for her journey back home. Serenity hugged her tightly. "Tell everyone I miss them, and I'll visit soon," she told her.

Rielle nodded. "I will." They pulled apart both trying to keep from crying. Rielle hugged Kang-Dae next.

"Thank you for helping to bring her back to me," he thanked her sincerely as they pulled away.

"Just keep making her happy and we're even," Rielle told him.

"Always," he swore.

Rielle glanced over at Jung-Soo who was speaking with Hae-In and Tae-Soo. She felt like she should say something to him but in the end, she chose not to.

"You guys ready?" she called out to Tae-Soo and Hae-In. The two men looked over at her and nodded. Tae-Soo helped her onto the horse. Rielle had only been on one of those trotting pony rides when she was little so she knew this trip was going to be interesting.

Rielle had considered staying a little longer, maybe giving the land a chance to show her its less violent side. But she was still having nightmares about that horrible night. When she woke up in the dark she could never go back to sleep, feeling someone would appear and attack her at any moment. She had wanted to give the place a fair chance. But it was difficult. Everything was so different here. Unable to stop herself she cast one more look at Jung-Soo who finally was looking back at her. She gave him a short smile and he nodded back to her. She said her final goodbyes to everyone, prodded her horse toward the open gate, and left with the two soldiers at her side.

# CHAPTER 97

Serenity stood on the balcony in her nightgown looking out into the night sky. Kang-Dae was holding her from behind. "Do you think they're okay?" Serenity asked. Kang-Dae knew she was asking not just about Rielle but the young boy Ami as well. It was only a day or so after Rielle's departure that the young boy had come to them, asking if he could return to his village. Serenity had wanted the boy to stay with them even if it was just for a little bit but he had wanted to return to the home he had lived in with his aunt. Kang-Dae sent him with some men and some gold, knowing Serenity would want him taken care of. After telling Kang-Dae how the boy had assisted her when she was trapped with Katsuo Kang-Dae was willing to give the boy whatever he wanted. The teen had been humble, not asking for anything but a small memorial for his aunt. Kang-Dae obliged.

Now it seemed Serenity was feeling sentimental. Kang-Dae noticed she had become more so with the pregnancy. Since being back, he noticed she was showing beginning to show. According to the healer Medhi she would be due in the spring.

"They will be alright," he assured her.

"What about everyone out there?" she asked. "Will they be alright?" They had gotten rid of Katsuo's main army but the smaller troops were still scattered about the country. And they still had to deal with the traitorous lords who chose to support Katsuo. Kang-Dae had his men going throughout the land to root them out and expel them all. He did not fear though. Without their leader, they were aimless and less dangerous. Before long, their country would be peaceful once more. The cities that had been occupied had quickly been abandoned at the news of Katsuo's defeat. All the captured civilians and children had been found and returned to their homes and family.

"They will be fine. We all will be fine."

"I think we'll be better than fine," she said. Kang-Dae could hear the smile in her voice. He kissed her cheek and led her back inside. Yes, they would be fine, better than fine, because now they were back together. They had their kingdom, they had their home, and they had their family.

THE SEER WILL RETURN FOR ONE LAST

ADVENTURE IN 2024